DISCOVERED

When he'd seen Roxanne running across the street he'd stepped into his trousers and prepared himself for trouble; the kind of trouble people came to the sheriff with. But when he'd opened the door and seen her face he'd known. Somehow—from the kiss, no doubt—she'd found him out. How had he ever thought he could keep this from her?

He waited for her to run away in tears, her worst fears confirmed with the utterance of a few words. But she didn't run. She stood her ground and looked him in the eye, and he, who could usually read her so well, couldn't tell what she was thinking.

The rain started to come down harder, and a gust of wind blew cold drops beneath the small overhang above his front door. It pelted Roxanne, and a few cold drops even found his chest and arms and face.

"It was you," she finally whispered.

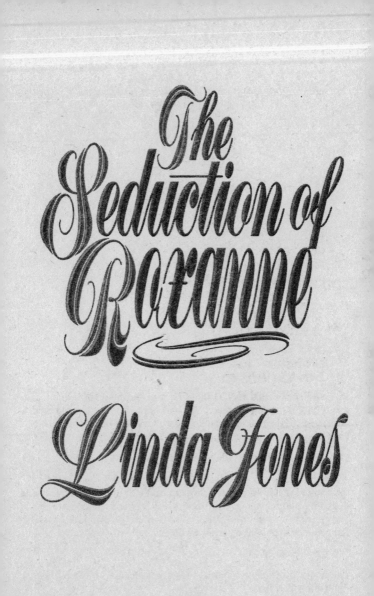

The Seduction of Roxanne

Linda Jones

LOVE SPELL BOOKS NEW YORK CITY

For Chris Keeslar.
For making me laugh and for (usually) understanding what
I'm trying to say. Thank you.

LOVE SPELL®

January 2000

Published by

Dorchester Publishing Co., Inc.
276 Fifth Avenue
New York, NY 10001

ISBN 0-505-52357-4

Printed in the United States of America.

The Seduction of Roxanne

Chapter One

Paris, Texas, 1868

Standing on the boardwalk, Cyrus leaned back against the wall of Nickels' Saloon to watch people and wagons and horses pass on the peaceful street before him. All was well here, as usual, the businesses prospering and the populace content.

It had been a quiet day so far, a good day. There was just a touch of a spring chill in the air to remind him of the winter that had passed, and at the moment there was only one prisoner in the Lamar County Jail, a local boy who usually managed to spend a day or two every month locked up for disturbing the peace. All in all he was a good boy, but liquor made him crazy. Soon as the kid sobered up, he would be contrite and apologetic.

Paris, Texas, was a good-sized town; not so big that everybody didn't know everybody else, not so small that the amenities that made life pleasant weren't available. Up and down this street, where Nickels' Saloon was one of three prosperous taverns, there was a dress shop and a bakery, a general store and a furniture store, a saddlery and the livery where Cyrus boarded his horse. There was a barber shop, a small café, and a decent hotel. Up near the town square sat the Lamar County Jail, the offices of several lawyers, and the Lamar County Courthouse.

The town was clean and prosperous, and beyond this street there were many fine homes, large and small, a park where the citizens gathered on occasion, and a number of churches. Paris was, all in all, a good place to live.

Most of the government rule, an authority that had been administered primarily by carpetbaggers and thieves, was finally gone, leaving the citizens of Paris to rebuild their lives after surviving a war that had touched them all in some way. Now and then Cyrus thought of moving on, heading west, but he didn't; and he wouldn't. He had his reasons for staying in Paris.

"Sheriff," Mrs. Fowler said as she passed close by, her booted steps crisp on the boardwalk. She nodded her graying head demurely.

Cyrus returned the subtle greeting, tipping his hat and muttering, "Good afternoon." Elizabeth Fowler had lost two sons in the war, soldiers Cyrus had served with in the Ninth Texas Infantry. She always looked at him as if she wondered why he'd survived when her boys hadn't.

After she passed, he absently ran his thumb over the scar that marred his left cheek. The texture was rough, the scar long and ugly. It ran from his jaw to just below his eye, and a small nick bisected his eyebrow with a scar so thin, so fine, that it was hardly visible. Still, every time he looked in a mirror he was reminded of how close he'd come to losing the eye. The blade of the Yankee's bayonet had barely skimmed past the eyeball. A half an inch closer, maybe less. . . . Well, Cyrus didn't look in the mirror any more than he absolutely had to.

Mrs. Fowler continued on without so much as a glance back, her head high, her spine just a bit too rigid. Yes, he'd be better off in a place where no one knew him, where he didn't see ghosts on every corner, in every pair of haunted eyes. But he had his reasons for staying.

A raised voice from inside Nickels' Saloon caused Cyrus's entire body to tense. His fingers flexed, his nostrils flared. Ah, he'd been right when he'd determined that the stranger who'd ridden into town and tied his horse up out front had smelled like trouble.

Sheriff Cyrus Bergeron had a nose for trouble.

With a sigh he pushed away from the wall and turned to enter the saloon. The short, broad-backed stranger leaned over the bar, threatening poor old Hamlin Nickels with a short, rusty knife.

"Is this the best liquor you've got?" the stranger shouted, knocking an empty shot glass aside. The blade of his short knife danced inches from Hamlin's frightened face. "Tastes like horse piss!"

Hamlin was a gentle, older man, with a narrow face and a ready smile. His abundance of well-kept dark red hair was shot with silver these days, and a number of deep lines bracketed the saloon keeper's mouth and eyes. Wide eyes in Hamlin's wrinkled face were fastened on the knife that threatened him, as he sputtered in defense of his whiskey and stepped away from the dull-bladed weapon.

"Get back here you lily-livered coward." The stranger reached out and snagged Hamlin's sleeve to hold the aging bartender in place.

Cyrus approached silently, closing on the bully. He recognized the stranger, even though he'd never seen him before. A little man with a big ego, the ruffian was looking for a fight. Men like this one never picked on those who might fight back.

"Let him go," Cyrus said softly.

The bully dropped Hamlin and spun around, hands raised, knife ready to strike. He was easily agitated, not too bright, and in bad need of a bath and a hair cut. He was also ready to fight—but not against someone who might actually prove a threat.

Pale, darting eyes swept over Cyrus, until the man's anxious gaze finally settled on a ravaged cheek. "This is none of your concern, scarface. Back away."

Moving very slowly, Cyrus lifted his hand and hooked two fingers around the edge of his vest, moving the leather aside so that his badge was revealed. "Everything that happens in this county is my concern."

He saw a hint of panic in the stranger's eyes, a moment of frantic assessment.

"I'm glad you're here, Sheriff," he said defensively. "This man tried to rob me. Charged me good money for whiskey and gave me horse piss instead!" The knife weaved and bobbed in a now unthreatening manner.

Hamlin backed into the safety of a corner to silently observe the confrontation. No one else was in the saloon at this time of the afternoon. In a couple of hours the place would be noisy and lively, but for now all was quiet.

Cyrus kept a careful eye on the knife. "You have business in Paris?"

The stranger narrowed one eye. "Just passing through."

"You got a name?"

The man hesitated, screwing up his face as if he were trying to decide if he should answer the question. "J. T. Johnson," he finally muttered.

"Well, Mr. Johnson, I think you'd better keep on riding through."

If the man was smart at all he'd hightail it out

of here without another word. Unfortunately, Cyrus didn't think he was going to be dazzled by Johnson's intelligence.

"You can't make me leave," Johnson breathed. "I ain't done nothin' wrong." The grip on the knife tightened, the muscles in the arm tensed, ready for attack. An air of indignity grew about the pathetic man, as he stood poised for attack, ready to defend his right to stay in Nickels' Saloon to harass and threaten its owner.

Cyrus moved so fast, his hand whipping forward smoothly and unexpectedly, that Johnson didn't even have time to flinch, much less react in defense. Before the ruffian knew what had happened he'd been disarmed, and Cyrus held the knife.

"If you're going to carry a knife," Cyrus said calmly as he studied the blade, "you should at least sharpen and clean it now and again. This is disgraceful."

Angered at finding himself so easily relieved of his weapon, Johnson reacted by reaching for the six-shooter he had strapped to his thigh. Once again, Cyrus was quicker than the man anticipated, beating Johnson to his own gun. He lifted the weapon so quickly and smoothly that Johnson's searching, short-fingered hand fell, too late, on an empty holster.

As Johnson cursed beneath his breath, Cyrus mindlessly twirled the six-shooter in his hand.

"You don't take any better care of your Colt than you do your knife," he said casually.

"What would you do if you ever needed to defend yourself? Beat your opponent with the butt of the Colt and saw at him with the dull edge of this blade, I suppose." It was clear to Cyrus that Johnson had never been a soldier.

"Give me back my gun," Johnson said childishly. He reached for the weapon and Cyrus moved it away; he reached again and Cyrus made sure the Colt floated just out of reach. Slow, fat fingers reached helplessly for the Colt that remained in constant movement; twirling, shifting, seemingly floating in Cyrus's hand. With every second that passed the ruffian became more frustrated. "All right, goddammit," he finally shouted. "I'll leave. I'll leave!"

"Hamlin," Cyrus glanced at the bartender. Hamlin had relaxed considerably in the past few minutes, and no longer cowered in the corner. "Did this gentlemen pay for his fine whiskey?"

"Yessir, he paid before I poured his drink." Hamlin busied himself wiping down the counter where Johnson had been standing moments earlier, as if attempting, already, to rid the saloon of any small reminder of the bully's presence.

With another controlled, lightning-quick movement, Cyrus returned the poorly kept six-shooter to the holster at Johnson's hip. The man twitched, obviously surprised, as the Colt landed smoothly home. Cyrus spun the knife one last time and offered it, handle first.

Johnson took the knife and returned it to the sheath at his belt, and with a wary eye on Cyrus he moved toward the door. His show of bravery returned with the familiar weapons close at hand. "You're some kind of peculiar, scarface," he said as he backed toward the sunlight. "I'll be right glad to keep riding out of this town."

Cyrus didn't trust the bully, so he followed. Johnson backed into the batwing doors, which swung open and allowed him to step onto the boardwalk. Cyrus caught the doors on a backward swing and tossed them gently as he exited.

Mumbling incoherently to himself, Johnson unhitched his horse and hoisted himself into the saddle. Cyrus was confident that the bully would ride out of town peacefully. Men like this didn't fight battles they couldn't win. They didn't take on men who were taller and faster and meaner than they were. They reserved their energies for frightened old bartenders and untested boys, for gentle women and soft men. There was no nobility in Johnson's heart, no honor buried beneath all that anxious hostility.

Cyrus had no use for a man without honor.

His gaze shot past Johnson's horse and landed on the gray-swathed figure that walked slowly down the street. If anyone else had wandered into his line of vision he never would have noticed, but he always noticed Roxanne.

Johnson noted the change in Cyrus's focus and turned his head. A low whistle followed. "Now, *that's* a woman," he said coarsely. Roxanne was still a good distance away, but her long strides carried her closer with every step. "Dammit, that is a lot of woman, and that is *all*-woman. Maybe I oughta introduce myself, take my chances and stay in Paris for a while longer." He smirked at Cyrus. "Overnight, anyway."

Silently, Cyrus slipped to the horse's side as the little man in the saddle returned his attention to Roxanne. Johnson never knew what was happening until Cyrus tightened the grip on a filthy shirt and pulled the ruffian halfway off the horse so he could look him in the eye. Cyrus knew that all he had to do was let go, and Johnson would surely fall on his ugly head.

"You don't so much as look at her again," he whispered, and for the first time since their encounter Johnson went white. He didn't look like a bully at the moment; he looked like a frightened, helpless, large child. Cyrus felt no sympathy for the wretched man. "She's a lady, you son of a bitch, and you don't lay your good-for-nothing eyes on her, you hear me? You ride out of town with your eyes straight ahead, and if I see you so much as twitch in her direction I'll shoot you in the back." He leaned slightly closer and lowered his already soft voice. "No one will miss you, J. T. Johnson." With that simple comment, the threat was accepted as fact.

With a hard shove from Cyrus's impatient hand, Johnson bobbed up until he was seated properly once again. He straightened his collar and rotated his neck as if working out a crick, but he didn't glance Roxanne's way. When his horse had taken a couple of steps down the street, when Johnson thought himself out of reach, he turned bravely to Cyrus.

"I'll bet a *lady* like that won't give the time of day to an ugly freak like you, scarface." Thinking himself safe, Johnson flashed a wide smile, revealing yellow teeth and one grim gap where another should have been.

Cyrus shifted his hand until it rested on his own holster. Johnson took the hint and galloped down the street. The man wasn't completely stupid, after all; he didn't turn his head toward Roxanne as he sped away.

Cyrus stepped back into the shadows and watched Roxanne's progress down the street. *All-woman* was right. She was taller than any other woman in town, taller than quite a few of the men. Using his own 6'2" and the times he'd been close to Roxanne as a guide, he figured she was a good 5'9" tall, maybe a little more. She'd been gangly as a kid, he remembered, all arms and legs. Somewhere along the way she'd grown into her height nicely, filling out in all the right places and learning to move those long arms and legs with unequaled grace. She now floated down the road like a queen, like an angel, as if her feet barely touched the ground she walked on.

She carried a short stack of books in her arms, and her eyes were trained unerringly straight ahead. This morning, when he'd watched her walk to the Paris Female Academy where she taught, her dark hair had been braided and twisted neatly around her head. But now a few strands floated around her face and shoulders, the ends of a few long, errant strands touching the silver gray fabric.

She'd been out of black for a while now, but he hadn't seen her in anything but black or gray or brown since he'd left to fight the Yankees. Sometimes it seemed that her mourning would never end, that she would never recover her life and her heart. There were dark moments when he was sure he would gladly give his right arm to see her smile again, his life to hear her laugh. Somehow, if Roxanne could survive, they all could. If she could heal, all would be right with the world. Foolish thoughts, but now and again he was so certain. . . .

Roxanne Robinette was, indeed, all-woman; she was also a young widow who'd grieved for her husband for three years, a teacher who gave her time and devotion to the girls at the academy, a dutiful niece who helped her frivolous aunt and demanding uncle manage their large home—and she was the reason Cyrus would never leave Paris, Texas.

Roxanne barely noted the rider who passed so quickly, leaning over his horse's neck as he sped down the road that headed south. She did, almost unconsciously, step to the side of the road so she was well out of his path. But she didn't even pay much attention to the dust his horse kicked up.

Her mind was on many things; tomorrow's lesson, Aunt Ada's cold, the petticoat that needed to be mended, the fine weather and the certainty that it wouldn't last long. Spring in Texas meant rain and thunderstorms. The thoughts that filled her mind were ordinary and calming, almost numbing in their familiarity.

In spite of her familiar thoughts, she knew that something was different this spring. With the departure of winter, something inside her was thawing. The thaw caused an occasional pang deep inside, as she rediscovered her own simple hopes and dreams. For three long years she'd thought her life was over. She'd watched the children and the young ladies she taught with the bitter bite of the knowledge that she'd never have babies of her own. Louis was dead, her dreams were gone, there was nothing left for her. That certainty seemed more painful than ever, these days.

But there was an occasional, unexpected joy mingled with the pain. She saw flowers this year, felt the sun, had begun to enjoy her students on occasion, to appreciate their smiles and their eagerness to learn. Easter was just a few days past, and Roxanne found herself experiencing a touch of wonder that spring was upon her and another year lay ahead.

Maybe her heart and her spirit were mending at last, maybe she could finally glimpse a hint of true hope. She would never have the life with Louis she'd always dreamed of, but perhaps she could find companionship with someone, eventually, and have the children she longed for.

Lately she'd begun to ponder, vaguely and with little energy, what she might look for in a potential husband. Her requirements were simple; he should be kind, of course, and have a stable and steady income. Love was impossible, but she would certainly have to *like* the man she married. They would be companions for a very long time. That wasn't too much to ask for, was it?

Movement in front of the saloon caught her eye, and she turned her head in that direction. While she couldn't see Cyrus's face in the shadows from this distance, his form was unmistakable. No one else in town was quite that tall, no other man carried himself just so. She turned in his direction, carefully looking both ways for more slapdash riders as she stepped into the street. She'd almost forgotten that Uncle Josiah had asked her to invite Cyrus to supper.

Cyrus didn't move as she crossed the street, advancing unerringly toward him. He just stood there, still and silent, waiting. She remembered a time when he'd been her friend, but perhaps her memory was faulty. Cyrus was older than she by seven years; he'd been a man when he'd marched off to war. She'd been a child, though she'd certainly thought herself a woman at seventeen. Perhaps she only remembered Cyrus as a friend because she had so few old friends left.

Well, the past didn't matter much, and these days Cyrus barely noticed her. He was a busy man, with more important things on his mind than a girl he used to know, long ago. In the years since his return from the war he probably hadn't said a dozen words to her.

He was a good sheriff, respected and dedicated; a good man, honorable and strong. When she allowed her thoughts to take such a dangerous turn, she wondered why he didn't have a woman, a wife. Even with the scar disfiguring what had once been a handsome face, he was a striking man. Cyrus Bergeron was everything most women looked for in a man, but he was always so alone. Perhaps it was by his own choice that he was a solitary man.

Nearly perfect as Cyrus was, he met all of her qualifications for potential husband but one— the most important. When she married again, *if* she married again, her husband would not be a man who lived by the gun. She'd lost one man to violence; losing another would surely kill her. Still, perhaps they could become friends again. She was beginning to think she needed friends in her life. Cyrus seemed a logical place to start.

"Hello," she said as she stepped onto the boardwalk.

Cyrus tipped his hat.

"Uncle Josiah would like you to come to supper tonight, if you're able." She shifted her books. They weren't heavy, but she'd been carrying them for a while.

Cyrus hesitated briefly before answering. "Sure."

"I think he wants to discuss building a new jail or something like that," she explained. "Besides, it's been a long time since you've had supper with us." In truth, she couldn't remember how long it had been. She remembered very little of the year after the war ended, the year Cyrus had come home without her Louis, the year she'd been widowed. She took a deep breath and closed her eyes briefly, little more than a long blink, as she willed her mind to return to thoughts of the weather and tomorrow's lesson and what they would have for supper.

"Yes, it has been a long time." Cyrus's voice was cautious, soft and easy; gentle.

"Six o'clock, then," she said as she re-arranged her books again.

Cyrus moved, barely shifting his weight in her direction. "Would you like me to carry those for you?"

"No," she said quickly, embarrassed that he thought such a small load was too much for her. He probably believed she'd been hinting all along for him to carry them for her, as if she wasn't capable of carrying her own small stack of books. "I don't need any help."

He returned to his post against the wall, stoic as always, untroubled by her curt refusal of assistance. She shivered once, deep and silent. Cyrus was a well-liked and effective sheriff, and an honored veteran of the war that had killed her husband. But he was also unbendingly hard and as tough as old leather. His eyes were too old for his face, and at times, like now, they were cold and emotionless. He hadn't been this way before the war; it had changed him, as it had changed her and everyone she knew.

"I should get home," she said as she backed away. "See you about six."

He didn't say anything as she turned and continued her short journey down the street. Aunt Ada would need her help with preparing supper, especially since she'd been feeling a tad poorly with that cold she'd been nursing.

She wondered, as she walked away, if Cyrus still liked apple pie.

The Scott Mercantile was a short distance north of the saloon, and Mrs. Scott was arranging a few things on a sidewalk display that included a table of notions, her broad hips swaying beneath a bright yellow skirt, her movements lively as if she felt the coming of spring as Roxanne did. As Roxanne stepped closer, she heard Mrs. Scott humming a gleeful tune.

Something caught Roxanne's eye and she stepped onto the boardwalk once again. Mrs. Scott said hello, but was immediately called inside to assist a customer. Just as well, Roxanne thought as she stood over a plank table of buttons and ribbons and lace. She wasn't in the mood for chitchat.

Spools of satin ribbons in bright colors were

arranged in a vibrant rainbow, and Roxanne balanced her books in one arm so she could reach out and touch a length of brilliant blue that caught just a hint of the afternoon sun and glimmered like a soft, tempting jewel. The length of blue was surrounded by other colors; emerald green, ruby red, a bright yellow and a soft pink.

How long had it been since she'd noticed color? She frowned as she fingered the blue ribbon. Years. Her life had been black and gray for so long, a bad dream she couldn't shake, a nightmare that stayed with her night after night, day after day. The bright blue ribbon slipped silkily beneath her fingers, inviting and beautiful.

Her heart beat too fast, and it had nothing to do with her brisk walk. Beautiful. This little bit of blue ribbon was *beautiful*. She hadn't seen beauty in anything in such a long time, she'd almost forgotten what it was like to simply admire a flower or a sunset or a bit of satin ribbon. For the past three years she'd drifted through her life in a daze, seeing nothing, wanting nothing. Was she waking up at last?

Did she want to?

Without moving from his post, Cyrus watched Roxanne. Johnson, the pitiable scum, was right. Roxanne Robinette was much too good for a man who was imperfect inside and out, who was scarred in body and in mind. He'd known this to be true as he'd watched over her for the past three years. Still, now and again he was assaulted by the most improper, impossible thoughts.

She seemed to be admiring something, lost in thought. With her head cocked to one side she stared raptly at an item on a table of odds and ends. He wondered what it was, wondered so hard that he almost stepped into the street to follow her path and discover what had grabbed her attention.

He didn't move.

She'd shuddered when he'd offered to carry her books, affirming what he already knew; she found him repulsive. He imagined it was the scar that appalled her, but it might be more. Perhaps she blamed him for failing to satisfy her whispered request as he'd prepared to march out of Paris in January of '62.

Watch over Louis, she'd whispered, her eyes wide and red from crying, her full lips trembling. She'd been a child, then. A bride, but still a child in his eyes. *I don't think he'll make a very good soldier. Don't let him get hurt.*

Cyrus had tried, and for years he'd been successful. He'd watched Louis's back, as the young man learned to be a good soldier. A fighter. A survivor. But in the end, in the final year, he'd failed.

Roxanne was too much a lady to voice her feelings of anger, to even hint at the fury that had to be in her heart. But Cyrus knew too well how he'd failed her. Surely she despised him.

Ah yes, his occasional impossible thoughts about Roxanne Robinette were just that. Impossible.

Chapter Two

The dining room in the Pierson house was as finely furnished as the rest of the large, elegant home. The long table and sturdy chairs were made of walnut, a gilt-framed mirror hung above the sideboard, and on the opposite side of the room hung a similarly framed portrait of a long-dead ancestor. The table was set with the best china and crystal, since they had company for supper, and the spring flowers in the center of the table had been picked and arranged in the porcelain vase by Roxanne herself, just an hour or so before Cyrus arrived.

Every now and again Roxanne caught Cyrus staring at the new blue ribbon in her hair. She wondered if he thought it disrespectful, too frivolous for a widow, inappropriate with her somber dress. She certainly couldn't tell what he was thinking by looking at him. There was no emotion at all on his face, not even when he caught Aunt Ada staring at the scar there. Twice.

Throughout dinner she had remained silent as Cyrus and Uncle Josiah discussed the need for a new Lamar County jail. They both knew the improvement was necessary, but it might be a while before the funds were available. Uncle Josiah had always been one for planning ahead.

They talked briefly about the new deputy sheriff who would arrive from Tennessee later in the week. Calvin Newberry had distant relatives in Paris and was coming here to settle. The relatives had recommended him for the job. Roxanne's mind was elsewhere; she cared nothing for jails or jailers, not tonight.

She cleared the table and carried in the apple pie she'd prepared that afternoon. It was still hot, and she protected her hands with a folded towel. The pie would be better after another hour or so of cooling, but this would have to do. She placed it in the center of the table and went to the sideboard for four dessert plates.

Before she could finish the simple task, Aunt Ada began to cough. She tried to contain it, but was quickly caught up in a violent coughing spell. Uncle Josiah helped his wife to her feet.

"She's got some cough medicine in her sitting room," Josiah said, his eyes on Ada's distorted face. "You two visit and we'll return shortly." Together, Ada, coughing spasmodically, and Josiah, supporting her lovingly, left the dining room.

All of a sudden a palpable awkwardness filled the air; a strained silence. Without Josiah to talk city business, and Ada to fill the empty pauses with bits of gossip, there was apparently nothing to be said. Roxanne sighed as she began to cut the pie. If she was going to wake up, if she was going to try to live again, she would need a friend or two.

"I hope you still like apple pie," she said as she carefully lifted a piece and set in on a plate. It steamed enticingly as she set it before Cyrus.

"Of course," he said quietly. "It looks wonderful."

She cut three more slices. "You might want to let it cool a few minutes," she said, sliding a piece onto her own plate. "If I'd known you were going to be here for supper I would have made it this morning, but Uncle Josiah didn't ask me to invite you until I was leaving for school."

As she took her seat, Cyrus lifted his eyes to her, following her every movement. "You made this?"

She nodded.

"Just because I was coming for supper?"

He seemed to have a hard time accepting the simple fact. "Yes, Cyrus," she said. Amazingly a small smile, a very small smile, teased the corners of her lips. "I made this apple pie just for you."

He lowered his eyes to the dessert. "Well,

thank you," he said softly. "It's been a long time since anyone made me an apple pie."

She desperately needed someone to talk to. Cyrus was sensible, and she could trust him to keep her musings to himself. He was not a gossip. In fact, she couldn't even imagine him at the barber shop or a saloon swapping tidbits of information with the other men of Paris. Her secrets would be safe with this man; she knew it.

He lifted his wine glass and took a sip.

"I want to get married," she blurted.

Cyrus apparently swallowed his wine the wrong way, for he immediately choked on the small sip. He coughed as viciously as Aunt Ada had, returning his wine glass to the table and leaning forward as he barked and shook.

Roxanne jumped from her seat and ran around the table to slap him on the back. He was so hard it was like slapping a brick house through a thin layer of cotton, so she whacked harder. Eventually, his coughing stopped and he very slowly lifted his head. She stepped back as he cleared his throat and rose to his feet.

"You want to do what?" he asked hoarsely. He didn't look so tough and mean at the moment, in spite of his narrowed eyes and hawk-like features. He had a nicely shaped, long nose and prominent cheekbones, one of which was marred by the long scar he'd brought home from the war. He still hadn't completely recovered from the choking spell, and his moss-green eyes watered as he stared down at her, ruining the fierce effect.

She realized, perhaps for the first time, that he was one of the few men in town who *could* stare down at her.

Oh, if Cyrus was taking the idea this hard, what would her aunt and uncle say? Damnation. Was she supposed to stay stuck in this terrible state forever? Lonely, grieving, never more than half-alive; the widow Roxanne Robinette who had nothing and no one, and never would.

She took a deep breath, for courage. "I want to get married," she said softly.

It wouldn't do for Ada and Josiah to return and hear this conversation; she wasn't quite ready to have the discussion with them. "Why don't we step outside for a few minutes?" They wouldn't be overheard there. Cyrus looked baffled and vaguely uneasy, but she didn't regret confiding in him. "You look like you could use a breath of fresh air, and by the time we return the pie will be cool enough to eat."

"Sure," Cyrus said softly. Very softly.

He followed her into the parlor and through the door there to step onto a small porch that overlooked the garden at the side of the house. There was a rocker there, where Aunt Ada usually spent an hour or so of her afternoon when the weather was nice, and a long bench that was barely protected by the overhang. Roxanne sat on the bench, leaving the more comfortable rocker for Cyrus. Instead of taking that seat he lowered himself to the opposite end of the bench, barely two feet away.

His cheek, harsh and jagged even in soft moonlight, faced her as she turned her head to look at his profile. She wanted to reach out and touch the scar, to ask him what had happened, but she did no such thing.

"Do you think Louis would be terribly disappointed if I decided to marry again?" She kept talking, not ready to hear the answer just yet. "You knew him better than anyone, perhaps even better than me after those years away from home. He mentioned you so often in his letters, and even before the two of you left for the war he admired you greatly."

There was a short pause before Cyrus answered. "He wanted you to be happy," he said softly, almost too softly.

Roxanne studied the garden by moonlight, as Cyrus did. "I won't ever be happy again," she said pragmatically. "I don't expect to be *happy*."

Out of the corner of her eye, she saw Cyrus turn his head. She could feel him watching her, but didn't turn her head to meet his gaze.

"Why do you want to get married?"

All her frustration, all her indecision, rose to the surface. "I can't live here forever, in someone else's house. I can't spend the rest of my life teaching other people's children. Aunt Ada and Uncle Josiah have been so kind to me, and they would never say they don't want me here, but I always feel out of place, as if I don't belong. I want my own home. I could buy a small house," she added, "or rent a room, but I don't want that either." She turned her head to find Cyrus staring at her. "I want a family, children, a home. I'm ready to get on with my life."

Again he paused before speaking. "Louis would want that for you," he whispered.

It was what she needed to hear, and maybe Cyrus knew that. Relief flooded her, rushed through her veins and her heart and her mind. She closed her eyes and drank in the cool night air.

"So," Cyrus continued. "Who's the lucky man?"

Her eyes flew open. Knowing what she wanted from life was one thing; specifics were another. "I don't know," she admitted. "A farmer, maybe, or a merchant. I'd like to stay in or near Paris, but. . . ." there were so many memories here, good and bad. Maybe she'd be better off without them. "Perhaps I should think about moving. There are mail order bride services—"

"Absolutely not!" Cyrus exploded, jumping to his feet as if he could no longer stand to sit.

After the soft voice he'd used all evening, the shout startled Roxanne so that she twitched. "It's just an idea."

"A damned bad one," Cyrus said just a bit more calmly as he reclaimed his seat. "You can't climb on a stage and take off for some unknown parts and some unknown man." She could hear the anger and frustration in his voice. "You might find yourself married to some . . . some. . . ." He seemed unable to continue.

"You're right," she conceded. "That is a foolish idea."

They sat in comfortable silence for a moment longer, both of them looking over the garden and enjoying the crispness of the air. Cyrus took several long, deep breaths before he spoke again.

"Why a merchant or a farmer?" he asked in a low voice.

Roxanne closed her eyes and leaned her head back slightly. "More than anything, I want to feel safe," she whispered. "I need a husband who leads a gentle life. No guns, no swords." She swallowed hard. "There can be no more war in my life. I lost Louis to violence, and even though I don't expect to love any other man the way I loved Louis, I won't risk losing another husband to the gun." *I couldn't bear it.*

Cyrus had no response to her reasoning, and for a moment longer they simply enjoyed the night. Roxanne lifted her face to accept a cool, gentle breeze. Now that she'd spoken the words aloud they made even more sense to her. Louis was gone and he could not be replaced, but she was ready to live again. It was time.

Cyrus smelled blood, heard cries loud and faint reaching above the clash of steel and the occasional explosion of gunfire. He fought the

Yankee with his bayonet, as he had fought the Yanks that had come before, slashing and stabbing, fighting to stay alive.

This battle for ground in Tennessee had quickly turned to hand-to-hand combat, vicious and desperate. There was no conscious thought as he felled one Yankee after another, just instinct and luck.

As the Yankee fell, wounded but not dead, Cyrus turned to Louis. The boy should've been right behind him, dammit, but he was far away, fighting hand-to-hand near the ditch the Yankees had been cowering in. Cyrus cursed as he turned and ran. Louis was a much better soldier than he'd been three years ago, but he still had a tendency to get lost in battle. The boy thought too much; he didn't always trust his instincts.

The Yankee who fought Louis was bigger and stronger; he was impossibly big and strong, a beast who couldn't be beaten. Cyrus ran faster, but he couldn't reach him. The faster he ran the further away Louis and the Yankee beast were. His heart beat so hard he could feel it, and all of a sudden he knew what would happen next. The beast would kill Louis, and then he would kill Cyrus. It always ended that way.

His feet were like lead, and no matter how hard he tried his movements were slow and difficult, like he ran through molasses; cold molasses that impeded his every movement and filled his mouth and his eyes and his ears. The sounds of battle faded and finally disappeared altogether, until there were only the three of them. Louis, fighting bravely, the Yankee, confident and aggressive, and Cyrus, running.

It seemed, for a moment, that he would reach Louis in time. Maybe this battle would end differently. A spark of hope worked its way into Cyrus's heart. Yes, he would reach Louis in time, kill the beast, and the nightmare would be over.

The Yankee slashed his bayonet fiercely, and in that instant Cyrus's hopes died and he knew he would be late again. Louis became still, and one hand settled over his ravaged midsection. It was a killing wound; they all knew it. Louis, Cyrus, the Yankee. Still Cyrus threw himself in front of Louis to take on the Yankee himself and in that instant, an instant that chilled him in his dreams and his memories, the bayonet that had killed Louis slashed up and across Cyrus's face.

Together he and Louis fell into the ditch. The long, slow fall stole Cyrus's breath. His eyes filled with blood that blinded him.

This was where he usually woke up. He knew, by this time, that he was trapped in a nightmare, a familiar nightmare formed of part memory and part nurtured fear. Always, as he fell he woke up. God, he wanted to wake up.

He continued to fall, and he and Louis landed softly in the ditch, not two feet from a dead Yankee.

"Cyrus?" Louis whispered as Cyrus rolled over to face his dying friend.

"Hang on," he said, lying and hoping and praying. "It'll be all right."

Cyrus made himself look down at the wound that would kill Louis Robinette in a matter of minutes. The wound was too deep, the blood flowing too fast. He laid his hand over the wound in a hopeless effort to staunch the bleeding.

"Promise me," Louis whispered, and then his voice died away.

"Anything," Cyrus said, willing the boy to live. "Anything."

"Take care of Roxanne. Tell her I was thinking of her when I died." He took a labored breath. "Make sure she's happy. I don't want her to . . . to. . . ."

"I know," Cyrus said.

"I was going to watch over her always, but now it's up to you, Cyrus. Take care of her."

"I will."

"Make sure she's happy."

"I will."

"Roxanne should have everything she wants."

What Roxanne wanted was this boy she'd grown up with and learned to love, this boy who had made her his wife while they were both little more than children. Goddammit, he didn't want to go home and tell her Louis was dead, that her husband had been thinking of her with his last breath.

But he couldn't say any of that to Louis. "She will," he promised. "Roxanne will have everything she wants."

Cyrus came awake instantly, sitting up in bed and taking a deep breath that burned his lungs. Drenched in sweat, his heart pounded fiercely. His blood ran icy cold.

He hadn't had the dream in months, had even hoped, once or twice, that it was gone for good. Tonight's conversation with Roxanne had triggered it, no doubt, with her concerns for what Louis would think about the fact that she wanted to take a husband again.

Running trembling fingers through his sweat-dampened hair, he left the bed. There would be no more sleep for him tonight. He wouldn't take the chance that the nightmare would be waiting for him on the other side of closed eyes.

Finding his way around his sparsely furnished one-room house was no problem. Too many nights he'd paced in the dark, until he knew his way well. Complete dark, eyes closed, it didn't matter. There was never a single misstep.

He paced now, toward the faint cast of moonglow in the front window, and then away. Past the cold fireplace and to the table and single chair where he ate his meals. To the pantry where he stored his foodstuffs and whiskey.

By the time he'd poured himself a short glass of whiskey, the trembling had stopped. The dream hadn't faded though; it never did.

He'd never told Roxanne that Louis had been thinking of her when he'd died. She'd been so damned sad for so long, it seemed cruel; not a comfort at all. He'd never been able to make himself walk up to her, look into her desolate eyes, and tell her how Louis had been killed, that his last thoughts had been of her. He certainly couldn't tell her now, as she was finally thinking of moving forward, of taking another husband.

While he'd failed in that request, he'd taken the other very seriously. He watched over Roxanne, made sure she was safe, anyway. He couldn't do much about the *happy* part. His secret guardianship was a duty he took as seriously as his job of sheriff, was more a calling than a duty, actually. He'd watched Roxanne cry and grieve, seen her pull deeper and deeper into her shell. He'd learned every nuance of her graceful motions, memorized every line of her face; the deep blue eyes, the arch of her eyebrows, the beauty of her high cheekbones and the fullness of her lips. He knew, by looking at that face for a split second, if she was having a good day or a bad one.

It had only been in the past few months that she had as many good days as bad ones. He should've known that eventually she would want more from life than living with her mother's sister, Ada, and Ada's husband.

But he hadn't expected this. Married! Dammit, he didn't like this development. He didn't like it one bit. He poured another splash of whiskey into his glass, his last for the night, and sat by the window in the main room of his small house so that moonlight fell on him and chased away the suffocating darkness of the night.

From here he could see the Pierson house, stately and majestic, surrounded by tall trees and well-kept gardens; a vegetable garden, an herb garden, a flower garden. Josiah had been insistent on adding lots of outdoor living space as well, including a large rear porch, the smaller side porch where Cyrus had sat with Roxanne a few hours earlier, and a couple of semicircular upstairs balconies that curved in an almost Italian style. One of those balconies was just outside Roxanne's bedroom, and while the leaves of a tall oak tree hid half of that space from view, he could see a portion of that balcony right now; it was one of the reasons he'd bought this particular house.

When had he become so completely obsessed with her?

He'd gone to war and left behind a young, scared, wide-eyed girl, and returned to a beautiful, desolate, solemn-eyed woman he watched over with great diligence. When he'd marched to war she had not been his, she'd been Louis's new bride. When he'd come home she had not been his, she'd been Louis's grieving widow. But somehow, in the past three years, he'd begun to think of Roxanne as *his*.

Any man, given the circumstance, might think on occasion of impossible kisses, and on a good night dream of having her in his bed. Any man might find a strange comfort in just looking at her face, in wondering what it would feel like to hold and comfort her on those bad days, to kiss her with abandon on the good ones.

He didn't dwell on his feelings overmuch. They weren't important in the scheme of things; they probably weren't even real. And even if they were it didn't matter. Roxanne wanted a husband, a kind, handsome, *safe* man. A stray thought flitted thought his mind, but he quickly dismissed it. A scarred lawman who couldn't shake violent dreams of war didn't meet any of her qualifications. She wanted a farmer or a merchant, someone who would be there for her forever, father her children, build a stable and loving home with her.

By God, Roxanne would have what she wanted. He'd promised Louis.

Like a wispy figment of his imagination from a kinder dream, Roxanne stepped onto the balcony. He wondered if a nightmare had awakened her, too, or if she simply couldn't sleep. So many nights he'd seen her step onto the balcony, had watched her sit there for hours, still as a statue. There had been fewer of those nights of late, as she began to heal.

She sat, as she always did, on the floor of the balcony, her hands gripping the wrought iron railing, her face resting against a bar. Even from this distance and by scant moonlight, he could see the white of her nightdress, the dark mass of her loosened hair falling over her shoulders.

He knew why he was wide awake at an hour long past night and not yet morning, but what kept Roxanne from sleep?

* * *

The bars in her hands and against her face were cool, almost cold, and the air that had been comfortably chilly earlier now had a bite that was anything but comfortable. Still, she didn't move.

Torn between the past and the future, she felt as if she didn't belong anywhere. There was no special place for her, no true home, no one person who truly needed her.

If only Louis had lived. . . . How many nights had she sat right here and begun her musings with those words? If only Louis had lived.

Louis Robinette had been an important part of her life from the day she'd come to Paris to live with her aunt and uncle. She'd been twelve at the time, and still grieving for her father. She sighed and closed her eyes. How much of her life had she spent grieving for the men she loved?

Louis had been her friend first. When they'd first talked about marriage . . . so young, too young . . . they'd planned a simple life on a farm near Paris, where they'd live comfortably and have lots of babies.

Her chums at school had been horrified when she confided in them. They all wanted adventure, romance, passion. Roxanne had only smiled at their protests. She was perfectly content to have her life with Louis ahead of her. What she wanted, what she needed, was a simple life, a man who was her best friend, and a family of her own. It was a life her father had not been able to give his only child, after his wife's death. Roxanne remembered too well moving from place to place, watching her father grow old before his time, until he died and left her to his late wife's sister, Ada Pierson.

Louis had been kind, familiar; she knew him so well. Their life was well planned, stretching before them with nothing but blue skies and happiness. Louis would farm and Roxanne would have babies. They would grow old together as they had grown up together; friends always. There was such warmth and security in those simple plans, they'd soothed Roxanne's heart. If not for the war they would have waited another two years to marry, but when it had come upon them everything changed.

For once, she didn't cry as she thought of this. She'd spent too many nights crying over what would never be, tearing her heart out over a thousand *what ifs*.

Down the street a short way Cyrus's brick home stood. Square and plain and well-kept, it was a nice little house on a small lot. She looked at the small square window near the front door, imagining Cyrus sleeping deeply somewhere beyond. Her memory of him wasn't faulty, she was certain. He *had* been her friend, and Louis's too, as much as a man could be a friend to two inseparable fifteen-year-old youngsters. Her first memory of him was as he'd chased away fat, greasy, stupid-eyed Rufus Russell, who'd decided to pick a fight with Louis in the middle of the square.

What had happened? It had been so long ago. All she could remember was being scared, Louis trying to force her to hide behind him, and then Cyrus Bergeron, a newly appointed deputy sheriff, appearing out of nowhere to take on the young man who'd been harassing them.

When Rufus had taken a swing at Cyrus, Cyrus had simply stepped out of the way, moving so quickly he amazed them all. Especially Rufus, who'd tried again; and failed again. Rufus had picked up a rock, but before he could throw it, Cyrus had plucked it from his hand. In the dark, Roxanne smiled. Oh, the look on Rufus's face had been priceless.

Cyrus had never laid a hand on Rufus who was, for all his size and bluster, just sixteen years old. Eventually the bully had run off crying. Her smile died. Rufus Russell had died in the war, too. Pneumonia, she'd heard.

After that day, she and Louis had considered Cyrus their special friend. They fed him fried chicken and apple pie when there was a church picnic, and whenever they were in town they made a point of stopping by to say hello. After all, Cyrus didn't have any family. No parents living, no wife, no family at all. Roxanne, who adored her aunt and uncle and had Louis forever at her side, had thought that very sad.

Now here she was, nine years later, still living with her aunt and uncle, marking time.

While Louis had been away she'd prayed, every night, for him to come home to her, and she'd been so certain he *would* come home. So certain they'd have the life they'd so carefully planned.

The lack of a real home left a hole in her heart. Oh, she did love Ada and Josiah, but she was forever conscious that they had taken her in, that she didn't really belong here. She wanted to fill her heart and her soul with her own family, to make her own special place in the world.

Maybe it wasn't too late for her to try again.

"I can make a family," she whispered to the night. "I will."

Chapter Three

Every afternoon on her way home from school Roxanne saw Cyrus. She'd noticed him on the day after her confession that she wished to marry, standing on the boardwalk casually. She wondered if he'd always been there as she passed, standing in front of the saloon or the saddlery, Fannie Rowland's dress shop or Uncle Josiah's furniture store. If so she'd passed unaware, as she'd passed most of the past three years unaware.

In the days since, Cyrus usually said hello and then asked how her day had gone. Sometimes he would walk part of the way home with her, as she told him about her students at the school. He never said much, and when he did his conversation usually consisted of a gentle prodding to keep her talking about school, or else a harmless comment about the weather. Other days he just watched her pass by, muttering a soft, friendly greeting as she walked on.

After just a couple of days she began to look forward to seeing Cyrus on the way home, and over the weekend she'd missed her walks through town. She'd actually searched for him, unsuccessfully, at church.

Today as she walked down the street she was searching for him still, peering into open shop doors as she passed by, glancing into long, narrow alleyways. It wasn't important that she see Cyrus, not really, and yet somehow she felt it *was* important. Her day would be incomplete without his comments on the weather and her best, or worst, students.

Finally he appeared just down the street, stepping from the barbershop freshly shaved and with a crisp hair cut. Roxanne experienced an unexpected wave of relief when she saw him. In his everyday dark twill pants, white shirt, and leather vest and polished boots, he was quite striking and masculine. He stood straight as an arrow, unbending and powerful as if nothing could ever make him sway or lose his balance, not even the most terrifying twister.

Long legged and broad shouldered, he simply cut a fine figure. He always had, hadn't he?

Settling her eyes on Cyrus, she suddenly felt better; lighter. What might have been a smile tugged at her lips, and if she wasn't mistaken the blood in her veins became warmer. Significantly warmer. Her step increased just slightly, as if she couldn't wait to reach him. As if she were *anxious* to be close to him.

The hint of a smile faded and her heart skipped a beat. She purposely slowed her step. Oh, she couldn't possibly like Cyrus that way! He was her friend, nothing more. A lawman would make an entirely unsuitable husband.

"Good afternoon," she said, as if she hadn't fully expected to see him on her way home, as if running into him was nothing more than a mildly pleasant surprise.

"Good afternoon." With a casual, almost lazy step, Cyrus joined her on the street, setting his wide-brimmed brown hat on his head. "You'd better hurry on home," he said. "Looks like rain."

At least Cyrus wasn't acting like a fool! Mentioning the weather, he steered the conversation down a safe and normal path, as always.

She cast a wary glance to the darkening skies. Spring storms could be violent and heavy, flooding the streets and the ravines, driving everyone indoors for hours or even days. Then again, sometimes the rains fell soft and sweet, watering the flowers and grass and clearing the air. It was impossible to tell what kind of storm this one would be. She increased her pace, just a little, and so did Cyrus.

Their long strides matched perfectly, quick and easy and comfortable. What a pleasure to walk with someone this way, unfettered and unchecked. For Roxanne, walking with Aunt Ada was always a chore, since shortening her stride to match that of her short-legged aunt took great restraint. Sometimes, some days, restraint was the last thing on Roxanne's mind. She thought of how perfectly her stride and Cyrus's matched, and dismissed her earlier foolish reaction. He was a friend, and that was all he could ever be. She looked forward to seeing him because he was her *friend*; nothing more.

They reached the end of the business district, and she waited for Cyrus to excuse himself as he usually did. A quick goodbye, a remembered appointment or chore usually came to him about here. But today he stayed with her, as the scenery changed from bustling businesses to quiet residences.

He cleared his throat.

"Merilee Smith is having a party tomorrow evening," he said softly. "Are you planning to go?"

She remembered receiving the invitation, wistfully recalling parties she and Louis had attended together, and then firmly setting the invitation and the memories aside. "No," she said simply. With anyone else she would've felt compelled to offer an excuse, but not with Cyrus. He understood; somehow she knew this to be true.

"Too bad," he turned his head to nod to Mrs. Upshaw, who was sitting on her front porch snapping beans. "If you're determined to marry, that would be as good a place as any to start looking."

"Oh," she breathed. "I hadn't thought of that." Deciding that she desired marriage once again, and actually doing something about it, were two very different prospects. She knew what she wanted: a fresh start, a new beginning, a break from the past. Where that fresh start would come from she had no idea.

She cut a quick glance to the man at her side. Cyrus would make someone a wonderful husband one day, but he was not the right man for her. There was too much of the past in his eyes, too much pain to match her own. He needed a fresh start himself.

He looked a little dismal, at the moment. There was no smile, no joy, no . . . ah, she knew this look too well. He really did need a fresh start.

"Why the long face?" she asked, leaning over slightly to catch a glimpse of his eyes.

"What?" He turned to her and raised his eyebrows slightly.

"It's just that you look a little . . . downhearted. That's all."

"I'm fine," he said absently, and she got the distinct impression that she'd embarrassed him somehow.

Friend or not, Cyrus apparently had clear and distinct limits. They could talk about the weather, their jobs, and her plans. His own personal life was apparently off limits. For now.

Roxanne heard the slowly approaching hoofbeats long before she and Cyrus reached the next corner, but thought nothing of it until a golden horse came into view from behind a tall growth of flowering bushes. The animal was extraordinary in size and color and beauty, but was nothing to compare to the magnificence of the man sitting on its back. She stopped dead in her tracks.

The man was as golden as the horse, with his softly curling blond hair and tanned skin. Broad shouldered and tall he held himself erect, like a Greek god leisurely surveying the kingdom before him. Apparently lost in thought, he didn't look to the side to see her and Cyrus standing there, but kept his eyes straight ahead as he rode through the intersection. His profile was startlingly handsome; nose razor straight, cheekbones and jaw chiseled and still warmly soft, lips perfectly shaped. As he passed, the wind caught his thick golden curls and lifted them gently, as caressing fingers might.

"Oh, my," she whispered as the man continued on his slow journey and all she could see were his broad back and golden head. "He's absolutely *beautiful*."

When the golden man was gone from sight she looked at Cyrus, embarrassed by her childish behavior. Staring at a stranger! Goodness, she'd practically ogled him. She lowered her eyes. What was wrong with her? First Cyrus and now this total stranger.

Roxanne thought of the blue ribbon, the way

the color had called to her. She was waking up at last, seeing beauty and brightness and *feeling* in ways she'd never thought to feel again. But this was ridiculous! If Cyrus was ashamed of her or embarrassed for her he didn't show it; but then, he always kept a tight rein on his emotions.

"Well, he is rather beautiful, you must admit," she said as she stepped forward, resuming her journey home.

"If you say so," Cyrus answered. There was a touch of bitter humor in his voice, and she remembered that he had once been beautiful himself, before the war had damaged his face and stolen the light from his eyes. He was still beautiful, in a way that only a hard man could be. She wouldn't tell him so, of course.

"Do you know that man?" she asked lightly. "I haven't seen him around Paris before." She would've remembered, surely, even in a dazed state of mind.

There was a short pause, long enough for her to glance warily to the side, before Cyrus answered. "That's my new deputy, Calvin Newberry. He arrived late yesterday."

"Oh," she said, hearing the disappointment in her own voice, feeling her heart sink. Again she reminded herself that a deputy husband would be completely unacceptable.

In the span of a quarter-hour, two men had made her heart leap, both of them lawmen. She resigned herself to the fact that it had only happened because she'd been thinking so much on her prospects for marriage. Other men would make her heart leap and bring a smile to her face, wouldn't they? She was certain they would. There would be no lawmen in her life; no guns.

She was almost home. Cyrus had never walked quite this far with her before, but she was glad of his company today. She felt anxious, unsettled, as if something wondrous and frightening waited around the next corner. Or perhaps around the *last* corner.

"He won't be a deputy long, I imagine," Cyrus said casually. "Once Calvin's certain Paris is the place he wants to settle, he plans to look for a parcel of farmland in the area."

Her heart lurched. "A farm?"

"That's what he said."

She stopped at the walk that led to the front door of her home, laying her hand on the low wrought-iron gate that swung open on flowering bushes and lush grass. A single drop of rain hit her face.

"Thank you for walking me home, Cyrus."

He shrugged off her thanks and glanced quickly to the blackening sky. "Calvin will be at the party tomorrow night," he said. "The gathering is meant, in part, to welcome him to Paris."

Another drop hit her arm, soaking through her cotton blouse. "Well, perhaps it would be rude of me not to attend, in that case."

He took a deep breath and exhaled slowly. "If

you'd like, I'll come by and we can walk over together."

The beginnings of a smile tugged at her lips again. Cyrus was her friend, perhaps her best friend. She'd closed herself off from others for so long, but he was here for her. Perhaps he always had been, as she'd blindly passed him by. "And you'll introduce me to your new deputy, I suppose?" A few more drops fell, but she didn't run from them.

"If you'd like," he said, his voice low, almost a whisper.

She nodded once. Yes, Calvin Newberry was beautiful, but he offered much more than that. He was new here, and looking at him didn't cause an assault of memories that were more painful than good. She would never look at him and wonder if he'd seen Louis fight and die, never talk to him of old times that would never come again and be assaulted by that sharp pain in her heart that sometimes came when she least expected it. She was trying so hard to leave her former life, the good and the bad, in the past where it belonged. Perhaps Calvin Newberry, or someone like him, was her future. There was only one way to find out.

The rain fell softly and steadily as Cyrus reached the Lamar County Jail. He was soaked to the skin, cold, and angrier than he had a right to be as he threw open the door and stepped into the front room. All he wanted was to make it to his office and close the door.

But of course it wasn't to be that easy. Three deputies talked and laughed loudly in the front room, and Calvin Newberry was one of them. The other two were familiar men, old friends, good deputies. Will Haller, short and stocky and compact in build, gave Cyrus a crooked smile and a quick hello. John Branden, a few inches taller than Will and skinny as a fence post, nodded his head in Cyrus's direction.

Cyrus ignored them both and stared at the newest addition to his staff.

This was what Roxanne wanted, he reminded himself as he slammed the door behind him. Beauty and light. Safety and security. If he could give it to her he should. It's what Louis would've wanted, what Roxanne deserved.

"Calvin," he said as the new deputy lifted his head. "My office."

Calvin followed obediently, only tripping over his own big feet once on the short walk down the hall from the front room to the sheriff's office. Cyrus didn't see what happened but he heard the stumble from the big man behind him, the clatter of big booted feet against the plank floor, the surprised exhalation of breath. He'd seen Calvin trip over his own feet enough in the past day to know what had happened.

A clumsy deputy. It was just as well that Calvin didn't plan to make peacemaking a career; he was likely to shoot himself in the foot at any time.

"Have a seat," Cyrus said as he took off his wet hat and reached for the bottom drawer of the small dresser at the back of his office. He'd spent many nights here, and was always prepared with a change of clothes and a washstand and towels. There had been too many wet, cold nights during the war when he'd only dreamed of a dry towel and warm clothes.

Funny, how little things could become so monumentally important. After spending days in clothes that refused to dry, marching on wet feet, watching the rainwater drip off a hat before his very eyes, a man could begin to think he'd never be dry again. He could feel every drop of cold rain on his already drenched skin, every brush of wet fabric across his flesh as he moved, until it seemed like his skin was no longer a part of him. He'd dream of a warm fire and a sturdy roof and dry warm clothes, hoping those fantasies would get him through another wet day.

Cyrus shook off the bad memories. For the moment he had to be satisfied to dry himself with the towel. The change of clothes could wait a few more minutes.

Calvin took the seat before Cyrus's desk, fidgeting nervously. Maybe the kid thought he'd already done something wrong; maybe he thought his career as sheriff's deputy was going to be even shorter than he'd planned.

"What do you think of Paris so far?" Cyrus asked, trying to maintain a purely conversational tone.

Calvin nodded his head once, barely moving, as his pale blue eyes fastened onto Cyrus's face. A hint of fear flickered in those eyes. Cyrus wondered if he really made such a fearsome sight. Maybe so.

"The people have been right nice," Calvin said in his melodious Tennessee accent that had just a hint of the hillbilly in it. "And I surely do like my room at the boarding house. It's a right big town, though," he muttered with a shake of his head. "I got myself lost this afternoon. Took a wrong turn somewheres and ended up taking the long way 'round to the square."

Cyrus nodded as if he understood and was sympathetic, but in reality he withheld a disgusted groan. Paris was a good-sized town, but it would be difficult to get lost between the boarding house and the square. Apparently not so difficult for Calvin.

"Newberry," Cyrus said as he stepped around the desk to close the door to his office. It wouldn't do for this conversation to be overheard. "I understand you don't plan to be a deputy for very long."

Calvin shot to his feet and spun to face Cyrus. The two men stood nose to nose, eye to eye. While Calvin was a bit broader in the shoulders, Cyrus figured they'd be a fair match in a fist fight.

"Now, I sure enough made that clear in my letter, Sheriff," Calvin said defensively. "But just because I don't plan to be a deputy forever that doesn't mean I can't do the job while I'm here."

Cyrus gestured impatiently with his hand. "Sit down," he growled. "I'm not trying to get rid of you." *Yet*.

Calvin carefully resumed his seat, and Cyrus took his own seat across the desk.

"You plan to be a farmer, I understand."

Calvin nodded once. "Yep. All the Newberrys were farmers. My daddy and my granddaddy and my great-granddaddy." All of a sudden the handsome young man looked deadly serious. "Things in Tennessee ain't what they used to be, and after Ma passed on I figured a new place and new people was just what I needed."

Cyrus understood all too well the craving for a new place and new people, the need to turn your back on the past and ignore it. Calvin was lucky; he could do just that.

There was no reason to beat around the bush. "I imagine you've given some thought to getting married, eventually."

Calvin blushed, his cheeks turning bright pink as he cast his eyes down. "Well, yessir. I'll need a wife, and younguns to help work the farm. A home ain't complete without a woman and lots of younguns."

While Cyrus had to admit he didn't see this young man as *beautiful*, as Roxanne did, there was an air of innocence and hope about him.

His dreams were simple; a farm, a wife and younguns. Goddammit, Calvin and Roxanne would be perfect for one another.

"Got anybody in mind yet?"

Calvin, slow as he was, finally became suspicious. He narrowed those startling blue eyes. "Are you figurin' on doing some matchmakin,' Sheriff?"

"I usually try to keep my nose out of other people's personal business," Cyrus muttered.

Calvin answered with a wide smile. "But not this time, right? Well shoot, there's no reason to be bashful about the dealings. Just tell me her name and point me in the right direction, and I'll be happy to spend a little time with her and see if we suit."

A matchmaker. If this was right, why did a knot sit heavily in his gut? It didn't take much pondering to come up with the answer. Even though Roxanne wasn't his and never would be, he was reluctant to let her go. Watching over her, dreaming about her, had become too much a part of his life. He dismissed his foolishness and remembered his promise to Louis. Even more clearly, he recalled the spark of sweet delight on Roxanne's face as she'd talked about a family of her own. Safety. Security. Beauty.

"Her name is Roxanne Robinette, and she'll be at the party tomorrow night. I'll introduce you there."

Calvin's grin widened as he stood. "I do

appreciate this. Why, just imagine it. The sheriff hisself fixin' me up with a woman."

There was nothing disrespectful about the way the words were said, but Cyrus felt compelled to lean over his desk threateningly. "Roxanne is a fine lady, not a woman I'm fixing you up with," he said in low tones. "You'll meet her, and if you think she might suit you as a wife, we'll go from there. She is not a woman to be taken lightly."

Calvin's smile faded and he took a step backward. "I understand. I didn't mean no disrespect. . . ." Another step and he caught his boot on the back leg of the chair he'd been sitting in. A shuffle, a prance, and a moment later Calvin landed on his backside. The whole room shook.

He popped up quickly. "I look forward to meeting this lady," he said as he backed away from the desk.

Cyrus stifled a groan. "Do you dance?" he asked as Calvin reached the closed door.

Calvin flashed another of those brilliant smiles. "Why, I'm a right fine dancer, if I do say so myself."

When Calvin was gone Cyrus dropped into his chair, wet clothes and all.

Roxanne sat on the balcony long after dark had fallen. Her feet were curled beneath her and her cheek rested against cool wrought iron. This had become her place of peace, a small corner of the world to call her own. While Ada and Josiah slept, while all of Paris slept, this was her refuge, her special place to sit and think and ponder and dream.

Tonight her thoughts and dreams took a new and startlingly unexpected direction. Apparently waking up from her long sleep included noticing men, remembering that she was a woman. The very sight of Calvin Newberry had been somehow exciting, and she could still envision his striking form as he rode past, unaware that she watched.

Calvin Newberry wasn't the only man on her mind. In the past week she'd thought of Cyrus so often it was downright frightening. This afternoon when she'd seen him step from the barber shop she'd actually felt a rush of excitement, a most improper thrill that had taken her by surprise.

She wondered what it would be like to have a man touch her again, even innocently. The shield she'd built around herself was an effective one; it kept everyone at bay. No one held her hand, or placed his arm around her shoulder, or kissed her. What would Cyrus's hand feel like in hers? Rough and strong, she imagined, hard and powerful and still . . . soft. His arm around her shoulder would be sheltering, wouldn't it? Warm and all-encompassing, protective and intimate. And if he were to kiss her. . . .

With a few deep breaths and a strength of determination, she forced her inappropriate thoughts of Cyrus aside; dismissed them as nonsense.

Be honest, she thought, *your reluctance to even consider accepting this afternoon's fleeting tenderness and this evening's fantasy about Cyrus as real and true isn't entirely because he's a lawman. In part, yes, but not entirely.*

Cyrus was and always would be too connected to the past, to Louis; that long-ago day in the square, the picnics, watching the two of them march off together. She thought of Louis when she looked at Cyrus, and dammit, thinking of Louis hurt. Not as much as it once had, but still she felt the pain for what she'd lost.

Her eyes drifted closed as she tried to shut out the memories. She couldn't spend the rest of her life grieving for all she didn't have. A new beginning waited out there for her, somewhere. Maybe it rested in Calvin Newberry's hands, perhaps it would come with someone she hadn't yet met.

She would never love again, but there had to be something more to life than this. If she had to will away the past, she would. If she had to will away these strange thoughts of Cyrus, she would do that, too.

Chapter Four

The Smiths always threw the best parties. It had been years since Roxanne had been to a social gathering at the grand home, and in the old days it had been Merilee's mother-in-law acting as hostess. She remembered. How well she remembered.

Early in January of 1862, Hank Smith had gone to war with the Ninth Texas Infantry, along with Louis and Cyrus. A minié ball had torn through his hip and nearly killed him in the same battle that had killed Louis.

He'd come home to his lovely wife, Merilee Ashworth Smith, and a daughter he had never seen, a child who had been born eight months after he'd marched away from home. Not long after his return he'd taken over the Smith family business, a saw mill just outside Paris.

Linda Jones

A tall, lean man with a prominent Adam's apple and ears just slightly too large for his thin face, Hank walked with a pronounced limp and a cane, and always would. Merilee was all peaches and cream, short and shapely and fair, and she doted on her husband and her children. They made such a perfect pair it was sometimes painful for Roxanne to watch them; the way they looked at one another, the way they held their children. It reminded her of everything she'd lost.

Tonight there was plenty offered in the way of food and drink, on tables scattered inside and outside the big red-brick house. Lots of people, everyone important in town and a few faces Roxanne didn't recognize, were in attendance. They milled throughout the large house and past open double doors at the back, and visited on the lawn by the dying light of day. They wore their very best. The women had styled their tresses elaborately and the men had polished their boots and slicked back their hair. It wasn't Paris, France, by any stretch of the imagination, but the people of Paris, Texas, held their own.

A few of the party-goers, unaccustomed to seeing the widow Roxanne Robinette in a social situation, stared as she and Cyrus entered the house together. Even though she was tempted to literally lean on her escort for support she resisted the urge. They said their hellos, and soon she and Cyrus were just a part of the crowd.

Roxanne fidgeted, picking nervously at the overskirt of her dark plum-colored dress. She wished Aunt Ada and Uncle Josiah had been able to attend. Unfortunately Aunt Ada's cold, which was better but still an annoyance, had kept them both at home.

Now that she was here her mind was filled with *should'ves*. She should've worn gray or black. She should've come dressed in widow's weeds with her hair pulled severely back, instead of arranged in thick curls atop her head.

She should've stayed home.

Cyrus was unusually handsome this evening, dressed in a nice black suit and a white shirt that was stark against his tanned neck and face. She stood close enough to study the smoothness of his freshly shaved jaw, the taut muscles in his neck, the precise cut of his dark hair. As always, he had an air of one who was in command, of a man who could handle any situation. He wore his silver star on a vest beneath the black jacket, and when he moved just so it peeked out. Women stared admiringly, now and again, and with good reason. Cyrus seemed not to notice.

She usually tried diligently not to stare at the scar on his face, but tonight she found it didn't bother her at all. The mark on his cheek wasn't a symbol of anything evil or disheartening, it was just a scar. Over time it had become a part of who he was, a feature of his face as surely as his nose was.

Twice he had started to walk her over to Calvin Newberry and make introductions, but both times she'd stopped him, tugging on his arm and backing away. He followed her silent directions obediently, perhaps understanding that she wasn't ready. If the knots in her stomach were any indication, she might never be ready. Besides, Calvin was surrounded by a bevy of adoring young women, some of them Roxanne's own students. She would not make a fool of herself in front of the entire town, would not have her students laughing at her behind her back.

After saying hello to several old friends, she and Cyrus piled two plates with meats and bread and vegetables and found a place to sit, a rather private table at a corner of the brick patio. The secluded spot was just right for her mood.

What had she been thinking to come here with the intention of meeting a man? With her stomach twisting and knotting she could barely eat, and Cyrus was so silent he wasn't helping the situation at all. Where was his mindless chatter about the weather and her students? She could certainly use a little chitchat right now. Goodness, to look at Cyrus you'd think he was at a funeral instead of a party, and she didn't imagine she looked any cheerier than he did.

Soon they had company. Merilee's oldest child, Mary Alice, was a rambunctious five-and-a-half years old. An adorable girl with pale blond hair and large brown eyes, she hefted a small plate to the table next to Cyrus's and climbed into the vacant chair at his side. Mary Alice was a friendly child who had never met a stranger, and she was never at a loss for words. Thank goodness!

"I'm starving," she said as she lifted her fork, her voice high-pitched and musical. "Edith Terry made me play all afternoon. She even tried to make me climb a tree, but I said no, Edith Terry, this is my very best dress. I can't be climbing no trees."

It was clear, from a smudge of dirt on the smocking of her pink dress and the tiny tear in the lace at her throat and the small green leaf in her hair, that Mary Alice hadn't said *no* soon enough.

Cyrus pointed his fork at the pile of green beans on the little girl's plate. "The beans are good." He leaned slightly toward the child. "There's lots of good, tree-climbing energy in those beans." His fork waggled above her plate. "And in the potatoes, too, and the ham." He paused thoughtfully, studying the large serving of what was obviously the girl's favorite vegetable. "But especially in the beans," he added.

Mary Alice attacked her green beans with a decidedly unfeminine verve.

Cyrus smiled down at the child, and in that moment his face softened—just a little—and Roxanne felt her heart and her resolve soften along with it. He should have little girls of his own, she decided. And little boys, too. He

71

should live in a house full of children who would make him forget. . . .

She looked down at her plate and played with her own green beans. A friend, she reminded herself. Just a friend. If she'd allowed herself to get close to anyone during the past three years, she surely wouldn't be feeling so uncommonly possessive and . . . and *twittery* about the sheriff. She was in the process of turning her life upside down, so it was only natural that she'd experience a few moments of irrational thought.

That decided, she felt better. Calmer. She began to think that perhaps when she settled on a husband for herself she'd find a suitable wife for Cyrus.

Before they had finished their meal a small band began to play. The house was large, but not quite spacious enough for this crowd, so party-goers began to dance on the lawn. The light of day was quickly fading, but lanterns hanging from trees and on sparsely placed posts provided enough illumination to see the dancers through the night, to light their untrained, joyous steps.

Calvin Newberry was quickly claimed for a dance, and Roxanne sighed with relief. There wouldn't be another chance for introductions, not tonight. The handsome deputy was so popular she probably wouldn't even get the chance to speak to him. A cluster of beautiful young women waited nearby to claim the next dance and the next. Just as well; she evidently wasn't as ready to move on as she'd thought.

As Mary Alice finished her supper, her mother appeared. Merilee was an attractive woman just a few years older than Roxanne. She had a pleasant round face with apple cheeks, and was blessed with thick, pale hair and a buxom figure. She stood not quite five feet tall.

"Time for bed, Mary Alice," she said sweetly, casting a quick glance to Roxanne and then to Cyrus.

"No," Mary Alice groaned. "I want to stay up for the party."

Merilee leaned closer to her daughter. "Remember what I said?" she whispered. "Since you're the oldest you were allowed to attend the first few hours of the party. But now it's time for you to go upstairs and join your brother and sister and get to sleep."

Mary Alice pouted. "They're babies. I'm not a baby." She looked past her mother to the spirited crowd. "Besides, I want to dance."

"You're too young to dance." Merilee's patience was fading. "Now, up to bed with you."

Mary Alice's eyes filled with tears that didn't fall, and her lower lip trembled threateningly. Merilee glanced around, perhaps looking for Hank to interfere before this quiet rebellion turned into a minor disaster.

Cyrus placed his napkin aside and turned to

the little girl. Roxanne wondered if he'd play the surrogate father and sternly order Mary Alice to obey her mother; she wondered if a command from the sheriff would frighten little Mary Alice into doing just as her mother asked.

He surprised her. "Merilee," he said, his eyes on Mary Alice as he spoke softly, "Might I have one dance with your lovely daughter before she retires for the evening?"

Mary Alice's tears dried, and she turned an excited face to her mother. "Can I? *Please*? Oh, *please* let me dance with Sheriff Cyrus."

In resignation, and perhaps relief, Merilee agreed.

Cyrus stood and offered a gentlemanly hand to Mary Alice, who slipped from her chair and presented herself, head raised, at his feet. He took her small, soft hands in his and directed, in a low voice, that she should stand on his boots.

She did, stepping up so that her white leather slippers rested atop his big black boots, as stark a contrast as her tiny, pale hands in his. Cyrus took a careful step, and Mary Alice smiled brightly. He took another step, and then another, and then a series of small, cautious steps that matched the music. Once, he spun around slowly, and Mary Alice giggled in delight.

Watching Cyrus, whose attention was entirely on his tiny dance partner, Roxanne felt that strange tug at her heart again. He really did need a family of his own. A man like Cyrus would make a wonderful husband and father; she saw the tenderness he tried to hide, the heart he didn't easily reveal. Why hadn't he married? Scar or no scar, he was a fine-looking man. More than that, he was strong and valiant and gentle. What more could a woman ask from a man? She wasn't the only one who noticed Cyrus's attributes. He'd gotten his share of admiring looks this evening, though he certainly seemed oblivious to them.

She forgot, for a moment, that he was a lawman whose life would always be at risk, and simply admired him for what he was; a rare, good man.

When the music ended he placed Mary Alice on her feet and bowed to her as any fine gentleman might. The child answered by throwing her arms around his neck and kissing him soundly on his unmarred cheek, and for a few seconds he was trapped there, leaning forward awkwardly with Mary Alice draped around his neck.

Roxanne smiled. The smile came to her unexpectedly, wide and natural and unstoppable. What a sight the two of them made! Oh yes, Cyrus should definitely have little girls.

With Merilee's help, Mary Alice's arms were disengaged from Cyrus's neck, and the little girl whispered an adoring "good night." Cyrus might not know it, but he'd just made a friend for life.

As Merilee and her daughter entered the house through the patio doors, Cyrus turned to face Roxanne and stopped dead in his tracks.

"What is it?" he asked as he sat beside her.

"What's what?"

He leaned just a little bit closer. "Why are you smiling like that?"

Oh, she must look a fool. In years past, Aunt Ada had often told her that her smile was too wide, too large, too much, and never ladylike. And she was not about to tell Cyrus that he looked adorable with a child hanging around his neck.

"I've been watching your new deputy dance," she said, taking a peek to make sure Calvin Newberry was, indeed, still dancing. He was. Badly. "He's rather clumsy, don't you think?"

Cyrus rolled his eyes. "Tell me about it," he muttered.

Together they watched the new deputy dance with a red-haired young lady who was one of Roxanne's better students. He did move rather awkwardly, always a half-beat behind. While the rest of the dancers moved closer together, a clearing grew around Calvin and his partner. Roxanne wondered how many people he'd already run over.

"Do you still want to meet him?" Cyrus asked softly.

"Of course. Being able to dance well isn't a requirement in my mind. But perhaps not. . . ." *Not tonight*, she'd planned to say. She never got the chance.

Cyrus stood and offered his hand, silently asking her to dance. Wordlessly she laid her hand in his and rose from her seat. One dance wouldn't hurt anything, wouldn't change her mind or affect her plans in any way. Perhaps she did have inappropriate feelings for Cyrus, but that didn't mean she had to act on them. He was a friend, she reminded herself as he led her to the grassy dance floor. *A friend*, and nothing more.

The music ended, and for a moment they stood there poised and waiting. She held her breath until the music began; a slow, simple waltz. Cyrus danced well, gracefully and with natural ease. So many of the men here were shorter than she, and most of the rest were about her height. But she had to tip her head back slightly to look at Cyrus as they danced.

They moved well together, as if they'd danced before. The rightness of the dance made her slightly uneasy, but at the same time she didn't want to give this up. Not yet.

It had been so long since she'd let a man touch her, hold her, she'd forgotten what it felt like; the warmth, the strength, the strange energy that sometimes swirled between a man and a woman. She felt and savored it all, ashamed and thrilled and guilty and elated, all at the same time. She'd been right in her silly musings; Cyrus's hands were strong and hard, and yet soft. Tender.

She had to distract herself from these feelings before they got out of hand, and the best way to do that was to think about her plans. A fresh life with someone new, a home, a family. Once she'd settled on a husband, she'd have to see about finding a wife for Cyrus. Her eyes flitted over the dimly lit dance area, looking for possible candidates.

Rose Wells was a war widow, like herself, and would make someone a fine wife. Jane Rice might be only twenty, but she was a level-headed young woman and eleven years difference wasn't really too much, not if the parties were well suited. In her mind there were several women in town who might make Cyrus a suitable wife.

What would he think of them? He'd been a ladies' man of sorts before the war, but since his return he hadn't courted a single woman that she knew of. Surely he wanted what she did: a home, children. Someone to hold at night; someone with whom to cry and laugh.

As he spun her around she could see it too well; everything she wanted, everything Cyrus surely wanted as well. "All this work just to find me a husband," she said, her voice purposely light. "Well, when we're done with my matrimonial plans we'll work on you."

He literally twitched in her arms. "What?"

"We'll find you a wife, someone—"

"No," he interrupted in a low, harsh voice. "I don't plan to get married."

She locked her eyes to his. "Never?"

"Never," he whispered, his voice so dark and determined she believed him instantly.

"Why not?"

For a moment she thought he wouldn't answer. His lips formed a hard straight line, his jaw tensed, his eyes glittered. Even his hands were somehow harsher, more remote. "Seems to me the only reason to get married is if you want a family, and I don't."

Her heart skipped a beat. "Why not?"

He didn't hesitate this time. "Kids," he said. "When they're little they're noisy and bothersome, and when they grow up they're impertinent and annoying. Most folks I know who have kids just go from one crisis to another."

"Well, that's not necessarily true," Roxanne said softly. She'd just watched him dance, so sweetly, with Mary Alice. He couldn't really believe that children were nothing but a . . . a bother. "In your profession you do see the worst side of folks at times, I suppose, but there's more to family than enduring one crisis after another."

"Christ almighty," he whispered. "I take care of this whole damn town. Isn't that enough? What, you think I need a house full of sniveling kids to come home to at the end of a long day? No thank you. I live alone and I like it that way, so keep those nasty little matchmaking thoughts to yourself."

She swallowed. Hard. This was the most he'd said at one time all evening, so he must feel rather strongly about the subject. "You have a rather harsh idea of what family life is like."

He locked his eyes to hers, and she experienced a little jolt of awareness. Her heart beat fast, her breath came shallow, her hand—cradled easily in Cyrus's own large hand—seemed to tingle and grow warm. She was suddenly acutely aware, once again, of his palm against hers, of the roughness of his skin and the gentle way his fingers folded over hers.

He came to a standstill, and as Roxanne looked around she realized that all this time, during this entire dance, he'd been working his way across the lawn to Calvin Newberry. The music stopped, and Cyrus spun around to face his newest deputy.

"Newberry," he said in a businesslike voice that immediately commanded the younger man's attention. "I'd like you to meet Roxanne Robinette. Roxanne, this is Calvin Newberry."

Calvin's startling blue eyes lit up as he smiled. "Is this the lady you wanted me to meet?"

"Yes," Cyrus whispered as he moved away and left Roxanne standing before Calvin Newberry.

Oh, this was a mistake. Her heart stuck in her throat, and complete and total fear washed through her as she looked up at the grinning, handsome man. Whatever had made her think she could even consider marrying again? Why had she made a fool of herself over a man's pretty face? She should be home nursing Ada, not standing here staring dumbly at a complete stranger.

But the music began again and Cyrus backed away and the beautiful Calvin asked, "How 'bout a dance?"

* * *

He'd been hiding here, in the relative safety of the shadows, since Roxanne had begun her first dance with Calvin. During their second dance he'd made his way to the refreshments and poured himself a stiff shot of whiskey. During the third he'd fetched the bottle.

Between dances with Calvin, Roxanne visited with old friends, and searched the crowd for Cyrus. At least, Cyrus imagined she was searching for him when she lifted her head and raked her eyes over the throng of party guests.

He'd played the nice guy enough for one night, dammit. He'd introduced her to Calvin; he'd done what was right for her. Not once had he buried his nose in her hair and told her she smelled of sunshine and flowers. Not a single time had he laid his lips on her tempting neck, or her soft cheek, or that wide luscious mouth. He'd been tempted, dammit. He'd been tempted more than once.

He lifted the bottle and took a good long swig, wishing he could get drunk. It wasn't working.

If he'd had any doubts about what he was doing, the smile had killed them all. How long had it been since he'd seen Roxanne smile like that? Years. Many, many years. She didn't smile like other women, all soft and demure and somehow secretive. She smiled with her entire face, broadly and unrestrained. God, he loved the way she smiled.

From his hiding place behind a wide oak tree, he saw Calvin and Roxanne come together for another dance. Calvin stumbled slightly and Roxanne smiled again; not as widely as before, but it was still a rare smile for Roxanne. Cyrus tipped the bottle back and wished he could get good and drunk.

He hoped he'd managed to kill any ideas she had about finding him a wife. Heaven forbid. What woman would want a husband who had nightmares that woke him up in a terrified sweat, memories that kept him awake while the rest of the town slept? Besides, there had been more than a grain of truth in his protest. The last thing he needed was something else to tie him to this place; someone else to take care of.

A very slight tugging at his pants leg distracted him. He looked down and there was Mary Alice. Dressed in her nightclothes and with her long blond hair braided down her back, it was obvious that she'd sneaked from her bed for another glimpse of the party she'd been banned from.

"What are you doing here?" he asked, trying to sound just a little bit austere.

"I couldn't sleep," she whispered. "I looked out my window and saw you standing here, and I just wanted to know why you're hiding."

"I'm not hiding," Cyrus said, sternly and softly.

Mary Alice looked at the wide-trunked tree that shielded them both from the rest of the party, then behind them at the deeper shadows. "Yes you are," she said matter-of-factly.

"I got tired of dancing," he lied.

"Oh." She looked up at him, and he could see the hurt in her eyes.

"After all," he said, trying to mend the damage he'd unintentionally done, "You were my very best dance partner tonight, and once you went to bed. . . . " He spread his arms wide in the universal sign of surrender, bottle in one hand.

Mary Alice giggled softly, covering her mouth with a tiny hand to silence her soft outburst.

"How about one more dance," he whispered, setting the bottle of whiskey on the ground. The place he chose wasn't quite flat, and almost immediately the bottle tipped over, spilling the remains of the whiskey into the ground. Just as well, Cyrus decided without attempting to save any of the liquor. He'd had enough for tonight. More than enough.

The child took his hands and stepped onto his boots with her little bare feet. They barely moved, but it was a dance, of sorts, as he stepped this way and that. Mary Alice, balanced on his boots, felt so light it was almost as if she wasn't really here, as if he were dancing with air. Her hands rested in his, fragile and delicate and unerringly trusting. And what a smile she had; not even six years old and already you could see the heartbreaker in that smile.

When the music ended she stepped carefully from his boots, and this time as he bowed to her she curtseyed with great formality, taking the edge of her nightgown between two little fingers and dipping down gently. Already she was a perfect little lady. More than that, in her bare feet and crisp nightdress she was a perfect example of what was good and right in the world.

Instead of immediately righting himself, Cyrus lowered himself to the ground and leaned his back against the tree. He didn't really want to watch Roxanne and Calvin dance, didn't want to see her smile at him; not right now.

Mary Alice took a seat beside him and leaned against the tree herself, in an obvious attempt to copy his pose. There was just enough light from the lantern that hung on the opposite side of the tree to illuminate their hiding place; she the misbehaving runaway, he the reluctant matchmaker.

After a few moments, Cyrus whispered. "You'd better get back to bed before anyone realizes you're gone."

"I know." Mary Alice's tone of voice was resigned and very grown up, in spite of the high pitch. "If I get caught, I'll be in big trouble." Still, she made no immediate move to leave.

"You'd better run along, then," Cyrus suggested, closing his eyes and listening to the music that was so near and yet so faint.

Mary Alice wasn't content to slip back to bed as quietly as she'd slipped away. Without warning she piled onto Cyrus's lap. His eyes flew open and he found himself staring into big brown eyes mere inches from his.

"Goodnight, Sheriff Cyrus," she whispered.

"Goodnight, Mary Alice. Thanks for the dance."

She smiled and leaned over to kiss him on the cheek with lips as soft and light as butterfly wings passing by. And then, instead of climbing off his lap and running off to bed like a good little girl, she settled two delicate hands on his cheeks. The palm of one hand rested over the scar on his left cheek, and that's where her eyes went; to that damn ugly scar.

She tilted her head to the side and ran her fingertips over the tough ridge that marked his face. "Does it hurt?" she whispered.

So matter-of-fact, so casual.

"No," Cyrus said honestly. "Not anymore."

"That's good," Mary Alice said, and she sounded truly relieved.

No one, but himself and doctors long ago, had touched his face since he'd been wounded. Until now. Those gentle hands on his cheeks made him want to scream, to push the little girl and her good intentions away. But he didn't move, he hardly even breathed as her fingers explored the tough scar tissue.

"My Mama says a kiss makes everything better," she said as she raked her tiny fingers over his scar.

"Is that a fact?"

Instead of answering, Mary Alice removed

her hands from his face and kissed him again, this time on his ravaged cheek. She didn't seem to find anything repulsive in the innocent gesture; it was simply a kiss to make everything better.

Cyrus found himself wishing that life could be, just for a while, as uncomplicated for him as it was for Mary Alice.

Chapter Five

Calvin was as beautiful up close as he was from a distance, and this near, dancing with him once again, Roxanne admired the full potency of his startling blue eyes. He had a nice smile, too, and good white teeth and wondrously thick blond curls and even features that might have been carved on a marble statue, a study in perfection.

Unfortunately, he didn't say much. In fact, he'd been so quiet, she felt that even though she'd danced with Calvin Newberry several times she didn't know him any better than when she'd seen him ride past on his horse.

Calvin spun around and bumped into Thomas Eakin, and the impact sent Thomas and his partner Rose reeling for a moment. No one hit the ground, however, and after a very quiet but heartfelt apology from Calvin the dance resumed.

Where was Cyrus? Roxanne searched the dance area as Calvin very cautiously twirled her about again. She couldn't help but notice how the dance area cleared around them as they moved, thanks to Calvin's tendency to bowl over everything in his path. Her steps automatically followed his, as her eyes raked over the crowd. Cyrus was nowhere to be seen, and she could feel the beginnings of a frown and an accompanying headache coming on. She shouldn't be concerned. He might be inside, sipping whiskey and smoking a cigar while he chatted with a group of politically minded men. He was the sheriff, after all, and might even have been called away on an emergency.

Then again, perhaps he had found a woman to spend the evening with, and was at this very moment in a dark secluded spot sharing kisses and whispered promises. His voice would be low and soft and enchanting, his hands would be strong and gentle as they held the woman he kissed.

The headache and the frown hit Roxanne full force.

As the music ended and Calvin released her, she caught a glimpse of Cyrus moving from the shadows. Ha! So her musings had been right. She had a mind to march over there and tell Cyrus Bergeron exactly what she thought about his shenanigans . . . and, of course, to catch a view of whatever woman waited on the other side of that tree.

A deep breath restored her senses. What Cyrus did was none of her concern. She'd already deemed him unsuitable as a husband, and besides . . . he was too much a part of the past, too much of a reminder of who she'd once been. Calvin was new, and if she was to have the life she wanted, perhaps he would be a part of it. She just wished he would talk more so she'd know if they were compatible or not.

"It's been lovely," she said, working up a small smile for Calvin. It wasn't easy; in fact, the effort made her face hurt. "But I'm afraid I must be heading home, now."

She wondered if he would offer to walk with her, and wondered just as well what she would say if he did. There was no reason to worry about her response; Calvin just bowed and said in his soft Tennessee voice,

"It's been a pleasure, ma'am."

Roxanne made her way to Cyrus, who stood leaning against the tree she'd seen him step from behind. He appeared to be so calm, so casual. His eyes, as she drew closer, told her nothing, darn his stoic hide. Was there a woman behind that tree? She tried to crook her neck to see more, without being obvious, but she saw nothing.

"Where have you been?" she asked, softly and yet more harshly than she'd intended. She took a very small step to the side and tilted her head slightly, in a sly attempt to get a better look behind that tree.

Cyrus raised his eyebrows, in an apparent combination of amusement and confusion. "I've been dancing."

She saw nothing behind the tree, not even a flash of color to suggest a full skirt, no hint of movement. Still, she was certain she was right. Cyrus had been dancing with some woman in the shadows, perhaps holding his partner too close, stealing kisses. What other reason was there to dance in secret? Her heart sank. "Would you take me home?" She tried to be pleasant and reserved, but her efforts were useless. She sounded tired and petulant.

"Is everything all right?" he asked as he moved away from the tree to join her.

She started to lie, to tell him that everything was fine. "I have a headache," she said.

Without another word he took her arm and together they said goodbye to Merilee and Hank and a dozen other people they passed on their way across the lawn and through the house. They didn't say goodbye to Calvin, who was engaged in an energetic dance with a young lady who was being flung about very much like a rag doll.

Moments later, she felt great relief to be down the street, away from the music and the noise and the crush of people. She slowed her step and took a deep breath of the cool night air, and her headache miraculously vanished. Cyrus slowed his step to match hers, and out of the corner of her eye she saw him turn his head in her direction.

"Well?" he prodded before they'd gone far. "What did you think of Calvin?"

"He's very. . . ." she searched for words that would be truthful and kind. She couldn't very well tell Cyrus that in spite of his efforts she still didn't know Calvin Newberry at all, and she couldn't very well tell him that after their one waltz, dancing with Calvin had been less than wonderful. How could she have known that one dance with Cyrus would spoil her for anyone else? She made herself remember what he'd said during that dance, about marriage and children and family . . . everything she wanted.

"He's nice," she finally said. "Polite, and handsome, and very agreeable."

A non-committal humming noise rose from the throat of the man beside her.

"He didn't talk much, though," she added. "So I can't say that I really got to know him well."

Cyrus just nodded.

"What about you?" Roxanne asked casually. "Who did you spend the evening dancing with? I swear, I didn't even catch a glimpse of you until I was ready to leave. Why, one might think you had something, or someone, to hide," she said teasingly, waiting for his answer, his reaction.

There was no immediate response.

"So," she prodded. "Who was she? Who was

the woman you were dancing with behind that tree?" The last of her limited patience fled, as a rush of something akin to anger rushed through her blood. "You were dancing back there, weren't you?" Dancing or . . . something else.

"A gentleman never tells," he offered softly and with a teasing lilt.

Roxanne emitted an uncontrollable, hot-tempered huff. She shouldn't have bothered attending Merilee's party. The entire evening had been a waste of time. She didn't know Calvin any better than she had before, and at the moment she was just incredibly frustrated. Frustrated and irritated and . . . well, she couldn't be jealous. She absolutely, positively, *couldn't* be.

But the very idea of Cyrus dancing intimately with some unknown woman in the shadows made her blood boil. If only she couldn't *see* it so well; the way Cyrus would tower over his secret lady friend, the way he would touch her and whisper in that pleasant voice of his, his mouth so close to her ear she would no doubt feel his breath on her skin. Roxanne shivered.

Too soon they were at the gate of her uncle's house, and Cyrus was telling her, very politely and distantly, goodnight.

What would he say if she reached out, took his face in her hands, and kissed him? Just once, just to know what it felt like. Perhaps there was no future for them, perhaps he didn't want the same things from life she did, but that didn't mean they couldn't share one innocent kiss, just to satisfy her curiosity.

"Goodnight," she said without giving in to the ridiculous notion. With her head high, she walked to the front door without looking back.

Cyrus sat by the window, wondering if Roxanne would come out tonight or if she already slept peacefully in her bed. He hadn't even undressed yet, didn't know why he should bother. If he slept, it would only be fitful bits and pieces filled with dreams he couldn't bear.

For a wild moment, as he'd been walking Roxanne home and she'd asked about his secret dance partner, he'd had the ridiculous notion that she was jealous. He quickly put it aside. Roxanne was just curious, that's all, like all women. Maybe he should've told her that he'd been dancing with Mary Alice again, that there was only one woman he wanted to hold, that his one dance with her had been more wonderful than he'd even imagined. No. Touching her, even so innocently, wasn't the way to cure his obsession. Telling her the truth was out of the question.

Roxanne wouldn't laugh at him; she had too much class for that. But he was sure she would feel sorry for him, the pathetic scarred man who had no right to so much as dream about beautiful women like her.

She wanted beauty and safety, and she

would eventually find both with Calvin Newberry. Of this he was certain.

The figure that passed by his window startled him and interrupted his bitter musings. What the hell was Newberry doing on this street? The passing shadow of a man was definitely Calvin, unmistakable in his broad brimmed white hat and the butternut duster that flapped around his long legs.

Maybe he was going to call on Roxanne. In the middle of the night? Cyrus rose from his chair just as Calvin walked past the window again . . . heading in the opposite direction.

Cyrus threw open his front door. "Newberry," he snapped. "What the hell are you doing?" One look at the young man's confused face, and Cyrus had his answer. Calvin was lost again, trying to find his way home.

He stifled a groan as he opened his front door wide and asked the deputy to come inside.

"I think I took a wrong turn back thataway," Calvin said, motioning with a finger as Cyrus closed the door.

"You want a drink?" Cyrus lit a lamp and set it on the single table in this simply furnished room. A soft light was cast on Calvin's beautiful face as the man removed his hat.

"No, thanks. I reckon I've had enough already tonight."

"Me, too," Cyrus confessed. He wasn't drunk, but he certainly felt the effects of too much whiskey. His head swam, ever so slightly, and his eyelids drooped heavily.

"If you'll just point me in the direction to the boarding house," Calvin said as he wrung the brim of his hat. "I'd be right grateful."

"Sure." Cyrus folded his arms across his chest. "But first, why don't you tell me how things went with Roxanne tonight?"

Even in the dim light, he saw Calvin blush. "She's right purty, ain't she?"

"Yes, she is," Cyrus agreed lifelessly.

"And a fine dancer," Calvin added.

Cyrus nodded once.

Calvin screwed up his nose in an almost childish manner. "I tried not to say much, on account of I didn't want to sound stupid. Roxanne seems kinda smart."

"She is," Cyrus said impatiently. "She's a teacher."

"I know." Calvin gestured with his hat. "I never had me a schoolteacher that looked like Roxanne. Why, all my teachers was ugly old maids 'cept for this one prissy perfessor fella that moved in—"

"Newberry," Cyrus interrupted. "Did you like her?"

Calvin gave this some thought and finally nodded his head vigorously . . . rather like a snorting horse. "I like her right fine. She's purty and agreeable and I reckon I could learn to live with a smart woman, if it come to that."

Cyrus glanced through the window toward the Pierson house. With the light burning in this room, he couldn't see if Roxanne was sitting on her balcony or not. "Well, if you expect anything to come of this you're going to have to talk to her."

Calvin shuffled his feet. "I know that, but purty women make me a bit tongue-tied. I open my big mouth and say something dumb, or else nothing but gibberish comes out. In my head, the words are all right, but when I say them out loud they jest don't sound the same as I mean for 'em to. It's right embarrassin'."

"I imagine it is," Cyrus muttered.

"If I could just talk to Roxanne without actually looking at her . . . maybe talk to her from a distance or close my eyes and pretend she's not really there or something," Calvin suggested dreamily. "Then maybe I could be as smart as she is."

Cyrus glanced to the window and the darkness beyond, and a glimmer of inspiration came to him. Inspiration, hell, it was a stupid idea. A really, really stupid idea.

But he couldn't make himself dismiss the notion. It might work. There was no reason it shouldn't. Dammit, he'd do anything to make sure Roxanne got everything she wanted, and if this dim but beautiful boy was her idea of the perfect husband, then she'd have him.

"Newberry," Cyrus said softly. "I have a plan."

* * *

Standing beneath Roxanne's balcony, his flash of inspiration seemed like an incredibly *bad* idea. If Calvin had agreed to do this on his own it would be different, but since the young man couldn't seem to remember even the simplest compliment Cyrus had suggested he convey, this close involvement was inevitable.

"Now," Cyrus said softly to the man who stood just a few feet away, beneath the balcony but in clear view of anyone who stood there.

"Psst!" Calvin lifted his head and made a noise that was jarringly loud in the deep quiet of the night. "Hey," he added quickly. "Roxanne!"

Cyrus could only pray that Josiah and Ada were sound sleepers. He motioned for Calvin to keep his voice down, but as he did he heard and felt Roxanne step onto the balcony above his head.

"Who's there?" she asked sharply, alert enough for him to be certain she hadn't been sleeping.

"It's me." Calvin removed his head and lifted his head. "Calvin Newberry."

Roxanne paused, not moving, not speaking, and then she whispered a softly puzzled, "What are you doing here?"

Calvin worked the hat nervously in his hands. "I didn't get to say everything I wanted to say tonight," he said. "So I just figured I'd mosey on over and say howdy."

"Oh," came a soft sigh from above Cyrus's head.

"You sure was purty tonight," Calvin added.

Roxanne cleared her throat uneasily. "Well, thank you, Calvin."

Calvin looked to Cyrus for help.

"Tell her she's beautiful right now." Cyrus whispered.

"Oh, yeah." Calvin's head snapped up to look at Roxanne again. "You look good now, too. You're as fine as frog's hair," he added enthusiastically. "I imagine you look right nice all the time."

Cyrus closed his eyes. *Right nice? Fine as frog's hair?* "Tell her she has eyes like sapphires and skin like pearls," he whispered. "Tell her she has hair like the darkest moonless night, and a laugh that makes angels sing and fairies dance."

Calvin screwed up his nose before lifting his head to Roxanne again. "You've got right nice eyes, too."

"Tell her you get tongue-tied when you speak to a pretty girl," Cyrus suggested.

"You get . . ." Calvin began, "I mean, I get tongue-tied when I talk to a purty gal."

"You are such a moron," Cyrus seethed.

"You are such . . ." Calvin managed to stop himself before he went further. "I'm a moron," he finished.

"Goodnight, Calvin," Roxanne said, and dammit, Cyrus could hear the laughter in her voice, the joy.

He lifted a hand and crooked a finger to call

Calvin closer. "Tell her to give you a moment to collect your thoughts."

Calvin gave Roxanne a brilliant smile that would surely make any woman do as he asked. "Don't run off on me just yet. Give me a minute to gather my thoughts and I'll be right back."

A very small basket would be sufficient to gather all of Calvin's thoughts, of that Cyrus was certain.

When Calvin stood hidden beneath the balcony with him, Cyrus took the white hat and jammed it on his own head. "Hand over the coat," he ordered softly, taking off his own jacket and dropping it to the ground, gesturing impatiently when it appeared Calvin didn't understand.

Calvin shrugged off the duster and handed it over, and Cyrus slipped it on, turning up the collar to hide the lower portion of his face. His heart beat too hard, his mouth went dry. Dammit his hands were trembling. Could he carry off the hillbilly accent? Would Roxanne know the minute he opened his mouth that he was *not* Calvin Newberry?

But when he stepped into the moonlight all his fears melted away. This was a night to end all nights, the kind of night good dreams were made of. He'd waltzed with Roxanne, he'd seen her smile, and now he was finally going to get the chance to tell her exactly how he felt.

* * *

Roxanne smiled as Calvin stepped from beneath the balcony. She waited for him to lift his head and smile at her again, but he didn't. He kept his head down, so all she could see was the top of his white hat. Why was he wearing it now? He had such a lovely head of hair, such a lovely face. It was a shame to hide them.

She shouldn't be standing here, in her night-dress and wrapper, with her hair down and her feet bare. This was a most improper situation. But darn it, she'd been proper for so long. . . .

"I have a hard time speaking my mind when I'm looking at you." Calvin's Tennessee accent had softened, was not quite as harsh as before. Perhaps he'd relaxed a little since he hid under his hat.

"I can't see why." She grasped the railing and leaned over slightly. A burst of wind caught the tail of her silver-gray silk dressing gown and made it swing around her legs. The same breeze ruffled her loosened hair.

"You're so beautiful," he whispered. "Much too beautiful and fine and good for the likes of me."

"That's just sweet talk," she said, dismissing his claim.

There was a short pause, and then a soft, coun-trified voice drifted to her. "It's the truth. Never in my life have I seen another woman to compare with you, Roxanne Robinette. You have eyes like sapphires and skin like pearls. Tonight, when we were dancing, I wanted so badly to bury my nose in your hair and just stay there, to forget that we were not alone. I didn't dare."

"It's rather bold of you to say so," she said, flattered and shocked and confused. While they'd danced, Calvin had looked as if he had nothing more on his mind than the music and the calculated movements of his big feet. But now . . . right now he told her differently.

"Tonight I will be bold," he said. "Tomorrow . . . tomorrow I'll be cautious and polite again, and I'll hide behind propriety and what I know is right. Tonight I will say what I think and feel and want."

Roxanne's heart flipped in her chest. She didn't want romance, she didn't want love, but maybe for tonight she could pretend that she did. "What do you think and feel and want?"

There was a short pause, and Calvin began to pace beneath her. She could see him well enough, by the light of the full moon, and yet she couldn't see him at all. His long duster and white hat were almost bright in the moonlight, but he kept his head down.

"I think you are the perfect woman. Perfect not just because you're beautiful, but because behind the sapphire eyes and beneath the pearl-like skin there beats a fine, good heart and there rests a wondrously beautiful soul."

She ignored the fact that her heart skipped a beat. This was nothing but romantic nonsense from a man who'd obviously had too much to drink. "You don't know me well enough to say such things. You certainly don't know me well enough to know my soul."

"Trust me," he said so softly she had to strain to hear the words. "I do. May I continue?"

She should say *no* and send Calvin away. This encounter was improper, scandalous, and wrong. But somehow it felt very, very right. "Yes."

"I feel," he said. "I feel like my heart has been kicked and stomped on, battered and broken, and you know what? I don't mind at all. There was a time in my life when I didn't think I'd ever feel anything again. Not even pain. Certainly not affection. But not feeling anything at all is too much like death. Pain is better than being numb," he whispered. "I was numb for too long."

"So was I," she whispered, and tears sprang to her eyes. Somehow this man *knew* her. He knew her heart, her soul, her fears. *Pain is better than being numb*. Was that true?

"Calvin," she called, leaning over the wrought iron railing. "Why won't you look at me as you say these things?"

"I can't," he whispered.

"Are you really that shy?"

"I am right bashful at times," he conceded, his Tennessee accent suddenly more pronounced. "But I must confess that this is different."

"How is this different?"

There was a long moment of silence, but she waited patiently for him to answer.

"If I tell you what I think and feel and want,

and you laugh to my face, I couldn't bear it. I'd die inside again and then . . . maybe there would only be more numbness, and maybe it wouldn't go away this time, not ever."

"I would never hurt you or anyone else that way," she promised.

"Not deliberately," he answered. "I know that. But what if I. . . ." his voice faltered, and as she watched him pace he stumbled over a root of the oak tree, jumped slightly as he regained his balance.

Roxanne couldn't help but smile. Calvin was so clumsy. "What if . . . what?"

"What if I fall in love with you? What if I come to love you with all my heart, and you don't return that love? That would hurt worst of all, Roxanne."

She knew he spoke the truth, and yet she couldn't promise love to a man she barely knew. She couldn't promise love to anyone at all. Like Calvin, she was afraid of being hurt again, of losing again. He was right; the numbness was awful.

"You said you'd tell me what you think and feel and want. You've told me what you think of me, and what you feel." She swallowed hard. The darkness and the fact that Calvin continued to hide his face so far below made her as bold as he. "What do you want?" she whispered, afraid for this to end too soon.

He came to a standstill directly beneath her. "Don't you know, Roxanne?" he whispered.

She *did* know, and her heart fluttered and

her breasts tightened. Deep inside, a faint but unmistakable tremor surprised her. Physical desire, feelings she'd thought long dead, rushed through her. The knuckles of her hands turned white as she gripped the railing tight.

"I want you," he whispered, and then he stepped beneath the balcony and out of sight.

A moment later he appeared again, and this time he lifted his head. She searched his face for signs of the tenderness and desire she'd heard in his voice, but all she saw was moonlit composed perfection. How could he look so calm, when with a few words he'd just turned her world upside down?

There was no smile this time, as he said "Goodnight, Roxanne," and walked away.

She slowly sank to the floor of the balcony and watched him walk away. At the edge of the lawn he stopped, looked up and down the street, and then started walking at a brisk pace.

She sighed. Poor Calvin, he was obviously more affected by his romantic confession than he'd appeared to be; if he was going back to the boarding house he was heading in the wrong direction.

Cyrus waited patiently and quietly beneath the balcony. He heard Roxanne breathing, heard her moving above his head. The ground was hard, the air was cool, but here he would sit until she went to bed. It didn't really matter how uncomfortable he was or how long he had to wait; he wouldn't be getting any sleep tonight.

Finally he had told Roxanne how he felt, what he wanted. God, he was a coward, to hide behind Calvin's pretty face to reveal his obsession. To pretend to be someone else as he told her all his secrets and fears. It had been so easy. Too easy.

And she'd loved it, hadn't she? He'd heard the softening of her voice, the little sighs, the hope in her simple questions. *What do you want?* She might say she didn't want love and happiness, but she lied.

He leaned against the wall of the house and closed his eyes. She wanted love and happiness, and by God he would give it to her. If giving Roxanne what she wanted meant he had to tie up everything he felt and desired in the pretty package called Calvin Newberry, that's exactly what he'd do.

Chapter Six

By the light of day, last night's so-called inspiration seemed utterly ridiculous. Cyrus didn't know whether he should blame the whiskey, the waltz, Mary Alice's innocent kiss, or Calvin. He decided to absolve them all of responsibility and blame himself, instead.

Apparently Calvin placed blame at his feet as well.

"Sheriff," the young man said as he paced before Cyrus's desk. "I don't mean no disrespect, and I know you musta had your reasons for what went on last night, but don't you think," the big blond man came to a standstill directly before a seated Cyrus and placed his hands on his hips in a pose that screamed reproach, "that maybe you went jest a touch too far?"

Cyrus ignored the knowledge that this dim boy was right and he was wrong. "Whatever do you mean?" he asked calmly and with just a hint of sarcasm.

Calvin narrowed one eye. "All that talk about love and hearts and souls and such." He appeared to have a real distaste for the subject, screwing up his nose and mouth until he was anything *but* beautiful. "Eyes like sapphires and all that foolishness about her hair. Shoot, she'll most likely be expecting a proposal of marriage next time we meet, and I ain't made up my mind if that's what I want to do or not."

"What do you mean you *ain't* made up your mind?" Cyrus asked angrily. "You said you were looking for a wife, and we agreed that Roxanne would suit you perfectly."

"No," Calvin said sternly, surprising Cyrus. "*You* said that she suited me perfectly. I met a lot of sweet and purty women last night, and I reckon any one of them would make a fair wife. Roxanne is purty, that's a fact, but then so are Jane and Rose and Hannah. Why, I'd have myself a hard time picking which one was the purtiest."

Cyrus stood slowly. How could this moron even suggest that those other women could hold a candle to Roxanne? He wasn't about to let this dimwit ruin his carefully laid plans.

"You'd be a fool to marry any other woman in town when Roxanne is available and willing," he seethed.

"Know what I think?" Calvin placed two

beefy hands on the desk and leaned forward almost threateningly, showing more spine than Cyrus had seen from the boy thus far. He couldn't be sorry. The man Roxanne married had to be capable of taking care of her, of standing up to anyone and anything when the situation called for it. "Sheriff, I think you just ought to ask Roxanne to marry *you* and leave me out of it."

The suggestion was so unexpected, so farfetched, Cyrus felt like the younger man had kicked him in the chest. "That's ridiculous," he muttered.

"Don't sound ridiculous to me." Calvin's mood changed quickly and the boy flashed a winning smile. "I think you're right sweet on her."

Cyrus relaxed and resumed his seat. "Now, that is ridiculous," he said calmly. "Maybe I went too far in my matchmaking efforts," he conceded. "I had too much to drink last night and I got carried away. Just seems to me that you and Roxanne would make a good match. That's all. I figured a little sweet talk would get you started."

"A *little* sweet talk?" Calvin grinned widely. "If what I heard last night is your idea of a *little* sweet talk I pity the poor woman you fall in love with."

Cyrus ignored the good-hearted censure. "I was hasty," he admitted. "Last night I pushed too far too fast, and I said some things I shouldn't have. You need to get to know

Roxanne better before making any important decisions. I understand that."

Calvin nodded once.

Yes, he'd moved too fast. Cyrus was willing to admit to that. But the admission didn't mean this was over. Not by a long shot. "There's a church picnic tomorrow, and I imagine Roxanne will be there. How about you make a point to attend, and you and Roxanne can sit together and get better acquainted."

The young man very seriously considered the proposition for a moment, then nodded his head once. "All right, but you come with me, all right? At least for a while, in case I can't think of nothing to say. You can jump in and do some of that fancy talking of yours. Not that sweet talk or anything," Calvin added hastily. "Just . . . talk."

Cyrus sighed. "You need a nursemaid to court a woman?"

"Just a little help gettin' started, that's all," Calvin said sheepishly. "Roxanne does make me a mite nervous. Shootfire, of course she makes me nervous. She's purty *and* smart." Calvin lifted innocent, pleading blue eyes. "You'll be there, won'tcha Sheriff?"

Cyrus almost contained a despairing sigh. He'd never intended to get in this deep, to become this involved. It was hard enough to watch Roxanne fall in love from a distance. To be right there with her and Calvin while his plan fell into place. . . . It was almost too much.

"All right," he agreed reluctantly. "I'll stick

with you for a while, but if it looks like you're doing all right on your own I'll disappear."

Calvin nodded at this agreeable idea. "Fine. Just don't ask her to marry me over vittles. Deal?"

Cyrus couldn't help but smile. "Deal."

Roxanne walked toward downtown with a languid, easy smile on her face. She didn't want to ponder exactly where the smile came from, but it felt good, natural, even though she hadn't smiled much at all in the past few years.

Perhaps she didn't want to ponder where the smile came from, but she knew too well. Calvin Newberry and his honeyed whisper hadn't been out of her mind since he'd walked away last night. She'd tossed restlessly in her bed as she thought about those adoring words. She'd dreamed of them, woke remembering them.

It had been so long since she'd really felt like a woman; loved and desired, admired and adored. Calvin, with his whispered confessions, had made her feel all that and more. For the first time in a long, long while, Roxanne harbored a twinkling of hope that perhaps she could find love and happiness again.

Everything he'd said had been wonderful, memorable and worth cherishing in her heart. But one statement stayed with her more than the rest. *Pain is better than being numb*. It was as if he knew that she'd been paralyzed for too long, as if he only had to look at her to understand that she was afraid of the hurt that might come if she dared to love again.

111

Waking up, allowing herself to hope again, was the bravest thing she'd done in years.

On Saturday the business section of Paris became a busy place. Saturday was usually a busy day for Roxanne. She baked bread, and did laundry and the heavy cleaning that was such a chore for her aunt. Ada refused to employ live-in help, judging it a luxury, and the girls she hired to come in and clean once a week were unable to keep up with everything that needed to be done. Roxanne always had chores to do on Saturday.

But today she felt much too restless to stay at home. She needed to walk off some of this unusual energy, to breathe fresh air and feel the April sun on her face. Thanks to Calvin, she thought as she lifted her face and closed her eyes.

Without conscious thought, she found herself standing before the dressmaker's shop. People walked by, saying hello and waving, if their arms weren't full of purchases. Roxanne smiled and waved absently, but her eyes were on the door of the dress shop. She waited a moment before stepping forward and opening the door, looking in on two shoppers and a very busy Fannie Rowland.

Roxanne held her breath. What was she doing here? She glanced down at the plain brown dress she wore and expelled a long, solemn sigh. She'd loved Louis with all her heart, and for so many years she'd known that they would spend their lives together. Such plans they'd had, for children that would never be, for a simple life of hard days and quiet evenings in their own part of the world. It wasn't much to ask, was it? Roots, family, her own corner of the world. She'd grieved for that lost life as much as she had for Louis, she decided, she'd mourned for dreams that would never be fulfilled, babies that would never be born.

Louis was gone. Was she a selfish fool to crave other dreams? Another life?

She took a deep breath to calm and fortify herself, as she lifted her head and closed the door behind her.

He hated Saturdays. Every farmer and rancher from miles around came to Paris to shop and visit, and there wasn't a Saturday to pass that he didn't end up throwing someone in jail. There were fights in the streets and in the saloons, arguments in the general store and the saddlery that occasionally got out of hand. Sheriff Bergeron was expected to be there to smooth all these disagreements over before there was bloodshed.

Today had been no different. Terence Michaels and Adlai Hart had come to blows over a less-than-magnificent horse Hart had bought from Michaels. Cyrus had played peacemaker, and the two had walked away grumbling but unhurt. A fancy-dressing professional gambler who went by the name Sir Latimer had been accosted by a local drunk who claimed he'd been cheated. The drunk was in jail and Latimer had promised to leave town on Monday's stage.

There had been a number of other disagreements, but they were minor, everyday transgressions without the threat of bloodshed, and they were easily handled by him or one of his deputies. Even Calvin had done his part, breaking up an argument between two farm wives in from out of town.

They'd been fighting over a bolt of bright yellow fabric, and Calvin had stopped the shouting match with a smile and the gentle observation that Miz Martha would look best in the blue, and Miz Irene really ought to try that purty green that matched her eyes. No one had bought the yellow and both women had headed for home happy and half in love with the newest Lamar County deputy. Cyrus could only shake his head in wonder.

Even though the streets were crowded and she was far away, he saw Roxanne on the boardwalk. Her arms were filled with a large brown-paper wrapped package that almost matched the dress she wore. She stepped into the street and headed toward home, her pace slow but steady. Almost thoughtful. Cyrus took off after her, his step brisk.

He really should leave her alone, and he knew it. Last night he'd gotten carried away, but then he hadn't been himself last night. Too much whiskey and an innocent kiss from a child had addled his brain. Yes, it would be best if he left Roxanne alone. His step didn't even slow as he approached her.

"That looks heavy," he said as he came up behind her. "Need some help?"

Roxanne glanced over her shoulder and grinned. Ah, what a smile it was, wide and natural and bright. "No thanks. This parcel is big, but it's not heavy." She jostled the package so that the brown paper rustled. "I bought a new dress." She blushed as she revealed this bit of information.

Cyrus nodded his head. "Well, that's nice. What's the occasion?"

"No occasion, just . . . just. . . ." She stopped dead in her tracks. "Cyrus, are you busy?"

"Not at the moment."

"Would you like to join me for a cup of tea and a slice of Maude Hipp's apple pie in her shop? I'd like . . ." her smile faded a little. "I'd like to talk to you."

An air of importance hung between them, in the words she spoke so softly. This was a moment that would never come again, an opportunity he couldn't pass up.

Dammit, if he had any guts at all he'd tell her exactly who had sweet-talked her last night. Looking at her, with her cheeks pink and her eyes bright, those eyebrows like dark wings and her hair so perfect against her pale face, he was tempted to tell her the truth, to take his chances and lay his heart on the line, face to face.

"Sure," he said simply.

Maude Hipp's place was named The Dallas Bakery, since that was the city where she'd lived before moving to Paris. Most of her business was conducted over a long counter, but she had two small tables in the back, and was always happy to serve tea and coffee and lemonade with her fabulous sweets and breads. A spare, graying widow who looked as if she never took so much as a bite of her own cooking, she had enough energy for three women.

There were two ladies at the counter, but no one at the tables in the back. Cyrus's heart beat harder and faster as Roxanne led him there. Her smile made him think of breaking all his promises to himself and spilling his guts; her smile and the spark of new life in her eyes.

"Here," she said, touching one chair and leaving him the one that placed his back against the wall. She deposited her package on the table as Cyrus pulled her chair out for her, laid her hands on the cherished parcel as he took his own seat.

"Look at this," she whispered, peeling back a bit of the coarse brown wrapping paper to reveal a tiny square of rose-colored silk. "Isn't this a beautiful color?"

The importance of that scrap of revealed pink silk hit him square in the chest. Roxanne was out of mourning, or at the very least heading there one step at a time.

"Very," he said.

Maude shouted out that she'd be with them

in a minute, and Cyrus answered that there was no rush. There was no reason to hurry. He settled his eyes, calmly, he thought, on Roxanne's face.

She had something momentous to say. He saw it as clear as day, in the spark of brilliant life that shone from her eyes. He wondered if what she wanted to say had anything to do with what had happened last night, if his words beneath the balcony had affected her so greatly that she'd taken this grand step.

As he watched she bit her lower lip, glanced to the side, and wrinkled her nose. He waited.

"I have to talk to someone," she whispered, leaning slightly across the table. "Aunt Ada wouldn't understand, and I've cut myself off from everyone else for so long there's no one else but . . . but. . . ."

"But me," he finished for her.

She smiled again, a small and endearing curve of her lips. "Yes. I told you that I want to marry," she said, her voice lowered so that no one at the counter could possibly hear her. "And you said that Louis would want me to be happy."

"I did," he agreed softly.

"And I said I wouldn't ever be happy again."

"You did."

She unconsciously fingered the package before her, brushing long pale fingers over the brown paper. "What if I was wrong?"

If Roxanne found happiness his job was done, his promise to Louis fulfilled. There would be no more reason to watch over her, day and night. He didn't want to give up his responsibility, his obsession, but he did want to see Roxanne contented again. "I think that would be wonderful," he said.

Her smile faded away. "Then why do I feel so guilty? Like I don't have a right to happiness, like my life should've ended when Louis's did?"

"But it didn't," he whispered.

She settled her intense eyes on him, studying, searching. "I was a bride for three days, a lonely war wife for nearly four years, and a widow for three. I've spent all my life grieving, first for my mother and then for my father. I grieved for Louis's father, a wonderful man, who passed away while y'all were gone. Just a few months later Louis was dead."

"I know."

"Sometimes I'm so afraid that if I let myself fall in love again I'll lose that person, too, and I don't think I could stand it." Her eyes were bright, her voice low and anxious. She was opening her heart to him, revealing the deepest parts of herself in a way Cyrus knew he never could. "I don't think I could survive burying another husband."

He nodded, understanding. She'd said pretty much the same thing when she dismissed lawmen as potential husbands.

"But I think I can," she whispered.

"Fall in love again?"

She nodded.

"Calvin?" he asked.

His answer was a smile and then a small nod of Roxanne's head and a whispered "maybe" as Maude Hipp appeared.

"What can I get you folks?"

"Just coffee for me," Cyrus answered.

Roxanne bit her lower lip again, and the uncertain gesture made her look much as she had at fifteen. "Tea," she said. "And do you have anything chocolate?"

Maude grinned. "Only the best chocolate cake in Texas."

"That's what I want," Roxanne said.

He hadn't seen her like this for such a long time. Happy. Young at heart. Alive. And so he couldn't be sorry that he'd lied to her last night, couldn't regret what he'd said to her. He certainly couldn't ruin such a transformation with the ugly truth.

"Calvin," Cyrus said as Maude stepped away. "You think he's the one?"

Roxanne nodded. "I think . . . maybe."

"Why?" Maybe he shouldn't ask, but he had to know. If it was just the words, if it was nothing but what had passed, secretly, between them, then maybe, maybe. . . .

"Well, he is *gorgeous*," she said, confiding in him as if he were a sister or a lady friend. He didn't particularly like it. "And I've always wanted to live on a farm, to plant myself in one place and make it mine forever. It's what Louis and I planned, it's what I always expected my life to be. A farm is a good place to raise children, and I want lots of children."

She blushed, her cheeks turning a flattering soft pink.

"I grew up on a farm," he said, and immediately he regretted the words.

"You did?" Roxanne's eyes got big. No wonder. He never talked about his life before coming to Paris. Never.

"I hated it," he said softly.

Her face fell. He could see the disappointment in her eyes. "Why?"

"My folks passed on, and I ended up living with a cousin who didn't want me any more than I wanted him." Yes, cousin Gil had made his dislike for his new responsibility clear as day. Gil's kids hadn't been too happy about having another child in the house, and his wife hadn't cared much for having another mouth to feed. No one had wanted him there. No one.

"I was seven. Old enough to help out with the chores. Young enough to get into trouble on a regular basis." And brother, had he. But those were details Roxanne didn't need to hear. "Mostly I found farm life as dull as ditch water."

"Oh," she sighed. "I guess it was your cousin who gave you your distaste for family life."

He didn't want to talk about it, didn't know what had possessed him to speak of it in the first place. Ah, yes he did. She'd been talking about having a dozen or so of Calvin's children. No wonder he'd changed the subject.

"You could say that. Let's see," he said before

she could question him again. "We were talking about . . . kids."

She was reluctant to redirect their conversation. "Not everyone is as unkind as your cousin obviously was. Some people would've been delighted to have a wonderful child like you in their household." She smiled softly. "And I'm sure you were a wonderful child."

"Opinions differ on that subject," he said curtly. "Now, can we get back to your plans?"

She narrowed her eyes. "I suppose. It's just that, well, I certainly won't be happy to teach other people's children forever."

"Guess not," Cyrus mumbled.

"I want my own children," Roxanne added softly. "And Calvin is . . ." A dreamy expression stole over her face. "Much more than he appears to be. Beneath that simple facade there's a romantic, intelligent, well-spoken man."

"Really?" Cyrus drawled.

"Oh, I know he doesn't say much, but in the right circumstances, he can be quite . . . " She sighed. "Charming."

"Great."

Maude delivered coffee and tea and cake on a well-balanced platter. She placed a slice of cake in front of Cyrus. "Eat it anyway," she said before he could remind her that he hadn't ordered it. "You don't want to pass up a treat like this."

Roxanne enjoyed her cake and tea with a relish that had been lacking at the party last night, closing her eyes with the first bite of the rich sweet, licking a crumb off her lower lip. Smiling as she declared it, indeed, the best chocolate cake in Texas.

Cyrus ignored the sick tightness in his gut, the unexpected sense of loss that overwhelmed him. Well, he'd done it, hadn't he? Louis's dying wish was that Roxanne be happy, and at long last she was. She was even thinking of falling in love again, of risking her heart. After all these years the time was right, and the task had been accomplished with a few sweet words and a handsome farmer.

And so he couldn't be sorry.

Chapter Seven

Today the first combined church picnic of spring—Methodists and Presbyterians coming together after services to mingle and eat—would take place in Mallory Park. It was a tradition of sorts, something they'd done regularly for years, when the weather was nice. Roxanne hadn't attended one of these picnics in a very long time. Just a few weeks ago, she surely wouldn't have gone.

She was not yet brave enough to wear her new rose dress, but instead of her usual somber clothing she'd chosen a very pale mint green gown that was years out of fashion but not comically so, thanks to the simple cut of the bodice and the flattering drape of the flowing skirt.

The morning's attentions to her appearance

hadn't stopped with her choice of a pastel and flattering gown. Instead of pulling her hair back severely she'd gathered it up in a softer, slightly curling style, so that a few strands hung about her face. The entire process, dressing and styling her hair, left her feeling more than a little nervous. A new hairstyle and a pretty dress were simple changes, but she felt them to her very bones.

Ada's cold was much better, and she felt well enough to attend church and the picnic. This morning she'd said nothing about Roxanne's dress or hair, though she'd cast more than one wide-eyed glance at her niece. Uncle Josiah had made a point of telling Roxanne how nice she looked, and then he'd changed the subject as the three of them began the walk to church.

They noticed the change in her, she knew. Perhaps they were afraid to mention it for fear she'd retreat into her customary gray. Had she become so sensitive that her aunt and uncle were afraid to make note of such a simple, momentous transformation?

Uncle Josiah returned home to collect the picnic basket from the house and bring it to the park, while Roxanne and Ada visited with old friends, talking about the fine weather and gossiping in soft voices. Roxanne noted more than one curious glance cast her way, more than one inquisitive raised eyebrow.

Did they notice the inner change she felt so strongly, or only the outer, superficial change?

Out of the corner of her eye she saw Cyrus

and Calvin arrive together. Cyrus carried a sloppily folded blanket, and there was a small basket in Calvin's hands. When she saw Calvin, Elizabeth Fowler's tirade about the unacceptable behavior of a few of the rowdier young men in her neighborhood faded to nothing in Roxanne's ears.

The two lawmen walked side by side, their long strides in perfect harmony as they walked over soft green grass, past tall leafy trees that took them in and out of the sunlight. Roxanne took a deep, stilling breath. They made quite a sight, both of them of a height—a couple of inches over six feet—both of them dressed in their Sunday best; Cyrus in black and Calvin in brown. They were both hatless and wore polished black boots. They were also both armed. The observation caused Roxanne a shiver of unpleasantness to spoil the moment. She would be glad when Calvin quit his job and bought that farm.

It didn't take her long to notice that other ladies had noted the arrival of the sheriff and his newest deputy, as well. Openly admiring glances, as well as a number of surreptitious glimpses past wide brimmed hats, were cast in their direction. The two men seemed not to realize that they caused a stir.

As they were coming straight toward her she returned her attention, in part at least, to Mrs. Fowler. She couldn't very well stand here anxiously as if she were waiting for Cyrus and Calvin to come for her! Not even if it were true.

Linda Jones

Soon enough the two men were at her back, and the eyes of all the ladies in their circle settled on the lawmen.

"Good afternoon, ladies," Cyrus said charmingly, and Roxanne turned slowly around.

Calvin stood behind his boss, apparently as shy as he'd claimed to be. He muttered a low "howdy."

"May we steal Roxanne from you ladies?" Cyrus asked, already taking her arm. Roxanne couldn't help but notice how Rose Wells bristled, or how Aunt Ada gave in to an affectionate smile as Roxanne allowed Cyrus to take her arm and lead her away. Calvin allowed them to pass and then fell into step behind, all without saying a single word. Goodness, he really *was* shy!

Cyrus placed the blanket he carried beneath a leafy maple tree, straightening and laying out the blanket in one easy snap. Ever the gentleman, he took her hand as she lowered herself to the ground. "You look very nice today," he said softly, his eyes telling her as he delivered the compliment that he noticed the change as everyone else did. Only Cyrus was brave enough to comment. She nodded her thanks as she tried her best to be graceful and demure, attributes which were sometimes difficult to attain with her height; especially when she was overcome with an unexpected rush of nervousness.

Behind her, she heard a muted rustle and a low whisper, and a moment later, as Cyrus and

Calvin lowered themselves so she was sandwiched between them, Calvin finally opened his mouth.

"Yep, you look right purty today, Roxanne," he said energetically.

"Thank you," she said, glancing demurely in Calvin's direction.

Calvin sat on the edge of the blanket that was bathed in bright sunlight, while she and Cyrus remained in the shade. Sunshine on golden curls made him seem somehow brighter, bigger, more beautiful than she remembered. His eyes were a paler blue than her own, and they were startling in their brilliance. Almost as startling as the smile he flashed at her.

"We brought ham and biscuits," he said as he reached for the basket he'd been carrying, "and some of Miz Hipp's chocolate cake. The sheriff seemed to think you might like it."

She glanced at a silent Cyrus and smiled at him. He had no doubt realized how much she'd enjoyed the chocolate cake yesterday, and had bought this just for her. "How very sweet," she said.

Cyrus did not return her smile. In fact, he merely grunted, and looked at her as if he'd rather be anywhere else in the world but here. So much for his gentlemanly manners.

She turned back to Calvin. "How do you like Paris so far?"

He nodded twice before speaking. "It's a right fine place, I reckon. The folks are friendly." He squinted his eyes. "There are an awful lot of people in this town, though."

"Yes there are," she agreed.

"I mean, I got nothing against people or nothing, it's just that I'm accustomed to a bit more peace and quiet. The place I'm from in Tennessee ain't nothing more than a wide place in the road," he said fondly. "Once I buy my farm I 'spect I'll settle in just fine."

There was something odd about Calvin today. He wasn't as open as he'd been on Friday night. Even his voice was different; coarser somehow. And while he smiled at her wonderfully, she saw none of the passion and allure she'd heard as he'd paced beneath her balcony. His shyness, she decided, and the public nature of today's meeting, forced Calvin to hold part of himself back.

"When do you plan to buy that farm?" she asked casually.

"Soon, I reckon," he said. "There's a parcel for sale near my kinfolk. Did I tell you I got cousins nearby?"

She shook her head.

"Well, I do, and I'm headed out that way to have a look at the land that's for sale later this week."

"Really?" The sooner he put his guns aside, the happier she'd be.

He nodded, and looked at her as if he had something important to say. She stared, as anyone might stare at something or someone who defied nature and was absolutely, positively perfect. Perfect face, perfect hair, on occasion perfect words. She held her breath and waited.

"Can we eat now?" he finally asked. "I'm starving."

Cyrus sat back and listened to the conversation. His deputy was handling himself well, if not brilliantly. Roxanne and Calvin spoke of simple things: the weather, his farm, the food. Cyrus supposed he should slip away and leave these two alone, but he stayed put even after his ham and biscuits were gone.

Roxanne's attention was completely on Calvin as he talked about his plans for a farm. On this one subject, the deputy was competent and comprehensible. It was a shared dream, Cyrus realized, this simple farm Calvin and Roxanne both wanted.

Roxanne had more color in her cheeks these days, he noted as he stared at her profile, more sparkle in her eyes. She didn't love Calvin yet, but the idea certainly tantalized her. He saw unbridled need in her face, a need for companionship and stability and perhaps even adoration. She hungered for all that, perhaps, dreamed of the life she wanted and deserved. Calvin could give her everything she desired.

She smiled at something Calvin said, flashed that wide, unrestrained grin that brought out delicate dimples in her cheeks and a flush of new color, as well. Soon she wouldn't be his responsibility anymore. If he could succeed this time, if he could fulfill his promise to Louis, maybe he could forget about the promise he hadn't been able to keep.

"Sheriff?" The tentative, feminine voice came from nearby, surprising him. He'd been so intent on Roxanne that he hadn't even heard anyone approach.

Cyrus looked up to see Jane Rice standing over him, her eyes wide and her hand cradling a plate that was covered with a linen napkin. He stood quickly, jumping to his feet so that he towered over the girl who stood barely five foot two.

"Good afternoon, Jane," he said, wondering if there was a problem somewhere in the park or beyond that required his attention. "Is something wrong?"

She shook her head slowly and looked at the ground. "Nothing's wrong. I just thought you might like some of my lemon sponge cake." She didn't lift her head, but cut her eyes to him demurely. "Do you like lemon sponge cake?"

Why were women always trying to feed him? Roxanne's apple pie, Maude Hipp's chocolate cake, and now this. "Well, I'm pretty full right this minute."

Clear disappointment rushed across Jane's face, for some reason he didn't quite understand. Her hint of a smile vanished, and her shoulders tensed visibly. He cursed himself for being so curt.

"Perhaps I could save it for later," he suggested, taking the plate from her.

Jane's smile sneaked back as she released the plate.

Cyrus placed the plate of lemon sponge cake on the blanket, noticing that as Calvin continued talking of plans for his farm, Roxanne's attention was divided between the agricultural details and Cyrus's own conversation with Jane Rice. Jane offered a chance, he realized belatedly, of escape. Calvin was handling himself well, and Roxanne was well on her way to falling in love with the dimwit. Cyrus knew he was definitely not needed here.

"Would you like to take a walk?" he asked Jane. "Maybe that will help me work up an appetite."

She smiled brightly and took his offered arm.

Cyrus glanced down at Roxanne, only to find her looking up at him, unsmiling. "If you'll excuse us," he said, and without waiting for an answer he walked away with Jane Rice on his arm.

They were as alone as two people could be, and still Calvin went on and on about his farm. Roxanne knew what he would plant in the fall and what he would plant in the spring. She knew how many cattle he expected to have to start with, and what kind of house he wanted to build. Even now, with Cyrus gone and no one else within earshot, he didn't say a word about his feelings. It was almost as if he didn't have any.

How foolish of her to be disappointed that

his conversation didn't cause a thrill to rush through her blood. She hadn't come to her decision to marry looking for thrills, but for a home and family. Calvin obviously wanted that as much as she did. He was a nice man, and he knew what he wanted from life: his farm. If she had to settle for the occasional thrill, when the moon and the mood were right, that would be enough. More than enough.

She shifted her attention from Calvin to watch Cyrus, as she had often since he'd left their shared blanket. He walked through the park with Jane Rice at his side, saying hello to those they passed, leaning slightly to the side as he spoke to his companion. She'd bet everything she had that not once had he spoken of chickens or corn, cattle or cotton.

Was this the woman he'd danced with in the shadows at Merilee's party? Jane Rice? Surely not. No matter how hard she tried, she couldn't see them as a couple. Jane was too young, too short, too . . . ordinary for a man like Cyrus.

She watched them walk over the bridge that spanned the narrow creek, stopping to look down at the trickle of water over rocks far below. Cyrus leaned against the bridge and listened attentively as Jane went on and on about one thing or another. The young woman spoke with her small, delicate hands and laughed more than once, more lively than Roxanne could ever remember her being. Jane was obviously smitten with Cyrus, and he was loving every minute of her silly, undivided attention.

Roxanne forced herself to look at Calvin again. This was what she wanted. Right? A simple life on a farm. A new beginning. Still, when Cyrus and Jane began to wander back in this direction, she found herself watching them more and more, actually trying to read their lips. How pathetic!

Cyrus walked slowly, long, graceful strides bringing him back to the blanket. Roxanne felt every step as he came near, as if his steps were attuned with her heartbeat. Nearer and nearer he came, with Jane still in tow.

Without warning, Mary Alice came out of nowhere and practically attacked him, throwing herself at his legs. Nothing made Cyrus stumble; he caught the little girl and lifted her into his arms, and they were close enough for Roxanne to hear him say, "Here's my best girl."

Mary Alice tried to shove a tea cake into Cyrus's mouth. Laughing, he allowed her to feed him.

The three of them, Cyrus and Jane and Mary Alice, came to the blanket.

"Excuse us," Cyrus said softly as he set Mary Alice on her feet and reached for the sponge cake Jane had prepared for him. "I'll just take this and. . . ."

"Don't be silly," Roxanne said brightly. "Have a seat."

It was an order; sweetly delivered, but still an order. Cyrus saw Jane seated, and with the same courteous demeanor helped Mary Alice to the blanket as well. When he seated himself, sandwiched between Jane and Roxanne with Mary Alice at his feet, the blanket was quite crowded.

"So, what have you two been talking about?" Cyrus asked as he peeled the linen napkin away from the lemon sponge cake.

"Oh, farming and such," Calvin answered.

Cyrus shot a sharp, somehow censuring glance to his deputy. "Is that so?"

"It's fascinating," Roxanne said. "Calvin has such wonderful plans." She smiled, but it wasn't her best effort.

As they passed the cake around Jane remained silent, Calvin merely mumbled now and then, and Cyrus was apparently lost in thought. Thank goodness for Mary Alice, Roxanne thought as the little girl carried the conversation. They heard about her new dress, her new doll, and how Edith Terry was still trying to get her to climb trees when she knew she shouldn't do any such thing.

The little girl was clearly fascinated with Cyrus. She directed most of her excited dialogue to him, and after she'd finished off her sponge cake she placed a hand carelessly on his boot, searching for a connection of some sort, Roxanne supposed. She was almost tempted to do the same, to reach out and lay a hand on Cyrus; on his arm, his knee, his other boot. Unfortunately she was long past five and had no excuse for such behavior.

Mary Alice lifted her precious face to

Roxanne, but she didn't move those possessive hands from Cyrus's boot. "My mama said that in just a few months I can go to your school and you can teach me to read and write."

"That will be lovely," Roxanne said with a smile. "You're such a clever girl I'm sure you'll make a wonderful student."

Mary Alice beamed. "Papa says I'm smart as a whip."

"Of course you are," Cyrus said in a matter-of-fact voice.

Roxanne glanced past Cyrus to an apparently adoring Jane. Was he blind? Did he know that simply by being attentive and polite he was leading her on? Cyrus, who'd made it clear he had no use for marriage, really shouldn't be leading innocent young women on.

"You know," Roxanne said, "Jane was one of my very best students not so long ago."

Jane blushed as she glanced past Cyrus to catch Roxanne's eye. "Well, it has been a couple of years."

A touch of awkwardness filled the air, though Roxanne couldn't be sure that anyone but she was aware of it.

Soon the cake was gone, and Merilee came by to say hello and fetch Mary Alice. Jane's father came to collect her moments later, saying it was time they headed home. Jane seemed to be embarrassed that her father had come for her much as Mary Alice's mother had. That, together with the reminder Roxanne had provided, made it clear that she was still just a girl; and much too young for Cyrus.

Cyrus ignored Jane's embarrassment and thanked her for the cake and the company, and as Roxanne watched and listened something in her stomach tightened and twisted a little.

For a few long minutes the three of them, Roxanne and Cyrus and Calvin, sat silently on a rumpled blanket covered with scattered crumbs and a few bits of grass. The silence was as strained, Roxanne realized, as it had been when she'd made a point of reminding everyone how young Jane Rice was. She didn't want to ponder why she felt so awkward at this moment.

Calvin picked up the conversation where he'd stopped, she supposed. She couldn't for the life of her remember exactly what they'd been talking about in the minutes before Cyrus had rejoined them. "I'll be leaving Thursday, I reckon, and be gone several days."

Cyrus's head snapped up. "Leaving? What for?" Then he remembered. "Oh yes, you're going to check out that farm, aren't you?"

"Yep," Calvin said, comfortable again. "And to visit with the cousins. They don't make it to town often, and I really haven't had a chance to pay a nice long visit, like I should." He stared past Roxanne to Cyrus. "That won't be a problem, will it? I shouldn't be gone much more than a week."

"That's fine," Cyrus said absently, and they

fell into another bout of uncomfortable silence. Roxanne wanted to kick herself for being so foolish. Calvin Newberry was everything she required in a man, and yet it seemed that Cyrus claimed all her attention without even trying. Next to Cyrus, beautiful Calvin seemed downright dull.

When one of the other deputies came by to ask Calvin to come take a look at his horse's foreleg, Calvin seemed happy to escape.

Leaving Roxanne and Cyrus alone.

"Well," she said when Calvin was out of hearing distance. "She's a little young for you, isn't she?"

Cyrus was obviously surprised by her question. He looked at her without answering, for a long moment, then he responded, "Jane?"

"No," Roxanne snapped. "Mary Alice."

When Cyrus smiled at her she lost her temper.

"Of course I mean Jane," she hissed. "She's barely twenty years old and you're *well* past thirty."

"I'm thirty-one," he said, obviously amused.

"And she's twenty," Roxanne said gravely. She narrowed her eyes and did her best to stare Cyrus down. "Is she the woman you were dancing with Friday night? Really, Cyrus, you shouldn't trifle with the affections of such an impressionable young girl."

"All I did was walk her around the park," Cyrus said with a casual air, not a bit bothered by her anger.

"She's not the woman you were dancing with behind that tree?" Roxanne asked, giving away her suspicions.

A sly grin slipped across Cyrus's face. "Nope."

Roxanne took a deep breath and tried to calm herself. How ridiculous she was! She'd thought herself, on Friday night, that Cyrus needed a woman, a wife, had even briefly considered Jane a candidate. And here she was practically interrogating him about the women in his life—a subject which certainly was none of her business.

"I don't suppose it's any of my business," she muttered. "Jane just seems so . . . silly," she added softly, unable to help herself.

Just a few days ago she'd thought Jane to be a level-headed young woman and a possible match for Cyrus. Today, for no apparent reason, her opinion had changed. Besides, if Cyrus had no intention of marrying he shouldn't be dallying with the affections of a naive girl who was much too young for him.

Cyrus rumbled something unintelligible beneath his breath, making a noise that sounded comfortingly like agreement with her unflattering assessment.

Another long moment of silence passed, but oddly enough the awkwardness was gone. Roxanne watched the people in the park, the children running and playing, the couples talking with their heads together. Her senseless hostility faded, and she allowed herself to enjoy a moment in time when somehow all was right with the world.

"You know," she said, her eyes roaming the park, "you never did finish telling me about your cousin and the farm."

"My, aren't we nosy today?" Cyrus said lightly. "First you want to know who I was dancing with Friday night, and then you try to dredge up ancient history."

She laid her eyes on him and smiled. "Not so ancient. Why, you just made a point of telling me that you're *only* thirty-one."

"Feels pretty damn ancient," he muttered.

She leaned just slightly closer. "Surely you have at least one fond memory of growing up on that farm. I just can't believe that you hated it completely."

"If it had to do with animals, plowing, or picking, I hated it."

"Did little Cyrus have a lazy streak?" she asked devilishly.

He cut her a narrow-eyed glance. "Perhaps. Mostly, little Cyrus was bored out of his mind. If Jean, that was Gil's wife, hadn't loved books and allowed me to borrow one now and again, I would've run away long before I was thirteen."

She slapped him on the forearm, almost playfully. "You ran away at thirteen?"

"Not a moment too soon, and that's enough of this topic of conversation," he said, closing the door on his past with a mighty slam.

She sighed and looked away, strangely content. She had a feeling Cyrus didn't tell just anyone about Gil and Jean and the farm he hated. But he'd confided in her. He was her friend, her very best friend. The thought warmed her from the inside out. He trusted her.

Beside her Cyrus fidgeted a little, as if trying to make himself comfortable after sitting for too long on the ground. "Can I ask you something?"

Her heart skipped a beat as she turned to him. "Anything."

He looked into her eyes. "Why are women always trying to feed me?"

"What?"

"You, Maude Hipp, Jane, even Mary Alice. Do I look like I need fattening up?"

She laughed, briefly and softly, her anger long gone. She couldn't stay mad at Cyrus for long. "No, you don't look like you need fattening up." She scrutinized him, her eyes raking up and down critically, searching for faults and finding none. "But you do," she said, "look like a man who needs taking care of."

Her smile faded. Cyrus was looking her straight in the eyes again, in that penetrating way he had.

"Do I, now?"

She nodded once, in answer. For a moment she forgot that a lawman would make an unsuitable husband, she dismissed the idea of leaving Paris and settling on a farm far from town. She dismissed the idea that she didn't need thrills.

How could this have happened? How could she be attracted to two men at the same time?

Calvin, with his whispered sweet words and handsome face and simple plans, and Cyrus, on a level that was more physical and surprising, and certainly inexplicable. Cyrus, who didn't want a family, who wore a gun, who was a part of her painful past. Cyrus, who was her friend, who was always there, who was looking at her right now as if they shared a divine secret. In her mind, Roxanne knew that Calvin was right for her and Cyrus was not. Oh, but her heart . . . her heart wasn't quite so sure.

If only she could reach out and revive the man who'd paced beneath her window and opened his heart to her. That was the Calvin she was falling in love with, that was the man who had kept her awake half the night, who had given her good dreams for the first time in a very long while. Why did he have to be so different today, when she needed him to remind her of everything they could have together?

Cyrus, she reminded herself again, was just a friend. Her awareness of him was just another step in her awakening, just another step in her return from numbness. He wasn't right for her, he wasn't the kind of man who could ever open his heart to a woman the way Calvin had.

But looking at Cyrus right this minute, she had the most disturbing thought: if only he could love her. . . .

Chapter Eight

Cyrus hadn't spoken to Roxanne in three days, since the picnic in Mallory Park. That didn't mean he hadn't seen her, hadn't watched her, but he'd observed from a distance as he had for the past three years. Lately he'd gotten too close to her, and that closeness only fed his obsession. When he looked into her eyes all sorts of impossible thoughts taunted him, and he questioned his resolve to see that Roxanne got exactly what she wanted. That wouldn't do.

So he'd returned to watching her from afar, sure it was for the best. He'd even suggested to Calvin that he meet up with Roxanne on the way home from school and walk her home, and on one day the deputy had done just that. Cyrus spied on the meeting from the shadows until he'd seen Roxanne smile just once; then

143

he knew all was right with the world and he was no longer needed here.

Today, however, Calvin was not around. Cyrus cursed under his breath, figuring that the boy was probably lost again.

Even though Calvin was not around to do the honors, he didn't join Roxanne as she walked by. Standing on the boardwalk before the saloon, he even lowered his head as she passed, so that if she looked his way she'd assume he didn't even know she was on the street. He stood in shadow and her gaze was steady and straight ahead, so likely she wasn't even aware of his presence.

Roxanne seemed well on her way to being happy, and he was glad; but he also felt a strange sense of loss. He hadn't expected that giving up his obsession would be so difficult, that he'd begun to think of Roxanne as his reason for being, as his purpose in life. Once her dreams came true there would be a large, empty hole in his life, a void he didn't think anything—anyone—else could fill.

A sound that didn't belong, something not quite right, made him lift his head. He stepped forward, narrowed his eyes, and looked searchingly from one end of the street to the other. For a moment all was still, and then he heard more clearly the faint noise that had disturbed him. Horses. Coming fast.

He stepped into the sunshine, into the street, and felt as well as heard Roxanne turn her gaze to him. That gaze hit him as surely as the warmth of the sun on his face.

"Hello, Cyrus," she said, just a hint of surprise in her voice.

He didn't look at her. With his eyes trained on the emptiness at the end of the street he squinted his eyes against the glare of the sun. A coarse shout, a joyous, angry scream, joined the approaching thunder of pounding hooves as the dust at the end of the street rose.

"Get into the dress shop," he commanded, nodding once toward Fannie Rowland's place.

"But—" Roxanne began.

"Now."

She heard the urgency in his voice, perhaps, because she obeyed without another word. Hamlin Nickels stepped onto the boardwalk, and without turning, Cyrus ordered the old man inside as well. Up and down the street the word spread quickly, and people took cover.

Dust filled the street as the riders approached. Cyrus's heartbeat increased and his mouth went dry. Riders coming fast didn't necessarily mean trouble, but that single shout had been spine-chilling in its fury. His gut told him nothing good would come riding through that dust cloud.

Three horses appeared, still coming fast. It didn't take him long to recognize the rider in the middle as the man who'd introduced himself, a couple of weeks ago, as J. T. Johnson. The man he'd run out of town.

Cyrus waited in the street, alone. The warm spring sun beat down on his hat, his face, and the length of his body, and dust rose to tickle his nose. Muscles tensed in his neck and his arms, and he flexed his fingers without conscious thought. Everyone else was behind closed doors, perhaps peeking from windows and rooftops, but he soon forgot that he had an audience. All his attention remained on the three riders as they came to a halt in the middle of the street.

J. T. dismounted first, and the others followed suit. The three of them stepped forward defiantly, moving unerringly ahead. J. T.'s companions fanned out, effectively surrounding Cyrus.

"Fellas, this is the Sheriff Scarface I told you about. He was right unfriendly to me last time I passed through town." With friends backing him up, J. T. was braver than before, and that made him dangerous.

"You boys might as well get moving," Cyrus said calmly, his voice low. "There's nothing for you here."

J. T. took a step forward. "I'm here to call you out, scarface." His hand rested comfortably over the revolver at his hip. "You insulted me, throwed me out of town for no good reason, even threatened to shoot me in the back." He shook his head in apparent disbelief. "Ain't right. I tried to forget about it, but I can't. You done me wrong."

Cyrus glanced quickly to the two men who

had ridden into town with Johnson. They were apparently as mean and stupid as J. T., and that was a real shame. Cyrus found it damn near impossible to reason with a single mean, stupid man, let alone three of them.

Watching Johnson's hands, Cyrus swept his jacket back to clear his holster. He flexed his long fingers again. "You have one last chance to ride out of town. Think of it as a gift. I'm in a fairly good mood and I really don't want to kill anybody today."

Johnson grinned. "I ain't riding out of town this time until I'm good and ready." He smirked. "That might not be for a day or two. I 'spect once you're dead the three of us will find that tall gal I seen on my way out of town and show her how a real man treats a woman."

Cyrus suppressed the flare of anger that shot through him and narrowed his focus until all he saw were the armed men in the street. The horses behind them faded, the people he knew were watching were gone—unimportant. Johnson really was stupid. Did the moron think the man he called Sheriff Scarface would get frightened and run just because he was outnumbered? Did they think he would panic because he faced three guns?

Yes, there were three of them, but no matter what, Johnson was a dead man. He should know that just by looking at Cyrus's face. One or both of the others might—*might*—get off a shot, but that wasn't going to happen before Cyrus put a bullet through J. T. Johnson's heart.

"Last chance," Cyrus whispered, his hand hovering over the Colt at his hip. "If you plan to ride out of town sitting upright, now's the time."

Johnson twitched once and drew his six-shooter, trying unsuccessfully to get the drop on the sheriff who had driven him out of town.

From the moment he saw Johnson make his move, Cyrus didn't think; what came next was instinct, reflex. The butt of the gun fit his hand with a comfort that made it a part of him. The weapon slid smoothly from the holster, without a hitch, without a split second of hesitation, so fast Johnson's companions flinched. One of them cursed reverently beneath his breath.

Cyrus tightened his finger on the trigger. When the moment was right, he squeezed.

An expression of surprise flitted across Johnson's face as he lifted a hand to his chest and fell to his knees. *Stupid*, Cyrus thought.

As if through another eye, Cyrus saw the men beside him draw their guns as the horses reared and skittered back. He rotated and fired, the defensive motion smooth and quick as he fired to one side and then the other. A single shot was fired from a weapon not his own, but it went wild.

In a matter of seconds the confrontation was over. He hadn't consciously aimed and fired, hadn't even thought about what was happening. Now it was done. Survival instincts had kicked in, and Cyrus had done what he had to do, what he did best. He'd killed them all.

The reverberation of gunfire diminished in the suddenly still air as townspeople stepped from their businesses to get a better look. The horses ran, scared off by the sharp, violent blasts that continued to ring in Cyrus's ears. Three men lay dead in the street. All three had their six-shooters in their hands. Only one of them had managed to get off a shot.

Around him, people murmured; whispering words he couldn't quite discern. He didn't need to hear their words. He could tell by glancing at their faces that they were scared, impressed, horrified. Cyrus himself felt only slightly ill.

He took his eyes from the bloody bodies on the street, and discovered Roxanne staring at him. Her face had gone pale, so white she looked as if she might pass out at any moment. He took a step closer to her, planning to explain what had happened, but when he made that move she took a matching step back.

He stopped his forward progress as Hamlin clapped him on the back and Thomas Eakin appeared to congratulate him on a job well done. When he didn't respond, they moved away to see to the task of removing the bodies from the street.

Cyrus moved toward Roxanne again, a single step, and when he did she turned and ran.

* * *

She should've been asleep hours ago, but right now she felt like she'd never sleep again. Her heart pounded unnaturally fast and hard and had for hours, and her mind whirled with thoughts . . . none of them pleasant.

Roxanne sat on her balcony and grasped the wrought iron bars before her as if the very grip kept her from falling apart. She drank in the night air as if it could nourish her, as if the coolness would calm her blood and her heart until all was right again.

She'd never seen a man shot before, never seen blood flow from a man's heart, taking his life with it. When she closed her eyes she heard the discharge of guns so clearly she winced, just as she had this afternoon when shots had been fired. In her mind's eye she saw, again, the men fall, saw Cyrus standing calmly over it all as if nothing were wrong, as if this turn of events was right and natural. He'd killed three men in the blink of an eye.

Oh, it had happened so *fast*. One minute all was well, and the next . . . the next nothing was the same. Cyrus had killed three men without so much as a breath of hesitation.

Three guns had been pointed at him. Three men had surrounded him. When he'd drawn his gun and pulled the trigger, an answering shot had been fired. Dammit, he could've been killed.

Like it or not, she kept coming back to that.

Cyrus might have been one of the men on the ground, bleeding, dead. If that single shot had been well-aimed, it would've torn through his body in a heartbeat, tearing flesh, perhaps bringing that heartbeat to an end.

She clutched the cool iron bars in her hands and looked beyond to the dark and silent moonlit night. All was apparently peaceful here, and all around her the residents of Paris slept, safe and sound.

The peacefulness was false, though, she knew. There was danger everywhere, violence right around the next corner, at the end of the road. She closed her eyes tightly. How could she have allowed herself to feel anything for Cyrus when she knew very well who he was and what he did?

She knew now, more certainly than ever, that Calvin was the one who could make all her dreams come true. No matter what inappropriate feelings for Cyrus flickered through her, she knew in her heart and in her mind that he was not the man for her. She could list the reasons from memory now; the past that tied him to Louis, his dangerous career, his horrified insistence that he would never get married, that children—the children she wanted so badly—were annoyances to be avoided. She couldn't allow her feelings for Cyrus to grow. No matter what, she would have to learn to squash the admiration and jealousy and desire that flitted inappropriately to the surface now and again.

"What keeps you awake?"

Her eyes flew open and she looked down to see a familiar white hat and long butternut duster.

"Calvin?"

"Yep." His voice was soft and gentle, easy and soothing. "I couldn't sleep myself, tonight, so I decided to take a nice long walk. I was jest passing by when I saw you sitting here. What's wrong?"

Which Calvin stood below? Farmer or lover? Distant friend or adoring suitor?

"It's silly, I know, but I was rather upset by this afternoon's . . . episode." Goodness, she couldn't even say the word shooting.

He nodded his head as if he understood. "It can be kinda disagreeable to watch a man die, even a bad man."

"Is that what they were?" she whispered. "Bad men?"

He hesitated; for a moment he didn't even pace, but stood stock still in the moonlight. "Do you think the sheriff would shoot them if they weren't? Do you think he would've fired his weapon if he hadn't been defending himself and anyone else those criminals might have run across next?"

"I don't know," she whispered. "It happened so fast."

"You shouldn't think of such things," he said. "What happened this afternoon was ugly and horrible, and you shouldn't be exposed to such misfortunes. You should. . . ." he stopped for a moment. "You should only have goodness and beauty for the rest of your life. Blue skies, green gardens, happy children."

Her heart skipped a beat. "Children?" she whispered.

"Children."

He paced, head down, beneath her balcony. Oh, she wished he would look up at her and smile, just once, but since they'd been through this before she didn't really expect him to. Maybe one day, when he knew her better and didn't feel so shy in her company, maybe then she could see his face as she heard sweet words from his mouth.

"I'm so very glad," she said earnestly, "that you're not going to be a deputy for much longer."

"Are you now?" he asked softly.

"Yes," she breathed. "I can't . . . I just can't. . . . "

"I understand," he said, saving her from her ramblings.

"Roxanne?" he said her name very slowly, and she had the strange notion that he liked the feel of the word on his lips.

"Yes?"

He didn't speak immediately, but stalled as if waiting for the perfect moment to speak. The silence was deep, complete. She waited.

"All I want is for you to have everything your heart desires," he finally said, his voice uncommonly low.

She smiled. "That's all?"

"That's everything," he whispered, and then he began to back away, one slow step at a time.

"Don't go," she said, coming up on her knees. "Not yet."

Already she felt calmer, more herself. The panic and the horror were gone, just because Calvin stood there in the night, whispering kind, sweet words to her.

"I can stay for a few more minutes, I guess," he said reluctantly.

Roxanne stood. She wasn't even wearing her dressing gown on this warm night, just her nightdress. She should run inside and change, or else she should allow Calvin to walk away. But she did neither. She clasped the rail in her hands and looked down at that wide-brimmed white hat that hid everything from her.

"I'm coming down," she said impulsively, releasing the rail.

"No!" Calvin backed away a few more steps. "I can't talk to you face to face, not tonight."

"Why not?"

He cocked his head slightly to the side. "Unless, of course, you want to talk more about the farm."

"No," she said quickly, ashamed that the very thought distressed her deeply. "I don't want to talk about the farm, not tonight. It's just that you're so . . . so far away, and it's so dark tonight."

He paced silently for a moment, then stopped directly beneath her. "I have an idea," he said, and then he turned his back to her and walked to the oak tree that grew near her balcony. An old, gnarled oak tree, the lowest limb hung a good ways off the ground.

Calvin jumped up from a standing position and caught the lower limb in both hands, and then he heaved himself up with a grace she hadn't known he possessed. He tossed one leg easily up and over the limb, and then the other. She smiled, and her heart raced. There was strength and beauty in that simple move, masculine grace and heart-stopping power. He disappeared into the leaves, and she only saw his boots as he stood on that low limb and climbed higher, bringing himself directly across from her.

Leaves rustled for a moment and then were still.

"Calvin?" she whispered.

The answer came from mere feet away. "Yep."

Cyrus leaned against the tree trunk and stretched his legs out along the sturdy limb. Through a break in the leaves he saw Roxanne's face as she leaned over the balcony railing. He could imagine that she reached for him with her entire body; that she reached for *Calvin*.

It came to him, again, how very beautiful she was. Every feature perfect, strong and still somehow soft. How could Calvin say that she was no prettier than Jane or Rose or half a dozen other girls? The boy was apparently blind as well as stupid and clumsy.

Roxanne smiled, and his heart constricted.

Tonight she wore only her white linen night-dress. Did she know how it molded to her body? How her breasts pushed against the thin fabric, how the linen flowed about her long legs? A short gust of wind pushed the fabric against her body, for a brief second delineating every curve, every crevice. Every in and every out. Before him stood pure perfection, *all woman*, and what he wanted more than anything was to reach out and touch her. Ah, but not only was he hiding, she was too far away. Unless he wanted to reveal himself, unless he was ready to face her with the ugly truth, he would never be able to touch her.

Watching Roxanne, thinking about touching her, fantasizing about his hands on that body, aroused him. His response was immediate, complete, and not at all surprising. He was so hard, getting down from this damn tree anytime soon was going to be a real problem.

No wonder his physical response was so quick and painful. He hadn't been with a woman in a long time; too long. At this moment he finally understood why. He wanted Roxanne and only Roxanne, a woman he could never have, a woman he had no right to desire.

"Is this better?" he asked.

Her smile widened. "I don't know. You're closer, but I still can't see your face."

"Just as well," he sighed. "You know how bashful I am. Why shucks, you just look at me with those big blue eyes and I lose my tongue, and all I can think of to talk about is plowing and cows."

She cocked her head to one side and a fall of dark hair draped over her shoulder. It looked so soft, so tempting.

"You even sound different," she said, apparently only slightly puzzled. "Your voice is softer. The same, somehow, but still . . . different."

"Maybe I am different when I'm alone with you," he said. "Maybe I've changed because I know you. 'The face of all the world is changed, I think, since first I heard the footsteps of thy soul.'"

She sighed. "You know Elizabeth Barrett Browning."

"Sure," he said, wondering if he'd made a colossal mistake. "I went to school. Mostly we had these old maid schoolteachers, but there was this one prissy perfessor fella." He tried to mimic Calvin as well as possible. "If I remember rightly he was the one who taught us poetry."

When she'd run from him this afternoon, she'd been pale and sickly looking, but now she had color in her cheeks and a sparkle in her eyes. Even in the moonlight he saw the details too well. She was right; she could never marry a lawman whose life would always be touched with violence. She was too delicate for a life like that. She deserved better. She deserved more.

But if he could love her, just once. . . .

He put the impossible thought from his mind. "Do you know you look like an angel, standing there?" he whispered, the voice too much his own. Perhaps she realized something was wrong. Her smiled faded. "Shucks," he added, doing his best to sound like countrified Calvin. "You're fine as frog's hair, and that's a fact."

"You say that, but it's not true," she said, half in modesty and half in confusion. "I'm too tall, and my mouth is too wide, and I—"

"To me," he amended, "You're the purtiest gal in town and always will be. You are not too tall, you're stately and graceful in a way no woman of an average height will ever be. And your mouth. . . ." His insides tightened and impossibly he got even harder as he studied that particular feature. "Your mouth is perfect, Roxanne. Especially when you smile or laugh."

"*You're* beautiful," she whispered shyly. "Truly, impossibly beautiful." It was hard to tell in the moonlight, but it seemed she blushed. "That's very forward, I know, but it's only the truth."

Roxanne wanted and deserved *beautiful*. Still, he was in no mood to hear how much she admired Calvin Newberry's face. "Talk to me," Cyrus said. "Tell me about yourself and your life and what you want."

Roxanne stared intently, and even though Cyrus knew she couldn't possibly see his face he shivered as she seemed to look straight through him.

"I don't know where to start," she whispered. Cyrus made himself comfortable—as comfortable as possible in his present condition—stretching his legs along the sturdy limb and crossing his booted ankles. The hem of Calvin's duster hung over the limb, and his wide-brimmed hat scooted forward to shadow his face . . . just in case.

How fortunate that Calvin was forgetful as well as clumsy. Cyrus had found the hat and duster hanging in the jailhouse long after Calvin had gone home.

"Start at the beginning," he said softly. "What were you like as a child? Were you happy? Serious? Did you play with dolls or were you a tomboy? I want to know everything."

Roxanne told him about her rootless years with her father, and coming to Paris to live with her aunt and uncle after his death. She even spoke about Louis. She told him so much he didn't know, along with tidbits he knew quite well. After a while she sat on the balcony, perhaps tired at last, and leaned her head against the railing.

She talked more about Louis, how much she'd liked him when they first met at the age of twelve, how much she'd come to love him, how he'd died. There were no tears. She told him how sometimes she looked at Mary Alice Smith and realized that if she'd been pregnant when Louis had gone to war, she'd have a child just that age. It was a very personal, intimate, heart-felt observation, not the kind of secret to share with just anyone.

When she finished, she took a deep breath

and sighed slowly, as if she'd just expelled something bitter and was better for it.

"And what about you, Calvin?" she asked dreamily. "Tell me about your life."

"Another night," Cyrus said softly. "Besides, you haven't finished."

She fastened her eyes on the leaves of the tree. It was a wonder, in his mind, that she couldn't see him.

"What did I leave out?"

"What do you want?"

She smiled, a soft, sleepy, wonderful smile. "I want to live again. To have a home and family and children. I want peace at last, real peace. And I want to pass countless nights just like this one, talking while the rest of the world sleeps."

"You shall have it," Cyrus whispered, his voice so low he was almost certain Roxanne couldn't hear.

Chapter Nine

After an almost sleepless night, Cyrus arrived at Lamar County Jail earlier than usual. Hell, if he was going to pace and mutter he could do it here as well as in his own one-room house.

Going to Roxanne's last night had been a bad idea. He knew that, had reminded himself again and again of his mistake. No matter how hard he tried he couldn't regret going to her. Thanks to his late-night visit he knew her better than he ever had, could close his eyes and see her as a lanky little girl, could understand even better how close she and Louis had been. He knew her dreams and fears, her strength and courage.

Calvin was a lucky man.

Cyrus paced near the window, thinking again how fortunate Calvin was, when a sharp rap sounded on the door and it opened. The lucky man himself stood there. He'd collected his duster and hat from the rack in the main office, where Cyrus had replaced them early this morning.

"Just wanted to say so long before I hit the road," Calvin said with a wide grin.

"You're leaving already?" Cyrus snapped.

Calvin's grin faded. "Figured I might as well get an early start. I got a long day ahead of me."

"What about Roxanne?" Cyrus asked impatiently. "You can't just. . . ." He waved one restless hand in the air. "Just go off without a word."

Calvin stepped into the room. His beautiful face was marred by a deepening frown. "I told her a couple of days ago that I was taking this trip. Ain't that good enough?"

"No," Cyrus said through gritted teeth. After last night she'd expect more. Of course, Calvin wouldn't know that. "At least leave her a note."

Calvin screwed up his face at this suggestion. "Well, I reckon I could do that, if you think I should."

Cyrus fetched a paper and pen from his desk drawer, and slapped them on the desk. He allowed Calvin to sit in his chair and ponder the possibilities for a few minutes before he put pen to paper. The deputy wrote slowly and deliberately, and still the note was finished in a matter of minutes. Satisfied, Calvin folded the note in half and handed it to Cyrus as he stood.

"Give this to Roxanne for me, will you? I gotta get on the road."

Cyrus took the folded sheet of paper and muttered a grumpy goodbye to Newberry. He waited until Calvin had departed and closed the office door before he unfolded the note to read the crude, uneven writing.

> *Dear Roxann,*
> *I hav gone to see my cousins. When I get back to Paris, meybe we can do some corting.*
> *Yer friend, Calvin.*

Cyrus closed his eyes as he took his seat at the desk. This would never do! Roxanne would expect something different than . . . than *this*. She would expect legible writing, correct spelling, a modicum of intelligence and emotion.

He should've remembered the crudeness of Calvin's letter inquiring about the job of deputy. Instead he'd only been thinking about how disappointed Roxanne would be if Calvin left without a word.

What had he done? Any sane man would've introduced Roxanne and Calvin and then stepped back and allowed nature to take its course. They'd suit or else they wouldn't. A man should only interfere so much.

Oh, but the look on Roxanne's face when she'd seen Calvin for the first time . . . it had been extraordinary. Cyrus was determined that if she wanted Calvin, she would have him. One way or another.

He took a fresh sheet of paper from the drawer, lifted the pen Calvin had left on the desk, and after a moment's hesitation began to write.

Roxanne felt an extra spring in her step and the tug of a smile on her face. Her feet moved faster, her heart was lighter. Everything was brighter today, warmer, better.

Who would have suspected that beneath Calvin's handsome face and perfect physique there beat a heart as good as any on this earth? How many men would sit through half the night listening to her ramble on about her life, would ask the right questions and laugh in the right places and then ask for more? Did he know that last night had been a purging of sorts for her? A turning point?

Last night she'd talked openly about Louis without crying, without pain. She'd even smiled once or twice as she remembered good times. Finally, at long last, she'd put Louis in the past where he belonged, and even though there was a special place in her heart for him and always would be, she realized now that her heart was not closed. It was unexplored, open, ready to love again.

She was falling in love with Calvin Newberry.

"Roxanne?"

She came to a dead stop in the street, and

smiled widely when she saw Cyrus directly before her. She hadn't seen him standing there, and if he hadn't spoken she probably would've continued walking until she bumped into him.

"Good afternoon," she said brightly.

He did not return her smile. "Good afternoon." His voice was low, soft, somehow secretive.

Even though she considered Cyrus to be her friend, even though she had experienced a fleeting, strange attraction for him, she realized that she didn't know him at all, not like she knew Calvin. Cyrus Bergeron was a mystery, a closed door, an unknown soul. The little bits she knew about his life as a boy had been grudgingly shared. If she wanted to know more she'd likely have to wrest the story from him one miserly sentence at a time, a task which would likely take a lifetime. She wondered if Cyrus had ever dared to open his heart to anyone.

"Walk with me?" she suggested when he didn't move. "I have essays to read and grade this afternoon and tonight, so I really need to get home."

"Sure," he fell into an easy step beside her, his long strides checked only slightly to match hers. She glanced at him out of the corner of her eye. His jaw, dusted with a faint afternoon beard, was taut. His lips were hard, his eyes cast down. He opened his mouth to speak and then closed it again, and a moment later, "About yesterday—" he began awkwardly.

"Calvin explained," she interrupted, and then

she turned her head to further study Cyrus's solemn profile. He looked so desolate her heart lurched. "I hope I didn't disturb you by running away as I did. I was upset, but I'm fine now."

"Good," he said without looking at her.

Roxanne felt the need to wipe away the dismal expression on his face. She was, at least in part, to blame. "I know you do what you have to, to keep peace, to protect yourself and others." She shifted her stack of papers and slim books to the crook of her left arm, and reached out to lay her hand on Cyrus's arm. He tensed significantly, and she immediately withdrew her hand. "I hope I didn't hurt you," she said softly.

Cyrus looked at her then, stoic as always. "Of course not," he said.

Of course not. She smiled wanly.

They walked silently for a while. Cyrus had become a good enough friend that silence between them usually wasn't awkward. Today, though, Roxanne wondered if he had more to say about yesterday's events, if the way she'd run from him had hurt in a way she couldn't understand or apologize for.

The very thought scared her a little. So quickly, Cyrus had become a part of her life she couldn't live without. He was more than a friend; he was a shoulder to lean on, an anchor in a tempestuous time, a rock she needed to keep her steady as she reclaimed her life. Perhaps he was close-mouthed and dangerous and hard to know and understand, but she couldn't imagine her life without Cyrus in it.

Fannie Rowland vigorously swept the boardwalk just outside her shop. When she saw Roxanne she stopped sweeping and lifted her hand to wave energetically. "I got your dress ready early," she called as she resumed her chore. "Come on in and try it on. If everything's in order you can take it home today."

Roxanne looked down at the stack of papers in her hand. The very thought of the new gown excited her, as if she were a silly girl who'd never had a fancy dress before. The blue gown was an extravagant purchase Aunt Ada would not approve of, a beautiful luxury, a concrete sign that she was truly ready to move on. Suddenly, she was a little afraid.

"I really do have these papers to grade," she said, disappointment in her voice.

"Surely it can't take that long to try on a dress," Cyrus said sensibly. She could hear the hint of interest in his voice, a liveliness where, a few minutes before, there had been none. "Besides," he added in a lowered voice. "What would happen if you were a day or two late grading those papers?"

Roxanne pursed her lips slightly. "Nothing," she admitted. "Nothing at all." She headed for the shop, hands full of the papers she'd decided could wait. When she turned she saw that Cyrus hadn't moved.

"Come on," she said with a grin. "I'm going to need a man's opinion." She needed much more than Cyrus's opinion on her new gown; she needed him with her as she took this step.

After a very short pause he followed her. He only hesitated once, at the door, looking almost panicky for a split second. Roxanne smiled at him, putting aside her own anxiety for the moment. She imagined Cyrus had never set foot in a dress shop before, and his discomfort showed. He was out of place among the fancy hats and laces, ready-made dresses and bolts of brightly colored fabric that made his own earthy twill and leather seem downright dull.

Roxanne placed her papers and books on a table near a rack of lace as Cyrus stepped into the shop and closed the door behind him. To his left there sat a table that displayed a basket of fancy buttons and several spools of colorful ribbon. To his right, an arrangement of fashionable hats added more color and gaiety to the small shop. The feminine accessories surrounded Cyrus, making him seem bigger, harsher. He was definitely out of his environment, and judging by his evident discomfort, he knew it.

Fannie did her best to make Cyrus comfortable, pulling out a dainty chair for him to sit in while he waited. He lowered himself slowly onto a padded seat that was too small for him. Fannie then offered a cup of tea, which he quickly declined.

As Roxanne slipped into the dressing room she glanced over her shoulder to see him sitting in that small chair, his hat in his hand. He did not look happy . . . but he didn't look particularly unhappy, either.

The blue silk dress had begun as a ready-made, but with Fannie Rowland's skill it had been transformed into something extraordinary. Roxanne swallowed hard as Fannie removed the gown from a rack of colorful clothing and presented it with a contented smile; she knew her talents as a dressmaker were extraordinary, and that this creation was one of her best works.

For a moment, Roxanne felt certain she'd made a mistake. Her new rose dress was brightly colored and pretty, but it was also modest and conventional, suitable for a widowed school teacher. The blue gown was shockingly beautiful, the kind of clothing that would draw all eyes to it, if she were ever brave enough to wear it in public.

With Fannie's help, Roxanne shed her gray everyday dress and slipped into the azure gown.

"The neckline is too low," she protested as the dress fell into place.

"It is not," Fannie insisted. "It's quite fashionable for evening, and certainly appropriate for a grown woman who has her eye out for a certain man."

When Roxanne gasped, only slightly shocked, Fannie smiled. "Sheriff Bergeron is certainly going to like this," she whispered. "Why, if you didn't already have the man wrapped around your little finger—"

"Cyrus?" Roxanne interrupted.

Fannie realigned the sleeves and tugged at a

piece of wayward lace. "Don't play coy with me, miss," she said happily. "I see the two of you walking in the afternoon, dancing together, sitting together at the picnic. Why, it's about time you two—"

"Cyrus is just a friend," Roxanne insisted. "Just a friend."

Fannie's smile faded, but the sparkle remained in her eyes. "If you say so."

Roxanne frowned as Fannie tugged at the full skirt and realigned the embroidered sash. She and Cyrus had been spending a lot of time together. Perhaps it was only natural that a few busybodies who had nothing better to do than speculate would think there was more to their companionship than met the eye. Yes, just a few busybodies, surely.

But suddenly she worried if there were others who thought as the dressmaker did. Then a more frightening thought chased away her irritation at a little harmless gossip. Good heavens. Could Cyrus possibly think there was more to their newfound friendship than she intended? Oh, no, this was not good.

She shook her head and put aside her fears. Cyrus had introduced her to Calvin, after all, and he knew very well how she felt about his dangerous career. He had confided in her about his plans to remain unmarried and childless, the way one *friend* might confide in another. He couldn't possibly think they could ever be anything more.

Try as she might, she couldn't completely

dismiss this new concern. What if Cyrus had experienced the same unexpected and irrational feelings she had? Maybe he knew, as she did, that they were unacceptable, wrong, completely impossible . . . but maybe he couldn't dismiss them any more easily than she could.

A new and disturbing thought practically sent her reeling. She had the sheriff of Lamar County waiting in a dress shop to pass judgment on her new gown!

"It's lovely," she said to Fannie. "There's really no need for Cyrus to. . . ."

Fannie ignored her, whipping back the curtain that separated the dressing area from the front room. Roxanne felt as if she were on display. An actress on the stage or, more likely since she couldn't make herself breathe, a marble statue on a pedestal.

Cyrus rose slowly from his little chair, hat in hand.

"Come along," Fannie said impatiently, offering her hand as Roxanne stepped from the platform to the floor. "Let's allow the sheriff a good look."

She had no choice but to step into the front of the shop and smile and allow Cyrus to tell her what he thought of her new gown. She wished desperately for more fabric at the neckline, then wished even more desperately that the hot flush she felt rise in her cheeks wasn't horribly red.

"Magnificent, isn't it?" Fannie said proudly. "Such a lovely color."

Cyrus waited silently as Roxanne stepped forward. Goodness, his eyes were fastened intently on her face and she knew, she just *knew* that her cheeks glowed as red as a strawberry.

"It's the color of your eyes," he said softly, almost as if he thought aloud.

She wanted to look down to see exactly how much of her bosom had been revealed. Too much, she knew without glancing in that direction. She could actually feel the air on skin that was normally covered, could feel the rise and fall of her exposed chest. By force of will she kept her eyes straight ahead. There was no need to call attention to the most decadent feature of the gown by staring at it.

Cyrus's eyes flickered down and back up again, and he looked at her face so hard it was as if he were trying as desperately as she was *not* to look at her exposed flesh.

"Lovely," he said gruffly, and then he turned to Fannie. "You've done a lovely job, Mrs. Rowland."

Roxanne turned about, more than ready to escape to the dressing room and her own simple dress. What had she been thinking when she'd ordered this gown? She would never wear it, never!

Cyrus stopped her, calling her name, and she made herself turn around to face him again, hoping, praying that none of her anxiety showed.

"Calvin left a letter for you." He lifted one side of his vest, exposing his badge. He touched the inside pocket there, then lifted the other side of his vest and repeated the soft touch on another pocket.

There was something in each pocket, she could tell, spying the edge of an envelope in each one. Cyrus hesitated, then he returned his fingers to the first pocket and withdrew a letter.

"He's already gone?" she asked softly.

"This morning." He laid the envelope on top of her stack of books. "Sorry to run, but I really do need to see Hamlin," he said as he walked to the door. "He's having problems with professional gamblers again, and I promised I'd stop by and have a word with the worst of them."

"Of course," she said relieved and disappointed at the same time. "Thanks for delivering the letter."

Cyrus opened the door, but glanced over his shoulder before stepping onto the boardwalk. "It's a nice dress," he whispered, and then he closed the door behind him.

Roxanne took a deep breath as she returned to the dressing room to disrobe.

Cyrus walked right past the saloon without even glancing over the batwing doors. He really had promised Hamlin that he'd have a talk with a couple of disruptive professional gamblers who'd made his place their home away from home, but tonight would be soon enough.

He'd always known that Roxanne was beautiful; that wasn't exactly news. But when

Fannie Rowland had parted those curtains and he'd seen Roxanne standing there in her new dress, his heart had damn near stopped.

Bright, brilliant blue instead of gray or black or brown or dark plum, brought her face alive, made her look younger, happier. And that neckline—he broke into a sweat just thinking about it. Fetching as she was in her nightgown, it had covered her from head to toe, merely teasing him with promising curves.

The neckline of her new gown revealed creamy neck to swelling bosom, and he'd seen the flesh there rise and fall with every breath she took until it became a chore not to stare, not to reach out and touch.

This was a disaster of major proportions. The dance, the conversation beneath her balcony, last night's confessions . . . and now this. Dammit, he was falling in love with her, and that would never do.

He patted the letter in his pocket. Carrying his letter *and* Calvin's miserable note around all day, he'd mulled over his decisions of late, his mistakes. He had to stop pretending to be Calvin, no matter how much he enjoyed the pure freedom he felt when he stood beneath Roxanne's balcony and said whatever came to mind. Hiding behind Calvin's pretty face had become almost second nature. It would be too easy to let it happen again.

Last night he'd had a good excuse for going to her. The look on her face as she'd run from him had frightened him. He'd had to know if she was all right after witnessing the shooting. He *had* to know.

Those mistakes were in the past. He vowed here and now that there would be no more excuses, no more acting. He'd done the right thing, giving her the simple note Calvin had written. It was only right that she knew the real Calvin before deciding to marry him.

And he was quite certain that Roxanne planned to marry Calvin. They were almost perfect for one another, two beautiful, naïve people who wanted the same things from life. A shared dream was enough to build a life on, more than enough; a farm, a dozen kids, a wide spot in the road to call their own.

True, Calvin could be less than dazzling on occasion, but maybe Roxanne would find a rustic charm in his note, perhaps she'd see something he had not.

Cyrus didn't even see Daisy McKee and Jane Rice standing on the boardwalk in front of the cafe until he nearly collided into them. They jumped back to avoid being run over, and he managed to tip his hat and offer a mumbled apology without slowing his step.

When he was safe in the Lamar County Jail, he made his way directly to his office and slammed the door shut. Tired, for some reason, exhausted to the bone, he plopped into his chair.

Once Roxanne was properly settled with Calvin, maybe he would think about moving on. Other men would manage well as Paris's sheriff, and out west there were lawless towns that would probably pay a pretty penny for a fast gun to keep their streets safe.

A fast gun. That's what he was, that's all he was and all he ever would be. He had nothing to offer a woman like Roxanne, a sweet, tender lady who dreamed of peaceful farms and fat babies and new beginnings.

He drew the envelope from his vest pocket and tapped the edge on his desk. Yes, it was a good thing he hadn't given her *this* letter. How would he explain later that Calvin could hardly write, that he couldn't even manage to spell her name correctly?

The letter he'd written went into the trash, unopened, tossed there with a hearty flick of his wrist. It was best to dismiss what had almost been a colossal mistake, to forget he'd written the damn thing.

He tried to dismiss all thoughts of Roxanne from his mind. He had no luck. Hell fire, she looked extraordinary in that blue dress. He'd damn near stuttered like a schoolboy and tripped over his own feet like Calvin, making his way out of that dress shop. And all because of a length of blue satin cut and sewn in a particular pattern and draped over the right body.

Half a minute later, he fetched the letter from the trash and opened the envelope. It was a kind of self-inflicted torture, that he felt the need to look at those words he'd written again. One more reminder of what he'd said, and then he'd burn the damn letter. He couldn't very well allow this to fall into the wrong hands.

Thrill to the most sensual, adventure-filled Romances on the market today...

FROM 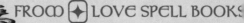 LOVE SPELL BOOKS

As a home subscriber to the Love Spell Romance Book Club, you'll enjoy the best in today's BRAND-NEW Time Travel, Futuristic, Legendary Lovers, Perfect Heroes and other genre romance fiction. For five years, Love Spell has brought you the award-winning, high-quality authors you know and love to read. Each Love Spell romance will sweep you away to a world of high adventure...and intimate romance. Discover for yourself all the passion and excitement millions of readers thrill to each and every month.

Save $5.00 Each Time You Buy!

Every other month, the Love Spell Romance Book Club brings you four brand-new titles from Love Spell Books. EACH PACKAGE WILL SAVE YOU AT LEAST $5.00 FROM THE BOOK-STORE PRICE! And you'll never miss a new title with our convenient home delivery service.

Here's how we do it: Each package will carry a FREE 10-DAY EXAMINATION privilege. At the end of that time, if you decide to keep your books, simply pay the low invoice price of $17.96, no shipping or handling charges added. HOME DELIVERY IS ALWAYS FREE. With today's top romance novels selling for $5.99 and higher, our price SAVES YOU AT LEAST $5.00 with each shipment.

AND YOUR FIRST TWO-BOOK SHIP-MENT IS TOTALLY FREE!

IT'S A BARGAIN YOU CAN'T BEAT! A SUPER $11.48 Value!

Love Spell ✦ A Division of Dorchester Publishing Co., Inc.

Get Two Books Totally
FREE —
An $11.48 Value!

▼ Tear Here and Mail Your FREE Book Card Today! ▼

PLEASE RUSH
MY TWO FREE
BOOKS TO ME
RIGHT AWAY!

Love Spell Romance Book Club
P.O. Box 6613
Edison, NJ 08818-6613

AFFIX
STAMP
HERE

Ready to face the most foolish part of himself, to torture himself with what he would never have, he snapped the single folded sheet open and read,

Dear Roxann.

"Oh, no."

Chapter Ten

Before leaving Fannie Rowland's shop, Roxanne slipped the envelope Cyrus had delivered
between the pages of the slim book of poetry
she carried with her students' essays. After last
night's quiet discussion, she couldn't wait to
read the letter Calvin had written to her. As she
walked home she wondered which Calvin
Newberry had written the letter; the romantic
man she was falling in love with, or the shy
farmer he became when she saw him face to
face. Anticipation almost made her dismiss
Fannie's ridiculous suppositions and the
expression on Cyrus's face as he'd left the shop.
Almost.

She said hello to Ada upon arriving home,
checked on the stew her aunt had started for
supper, and then very casually excused herself

to her room for a short rest and a chance to freshen up.

Her students' essays were deposited on the end of the bed, and with anxious fingers she plucked the envelope containing Calvin's letter from her book of poetry. She sat on the edge of the bed and slowly opened the envelope, sliding out the single sheet of paper. After last night, what would he say? With Calvin, one could never be certain. It might be all about the farm and his cousins, and then again. . . .

Dear Roxanne,

I wish I did not have to leave you, even if it is only for a short while. We grow closer every day, and I know, as surely and truly as I know nothing else, that when you are not beside me, when I cannot walk to your balcony and call your name, I will miss you.

After talking with you last night, I know you better than I ever thought I could, better than I have ever known another human being. It's as if your dreams have become mine, as if somehow you are already a part of me.

While we are apart I will think of you often, more often than you know. I will close my eyes and see you as if you stand before me, and take comfort in the very thought of you, as I always do. Think of me while we're apart.

Yours,
C

She read the letter three times, smiling more widely with each rereading. One would never dream, to look at Calvin Newberry, that he had such a romantic heart. He hid it behind his shyness and his need to present a masculine front, she supposed. Whatever his reasons, she wanted to teach him, to *prove* to him, that he could trust her enough to be himself to her face, to tell her, without fear, how he felt.

She fell back on the bed with the precious letter clutched to her chest. Her fingers were gentle, so as not to crumple the paper. She would save this letter forever, read and reread the cherished words a thousand times. Already she could close her eyes and recite Calvin's sweet words, they were so indelibly burned into her mind.

A soft, warm tingle teased her, reminding her that she could desire a man again; her heart pounded, a sign that she could fall in love again. The smile on her face suggested that she could once again be truly happy.

She owed Calvin a debt for this gift of warmth and hope and love, a debt she would happily spend a lifetime repaying.

Cyrus ran harder than he'd ever run before, pushing through the invisible forces that tried to drive him back. No matter how hard he pressed forward, Louis and the Yankee monster got further and further away.

Everything would be different if he could just reach Louis in time. The world would be better.

181

He would save himself and Roxanne and Calvin as well as Louis. He didn't know why or how, but in his heart this was a certainty.

Still, he wasn't surprised to watch the Yankee's bayonet rip into Louis, wasn't shocked when the bayonet slashed up and across his own face sending him falling back and back and back.

Cyrus came up with a hoarse shout that no one but he could hear. His heart beat so hard he could feel it pounding against his chest. A cold sweat drenched his skin.

He left the bed quickly, as if he could escape the nightmare by leaving behind scattered sheets and abused pillows, as if the place where he slept were a battlefield. One look at the rumpled sheets and the quilt that lay on the floor, and he knew he was right. Here before him was one battlefield he'd never escape.

The damned images stayed with him a while longer, as they always did. He paced the room, naked and trembling, trying to shake the dream. With the curtains closed the room was pitch black, but his instincts and his memory of the room's layout and his excellent night vision guided him as he stalked across the plank floor.

This nightmare had come too soon after the last one, dammit. Much too soon. The last horrific dream remained with him still, coming to him in bits and pieces he couldn't quite drive from his mind; and now this. He'd been having the nightmare less often over the past couple of years, the nightmare horrors coming to him further and further apart until he'd begun to hope that maybe one day he would be rid of them completely.

His time with Roxanne, he reasoned, had triggered the dream. Talking to her, as himself and as Calvin, as he walked her home and as he hid beneath her balcony, had become a torture all its own. Seeing her this afternoon, in a seductive dress that made her look like an anxious lover rather than a grieving widow, had been more than he could take.

Dammit, he'd seen her standing there in that dress and all he could think of was getting her *out* of it.

More than a single afternoon's fantasy haunted him. Roxanne had been on his mind more and more of late, as his obsession grew. All the hours he'd passed in her company, talking to her, listening to her, standing so close he could reach out and touch her if he had a mind to, had somehow made her a much larger part of his life than he'd ever intended.

Being a part of her life was much more entangling than watching from a distance.

Yes, when she was wed to Calvin and they had their damn farm, he'd wave goodbye and head west, leaving behind memories, obsessions, nightmares. Then again, maybe he shouldn't wait even that long. One thing he'd learned about Roxanne in the past couple of weeks; she wasn't as fragile as she appeared to be, she wasn't as delicate as he'd always assumed she was. Behind the pale mask of a grieving widow, beneath the quiet, withdrawn woman he knew, there was more strength than he'd ever imagined. She didn't need him to watch over her, not anymore.

He peeked through the curtain to the Pierson house. Roxanne didn't sit on her balcony tonight, sleepless and melancholy. She likely slept soundly, dreaming sweet dreams that would disappear on waking.

There would be no more sleep for him, not tonight. He lit a lantern and placed it on the rarely used desk in the corner. He opened all the drawers, searching almost frantically for what he needed. At last he found what he searched for: paper and pen in the bottom drawer.

He pulled a chair up to the desk and sat, and moved the paper so that the light from the lantern shone directly upon it.

My dearest Roxanne, he began.

She kept an eye out for Cyrus as she walked home from school, but he was nowhere to be seen. Just as well, she supposed. Perhaps he avoided her on purpose, as disturbed by yesterday's awkwardness as she'd been.

Perhaps it was impossible to be mere friends with a man, especially one like Cyrus. He was a good man, she knew that well, but he was also hard and restless, all male, a little lonely and maybe even a little lost. Lost inside, as she'd been lost for so long. Goodness, Cyrus didn't need a friend, he needed a woman. Someone to hold and kiss him, to make him a real home, to soften his hard edge and ease his restlessness. A rather surprising, deep shiver, shot through her body. She shook it off.

Thank goodness Friday was finally here. Tomorrow was cleaning and laundry day and with all this energy, she needed a place to expend it. She'd do some baking, too; fill the house with the wonderful aromas of baking bread and spice cake. Still, she could sleep late, if she wanted to, and retire early in the evening. She could steal a few quiet minutes here and there, perhaps a quiet hour or two, to contemplate her future.

For the first time in too long she could think of the future without pain, without bleakness.

Dismissing Cyrus firmly from her mind, she thought of Calvin instead. She pictured his lovely face, of course, but more importantly she went over the letter he had written, the soft whisper beneath the balcony. There was such wonderful promise in his words, such hope.

Their children would have blue eyes. . . .

He would've been wise to decline Josiah's invitation to Sunday dinner. Cyrus knew that full well even as he rapped on the front door of the Pierson house.

The further away from Roxanne he stayed the better off they'd both be. She wanted Calvin, the farm, a safe and happy life. He couldn't promise her safe *or* happy, so he had no right to even try.

Still, he wanted to see her again before Calvin came back to Paris and took over, before he finally gave up and completely handed the woman he wanted over to his dimwit deputy.

The meal was plentiful and delicious, as always, and Cyrus tried to be a good guest, complimenting everything that was placed before him and making small talk about the weather with Josiah and Ada.

Roxanne looked lovely, of course, in a simple white blouse and a brown skirt he'd seen her wear a hundred times. How could a woman make something so plain look so tempting? He wanted to unfasten every tiny pearl-like button himself, wanted to unfasten that brown skirt and watch it fall to the floor in a puddle. He stared at the food on his plate and tried to listen to Ada wish for a little rain for her flower garden.

Throughout the meal Roxanne remained distant, as if her mind were elsewhere. Of course her mind was elsewhere, Cyrus chided himself. She was thinking of Calvin Newberry and anxiously awaiting his return.

It occurred to him that he could always fire Calvin and speed the process along. Without his job as deputy, there would be nothing to keep the dimwit in Paris. Calvin Newberry and the widow Roxanne Robinette could be married and move to the country, just as they both obviously wanted.

He endured the rest of the meal, talked town

business with Josiah, and complimented Ada and Roxanne on the fine food he barely tasted. There was just one thing more he had to do before leaving this house for the last time. He didn't look forward to it, but he knew it had to be done.

Ada pushed back her chair, walked briskly into the kitchen, and came back with a spice cake she set at the center of the table.

"Cyrus," Josiah said as if he'd just remembered something important. "Ada and I will be out of town for a few days next week. My brother's having a big barbecue at his place in Honey Grove, and he asked us to come out and stay for a few days. We haven't been away in so long we decided we really should go. Keep an eye on things for us, will you?"

"Certainly." He glanced to Roxanne, whose mind was elsewhere. "The three of you are going?"

Ada shook her head as she served the fragrant cake. "No. Roxanne refuses to leave her students, even for a few days." She pursed her lips, making her disapproval clear.

"She is a grown woman," Josiah said sensibly.

"I'll be fine," Roxanne said in a monotone that suggested she'd said so a thousand times.

Cyrus waited through dessert, picking at the spice cake and eating little. When the meal was finally finished he stood and said his goodbyes to Josiah and Ada. Then he turned to Roxanne. She smiled at him wanly, almost absently, but still—it was a smile.

Linda Jones

"Roxanne," he said. "Could I speak to you privately? Perhaps on the side porch."

The widening of her eyes indicated surprise, but she stood without hesitation.

"School business," Cyrus said in an aside to Josiah, satisfying the man's curiosity with the simple lie.

Roxanne walked with him through the parlor to the side porch. Like it or not this was as alone as they were likely to get, with the gardens before them and the house at their back. He closed the door.

Roxanne turned to face him and waited, her eyes wide with curiosity and perhaps even a little fear.

"I wanted to tell you first," he said softly. "It looks like I'll be leaving town soon."

The news obviously puzzled her. Her eyes widened, and suddenly she was more alert, on guard. "Why? Where are you going? Have you gotten another job offer?" She took a step toward him.

"It's just time to move on," he said. "That's all."

She stopped an arm's length short of him. "I guess I just thought you'd always be here," she said softly. "You're as much a part of Paris as anyone in this town."

"Too much a part, maybe," he said.

Roxanne cocked her head to one side, confused by his decision. He couldn't tell her the real reason for his departure; he couldn't admit that he was leaving to escape her.

"I'll miss you," she whispered.

"Will you?" If he thought there was anything for them, any chance at all. . . .

She nodded and lowered her head, perhaps afraid to explore the notion any further.

He took the single step to close the space between them, and placed an uncertain finger beneath her chin. With a small amount of pressure, he forced her to look at him.

"I'll miss you, too," he whispered. "Too much."

She stood very still as he lowered his head slightly to kiss her, laying his mouth over hers, soft and hesitant. Their lips touched like two breezes blowing in from opposite directions, barely meeting, just passing by. Dammit, he couldn't leave without this, at least; one kiss to remember.

If Roxanne had responded quickly, if she'd wrapped her arms around him or pressed her mouth more insistently to his, the kiss might have grown into something more. But she didn't, and Cyrus backed away with no regrets.

"I hope you'll be very happy," he said.

"Thank you," she whispered, apparently deciding to ignore the kiss. "I . . . I wish you happiness, too."

To laugh bitterly at her would be cruel, so he didn't. "I have something for you," he said, his voice cool as he reached into his inside pocket for the small bundle he'd been carrying with him since early morning. "I ran into one of

Calvin's cousins at the feed store yesterday, and he asked me to pass these on to you."

He handed over the small packet, three letters tied together with a narrow strip of scarlet satin ribbon.

"Was Calvin with him?" Roxanne asked, and Cyrus couldn't help but notice that she held her breath as she waited for an answer.

"No. This cousin said Calvin was working hard to get finished up so he can get back to Paris as soon as possible."

That false news brought a weak smile to her lips. She clutched the tiny bundle desperately. "Thank you for delivering these letters."

"No problem," he said, backing away.

He could still feel her on his lips, even though the kiss had been brief. Time to get away from here before he did something stupid; like telling Roxanne that he'd written the letters she grasped.

"Cyrus?" she asked as he turned to leave. "When are you leaving town?"

"Soon," he said, glancing over his shoulder. "Real soon."

But not soon enough.

Still dressed in her blouse and skirt, Roxanne lay atop her coverlet with the unopened letters clutched to her breast. A single candle burned on her bedside table, and just a touch of moonlight broke through the open window at her balcony.

She told herself she simply savored the moment, relishing the anticipation of reading these letters, but after several minutes had passed she had to admit she was lying to herself.

How could she open these letters and enjoy them when she still felt Cyrus on her lips? When her heart still beat just a little bit too fast from that brief encounter? No, Calvin deserved her full attention, and right now . . . right this minute . . . she didn't have it to give.

A flash of anger exploded inside her. How dare Cyrus confuse her this way! Darn it, she *knew* what she wanted. What right did he have to kiss her and make her question everything she knew to be true?

She took a deep breath and tried to reason with herself. What nonsense for a fully grown, sensible woman much too old to allow a kiss to turn her head.

Logic, that's what she needed right now. *Logic*.

Perhaps it was true that Cyrus appealed to her baser instincts. Surely the man was possessed of an overabundance of some masculine element that made him turn her own body against her. How unfair! A simple kiss, no more than a grazing of his lips against hers, certainly shouldn't have the power to paralyze her, to make her question everything she wanted and needed.

But it had. Blast him!

She closed her eyes and thought of Calvin. He was sweet and romantic, and he appealed to her heart and her mind, not some traitorous part of her body. She was sure that if Calvin ever kissed her it would be just as wonderful. *More* wonderful, in fact.

When she married, and she was determined to see that happen, it would mean sharing a bed with a man again. In the past three years she hadn't so much as considered the possibility. Louis had been her husband, her partner, and the very idea of taking another man into his place had been unthinkable. It had been easier to forget everything, to close that part of herself off. When feeling hurt, it was best not to feel anything at all.

Laying on the bed with Calvin's letters clutched to her bosom, she thought of her three nights with Louis. It had been such a long time since she'd allowed herself to remember. Bittersweet memories rushed back, assaulting her with vivid images.

Their first night together, their wedding night, had been awkward and anxious and painful. They'd both cried a little; Roxanne because she hurt, Louis because he'd hurt her. The pain had faded quickly, and wonderful Louis had held her close throughout the night.

The second night had been better. They came together much more easily, without pain and without tears. Louis had tried his best to be quick and gentle, while Roxanne had prayed that they'd make a baby. She remembered loving the touch of his skin against hers, so intimate, so right.

And then came that third night, their last

night together. They'd decided to just kiss, to snuggle together beneath the covers and keep one another warm and talk all night. They had begun just that way, whispering, kissing, touching. Soon they kissed much more than they whispered. Louis fondled her in places she'd never been touched before, and she boldly touched him.

In spite of the cold she'd grown hot beneath the covers. Her body tingled, her thighs parted, and when he'd slid between them, come into her, it had been the most wonderful, most beautiful moment of her life. They'd truly come together that night, in heart and body and spirit, discovering joys they'd never known existed, unimaginable pleasures that surprised and delighted and exhausted them.

Roxanne squeezed her eyes shut and a couple of wayward, unwanted tears ran down her face.

God forgive her, she wanted that again. Cyrus promised pleasures like that, with his eyes and his kiss, and with his reluctantly whispered *too much*. But he didn't offer anything more. Not love, not promise, not the family she wanted so desperately.

She wanted to be close to a man she loved again, to reawaken that part of herself . . . but holding and loving and kissing weren't enough.

Calvin offered her everything she wanted. Everything! When he finally kissed her she'd surely experience the same thrill as she had in that moment when Cyrus had laid his mouth against hers and taken her breath away.

With determination, she lifted the first letter from the stack, carefully opened the envelope, and began to read.

Chapter Eleven

Certain phrases from Calvin's wonderful letters stayed with her, coming to her mind often in the days since Cyrus had delivered them. She found the words intruding when she should be teaching, and, on occasion, when she should be watching where she was going. The words were enough, she kept telling herself, to completely wipe Cyrus Bergeron from her mind.

The house was quiet with Josiah and Ada gone, but Roxanne enjoyed the solitude. She had time to think, to plan, to reread Calvin's letters wherever and as often as she liked. She usually took them out late at night, when her mind tended to take dangerous and unwanted turns.

When I'm not with you a part of me is missing.

Some days I'm sure that just looking at your face is enough to right the wrongs of the world.

I long to touch you.

I adore you.

Without you I'm nothing.

There were even a few quotes from Elizabeth Barrett Browning's *Sonnets from the Portuguese.* A couple of those lines came to her again and again, just as Calvin's own words did. "I think of thee!—my thoughts do twine and bud about thee, as wild vines, about a tree." And of course her very favorite: " The face of all the world is changed, I think, since first I heard the footsteps of thy soul."

The letters were so personal, so dear to her, that she knew no one but she would ever see or touch them. She'd taken the letters out so often she no longer needed light to read by, just the feel of crisp paper in her hands as she recalled the loving words. Calvin never actually wrote "I love you," but love lurked in the letters, in every line, in every carefully written word.

Thank goodness the envelopes had been well sealed before leaving Calvin's hands! She could be certain that neither his cousin nor Cyrus had so much as glanced at the love letters. They were for her alone.

On the way home from school she stopped by the mercantile and bought several new ribbons for her hair, all brightly colored. She stopped by Fannie Rowland's place and looked over several fabrics but bought nothing. She went into the Dallas Bakery for a pastry to take home with her. Cooking for one was rather boring, she'd discovered in the past two days.

When she left the Dallas Bakery and stepped onto the boardwalk, she saw Calvin on his golden horse, riding solemnly and magnificently into town. A wide grin grew on her face as she stepped into the street and waved.

Calvin dismounted with the cautious ease of a man who's been in the saddle all day. When he hit the ground—with obvious relief—dust rose up around his boots. Roxanne sighed. Heavens, he was splendid. His face, his body, his heart. . . .

If there weren't so many people around, she'd run to him and throw her arms around his neck and give him a big kiss. Unfortunately there were a dozen curious eyes in the vicinity, perhaps more.

"Welcome home," she said softly as he came closer, leading his horse by the reins.

"Howdy," he said with a grin to match her own. "What a purty smile," he added. "Now, that's a fine sight to come home to."

Howdy wasn't a particularly intimate greeting, but then Calvin knew, as she did, that this meeting was being closely observed from windows and passersby all around. "How did your trip go?"

"Fine," he said. "Found myself a good piece of land, and if the old man accepts my price, I'm set."

A farm, peaceful solitude, and romance with

Calvin. What else could a woman ask for? "Sounds wonderful."

"I do need to talk to you, though," he said, lowering his voice. "But maybe it would be better if we spoke in private."

Her heart lurched. "Certainly."

"Good afternoon, Mrs. Robinette," a chorus of young voices called, and Roxanne turned around to see a small contingent of her students passing by. Sarah Carlisle and Mary Elizabeth Sullivan were two of her best students, and they walked at the front of the group. Both fifteen years old, they were entirely too impudent for Roxanne's liking. The other girls, three of them, merely followed Sarah and Mary's lead.

The full skirts of crisp, youthful dresses in an array of bright spring colors, swayed as the girls walked by. They all slowed their step slightly to take a good long look at the handsome deputy. Sarah smiled widely, directly at Calvin, and the others followed suit.

"Good afternoon, girls," Roxanne answered, ignoring the knowing glances that made her want to blush.

When they were well past, they all giggled. Silly girls.

"We do need to talk," she returned her attention to Calvin. *Alone. Alone at last.* She found that she wanted to do much more than talk. All she'd thought about for days was what it would be like for this man to touch her. To hold her close. She craved a kiss with surprising intensity, yearned to have his strong arms around her. Once Calvin held her, surely she would forget about that silly, disturbing kiss Cyrus had surprised her with on Sunday.

Calvin nodded shyly, looking at the ground.

"Would you like to walk me home?"

Calvin shook his head. "I'd better not. Got to get Betsy to the livery." He patted the animal lovingly on the neck. "She's had a long day, too."

"Of course." She tried to hide her disappointment. Calvin was right. People all around watched this meeting, people who knew Ada and Josiah were out of town and she was all alone in that big house.

"I need to check in with the sheriff, too, I reckon. He didn't expect me back for a couple more days."

She smiled. He'd hurried home for her. " 'The face of all the world is changed, I think . . .' " she whispered dreamily.

Calvin stared at her and cocked his head closer, as if her words had been too soft for him to hear. "Huh?"

If she spoke any louder someone was bound to hear, so she did not repeat herself. "I was rather surprised to discover that you know Elizabeth Barrett Browning so well."

Calvin screwed up his lovely, perfectly shaped nose. "Don't think I've ever met her. Does she live in Lamar County?"

Roxanne laughed softly. Handsome, romantic,

and funny, too! What a treasure this man was.

The look on Calvin's face turned quickly from comical to serious. "We really do need to talk," he whispered, looking this way and that as if someone might be listening.

"I know," she whispered as well, leaning close. She swallowed hard, gathering all her courage. "Tonight." She looked deep into his beautiful blue eyes and thought of the words he'd written, of the secrets they'd shared by moonlight. Yes, this was right. "My aunt and uncle are out of town and I'm all alone in the house, so . . ." she took a deep breath. "It would be best if no one saw you."

Calvin's eyes got big. His lower lip trembled. Goodness, he was more worried about this than she was! His shyness would be a problem, she supposed. Well, it was a problem they would have to work around.

He might be shy, but the man who wrote those letters was also tender and loving and passionate. One kiss, and she was sure his shyness, and with it every doubt she still harbored, would melt away.

"Tonight," she whispered, and before her giggling students passed again on their way back from the confectioner's, she was on her way home.

Cyrus had to go searching for Calvin, having heard third-hand that the boy was back in Paris. Dammit, he was early, *days* early. This was a wrinkle he could live without.

The letters had to be explained before Calvin and Roxanne met. If Roxanne said something about the letters, and Calvin opened his big mouth and said, "What letters?" there would be hell to pay. A few words of explanation, that's all that was needed. Cyrus only hoped he was not too late.

After checking the boarding house, the livery, and the jail, he finally found Calvin in Nickels' Saloon. The boy leaned over the bar with his head down and a drink in front of him.

"Calvin," he said, stepping to the long bar to stand beside the kid. "I heard you were back in town."

Calvin lifted his head slowly, and settled desolate blue eyes on Cyrus's face. "Howdy, Sheriff." He slurred his words badly. The kid was obviously miserable. And drunk. "I'm glad you're here." He looked like he was about to cry. "I done messed up something awful." He downed his whiskey and pushed the short glass toward Hamlin for a refill.

Cyrus ordered a glass of whiskey of his own. One look at the kid's face and he figured he was going to need it

"What's wrong?" With two full glasses of whiskey before them, Cyrus waved Hamlin to the other end of the long bar so he and Calvin could have a little privacy.

"It was the note, I reckon," he said sadly. "I told Roxanne that we'd do some courtin' when I got back, and now I reckon that's what she 'spects."

Linda Jones

"So?" Cyrus asked impatiently. "What's wrong with that?"

Calvin shook his head. "Everything's different," he muttered. "And she . . . she asked me," he lowered his voice and glanced around, only to see exactly what Cyrus saw; people having a good time and staying well clear of the law. "She asked me to come to her house tonight. Said she was in that house *all alone*. I can't go over there and . . . and . . ." he blushed deep red. "You know. Hellfire, I'm not the one Roxanne wants. She wants the man who stood under her window and spun sweet words for her ears. I did some thinking whilst I was away, and I come to the conclusion that she ain't sweet on me at all. It's you, Sheriff, and I can't—"

"That's ridiculous," Cyrus hissed.

Calvin raised blood shot eyes. "No, it ain't. She likes you, and that's a fact. Hellfire, it's plain as the nose on your face."

The declaration hung between them, and in the dead, uncomfortable silence, Cyrus lifted his glass and downed the whiskey in one burning gulp. "You can give her what she wants, Calvin," he said as he placed the empty glass on the counter. "I can't. Now get over there and . . . and . . ." Oh, hell. The kid was drunk. No telling what he might say to Roxanne in this condition. Something stupid, no doubt. Maybe something that would give up the game they'd been playing.

"I tell you what. I'll head over there and

make your excuses." It made perfect sense. "Tomorrow you'll see things more clearly."

Calvin shook his head, but Cyrus ignored him.

On his way out of the bar he shed his brown hat and leather vest, and grabbed Calvin's white hat and butternut duster from the rack by the batwing doors.

The moonless night was black and cool with shadows so dark and deep they appeared endless.

Roxanne sat on the balcony, her head resting against the wrought iron bars. What a complete and utter fool she was! Calvin wasn't coming. It was long past dark, and he wasn't here.

She was an idiot, surely, for sitting here in her newest nightdress and gray silk wrapper, waiting much too anxiously for a man's heart-warming whisper drifting upwards to her eager ears. She was more the fool for thinking that maybe, just maybe, there could be more tonight. It had been so long since anyone had touched her, and tonight she felt as if she'd wither and die if Calvin didn't touch her soon. A kiss, a sweet caress. She wanted to *see* the passion he shared in his letters.

Blast him, Calvin Newberry was the most confusing man she'd ever met! One minute he acted like a friendly acquaintance, the next he spouted sweet words to her. One minute it seemed he didn't have a thought in his head beyond farming, and the next he revealed the intelligent, tender man he hid beneath that simple, beautiful exterior.

Was he really so shy that he couldn't stand to face her? Could he only bare his soul from a distance that made it impossible for her to touch him? What torture this was.

A nagging, almost painful thought came to her as she watched the deserted lawn below. Maybe Calvin didn't care for her at all. Maybe the letters and the nights spent talking in whispers were merely parts of an elaborate, cruel amusement.

No. She closed her tired eyes. The letters seemed so real, so ardent. Surely this courtship was not a game. Surely. She'd fallen in love with Calvin, reading those letters. They *had* to be genuine.

So where was he? He'd been away from Paris for days, and she'd missed him more than she'd thought possible. She'd missed the soft sound of his Tennessee accent, the loving connection she felt even though he kept himself so far away.

Perhaps she had shocked him with her boldness, asking him to come tonight, telling him that she would be in the house all alone, and he no longer loved her. Perhaps a shy man had no use for a brazen woman.

A chill ran down her spine. He'd never actually said he loved her, he'd never actually written those three words, *I love you*. Oh, but how could she doubt his love when the letters he'd written made his feelings much more clear than the utterance of any word ever could?

The night was so dark, if he'd been wearing black she wouldn't have seen him. At the edge of the yard she caught a glimpse of a white hat, a shimmer of a butternut duster, and a moment later she saw a dark figure moving slowly, very slowly, across the yard. Head down, every step was slow, and as she watched, he stopped.

He readjusted the hat on his head, shrugged once as if making himself comfortable in his own duster, and then he just stood there, head down, motionless.

What made him afraid to face her with his feelings? Perhaps another woman had broken his heart. Had some foolish woman spurned him and made him afraid? Roxanne's unshed tears dried and her heart beat fast with anticipation. She would teach Calvin not to be so shy; she would show him how she loved him until he had no fear of facing her with everything he wanted and felt.

While he stood there, hesitating, she left the balcony, ran through her room, and darted down the stairs on bare feet. He wouldn't woo her from a distance. Not tonight.

After an unhurried walk that included several long pauses, Cyrus finally stood beneath Roxanne's balcony. What would he say to her? He'd told Calvin he'd make excuses, but at the moment nothing plausible came to mind.

What had he done? Dammit, he'd stuck his nose into Roxanne's love life and made a royal

mess of things. All he'd wanted was to make
her happy, to see her smile and laugh; and he
had. But she wouldn't be laughing when she
found out that Calvin hadn't written those letters; and she would find out eventually, if
things continued. She wouldn't be smiling if
she ever found out it had been him beneath the
balcony and in the tree, and not beautiful
Calvin.

Maybe if he coached Calvin carefully, she
would never know. That would be best.

"Roxanne," he whispered, his head lifted to
the empty balcony. Once again he would play
the part he'd played so well, whisper a few
sweet words and then walk away. She was
alone tonight, and he wondered if she wanted,
expected, Calvin to walk in the front door of
the Pierson house and climb the stairs to her
bedroom. He actually wondered, for a long second, if he could pull it off, if he could sneak
into a dark house and into Roxanne's bed and
whisper a few sweet hillbilly words as she
opened herself to him. He could almost feel it,
her welcoming warmth, her tender arms, her
body under and around his. He closed his eyes
and tried to take a deep breath.

As much as it hurt him—and it *did* hurt
him—he knew he wouldn't touch her tonight
or ever. "Roxanne!" he called again when she
did not appear.

"Yes."

The whisper came from directly behind him.

She stood close, too damn close. As he stood there, frozen to the spot, soft arms encircled his waist.

" 'The face of all the world is changed, I think . . .' " she whispered.

" 'Since first I heard the footsteps of thy soul,' " he finished the verse in a low tone, automatically, and with just a touch of the hillbilly in his voice. Roxanne answered by squeezing him tight.

Calvin was solid and warm in her arms, and Roxanne took a deep breath and sighed with contentment. She'd dreamed of this, of holding him tight and pressing her body against his. He stiffened considerably, and she wondered again who had hurt him. He'd spoken, only once, of numbness and pain. Someone had broken his heart, and all she wanted to do was fix it. She wanted to fix everything for him.

"I thought you weren't coming," she whispered.

He took a deep breath she felt and heard. "I almost didn't. Roxanne, we can't. . . ."

Her arms encircled him gently, and she rubbed her hands across a tense, taut chest and belly, barely touching him. He shivered in her arms. "We can do whatever we want," she whispered. "What I want right now," she took a deep breath for courage, "is for you to kiss me."

"I . . . I . . ." he stammered.

"There's no reason for you to be shy with

me," she said softly. Her hands stilled on his chest. "You were so open in your letters, so . . . so romantic and dear." She began to slowly step around him, her heart beating so hard and fast she was sure he could hear it. His hat covered his head, the collar of his duster was turned up, and as she turned she caught just a glimpse of his jaw before he moved.

He turned slowly, just as she did, keeping his back to her.

"Come inside with me," she whispered. "I'll light a few candles and pour us some wine, and—"

"No," he said huskily.

She became very still, and her hands dropped. His *no* sounded so insistent, so final. Her heart died a little, and she chastised herself for making a fool of herself over this handsome, shy man.

"I've made a terrible mistake," she said, horrified by her blunder. "I thought you . . . I thought you cared for me, that you wanted me, but apparently you don't."

With what dignity she could muster, she walked away.

She didn't get far before Calvin stopped her. He grabbed her by the shoulders and propelled her beneath the balcony, into shadows so deep she could see nothing at all. His arms encircled and entrapped her, her breasts pressed against his hard chest, and she felt his long, strong legs brushing hers.

Without a word he gave her the kiss she

craved, clamping his mouth to hers and teasing her lips with his tongue, brushing it lightly and tenderly over her bottom lip. Her lips parted, and she drew in a heated, anxious breath. He tasted mildly of whiskey, and the smell and touch and taste of him overwhelmed her senses until she reeled. Her heartbeat increased; she melted against him.

One hand crept up her back and to her neck, fingers spearing through her hair, while the other continued to hold her tight. Trapped here in Calvin's arms, caught in his insistent embrace, she knew a moment of perfect happiness.

His mouth devoured her, hungry and demanding. His tongue slipped through her parted lips, danced with her own exploring tongue, and then plunged deep. The kiss was everything she'd known it would be, and more.

No man had ever kissed her like this before, demanding, insistent, hungry; as if he wanted to devour her alive. Her entire body tingled in response, a pleasant sensation that threatened to overwhelm her. The heaviness in her loins beat in a resounding, demanding rhythm.

The rhythm and the demand continued even after Calvin took his lips from hers.

"Don't want you?" he whispered in a voice that was so husky and distraught it sounded not at all like the happy-go-lucky deputy. He pulled her against him so she couldn't help but feel his insistent arousal. "I want you more than anything. I would give anything to have you.

But I can't," he took a deep breath, "have you."

All was dark here, so dark she couldn't see anything. Her eyes drifted shut. Ah, she didn't need to see. She felt Calvin's warmth, his body against hers, and she needed nothing else. "Why not?"

There was a long pause before he answered. "You don't love me."

She smiled in the dark. Her suspicions were correct. Calvin hesitated not because he was unsure of his feelings for her, but because some woman had broken his heart and he didn't quite trust anyone; not even her.

"Are you the man who wrote me those wonderful letters?"

"Yes," he breathed.

"Are you the man who spent an entire night sitting in that tree and talking to me about the past and the future?"

Another affirmative breath of air touched her ear.

She slipped her arms through his duster and around his waist. "Then you're the man I love, the man I will always love. If I didn't know it before you left town, I know it now. You put your heart in those wonderful letters you wrote, you made me long for you in a way no man ever has." She found his mouth and kissed him, swift and deep, trying to tell him with a caress what he meant to her. He answered her kiss with a searing demand of his own, a sway of his tongue, an insistent brush of his lips. She came away breathless.

"If I move too fast it's because you touched me so with your words." Her smile grew into a wide, unrestrained grin. "You make me impulsive."

"We can't—"

"Just kiss me and hold me, that's all I ask." She wanted more, she wanted it all; this man inside her, his hands on her naked body. Her desire was shocking and wicked and impetuous, but it wasn't wrong. Where love was concerned, it couldn't possibly be wrong. But if Calvin wasn't ready for more, she would do her best to be satisfied with his arms around her and a thousand or so kisses. She would show him how she loved him until he was no longer afraid.

"That's all you ask," he whispered, and then, after a moment's hesitation while his mouth hovered over hers, he kissed her again. For a disturbing second, she thought of Cyrus . . . and then with a flick of her tongue she put the sheriff from her mind.

Chapter Twelve

It was like a dream, where he could touch and hear and smell and taste, but not see. Roxanne's mouth fastened to his, her lips parted, her tongue boldly teased and tasted his. He answered with a delving swirl of his tongue and she moaned, a small catch coming from her throat, a soft sound that signaled a sensation so deep and fine it couldn't be contained. With her body pressed completely and warmly against his she shivered in his arms, telling him that she wanted what they couldn't have as badly as he did.

It would be best to break away, to quickly blend into the night's shadows and disappear without another word. But Cyrus knew too well that this opportunity would never come again, that he would never hold Roxanne this way again, so he planned to realize a few of his fantasies.

As he kissed her senseless, his hand slipped through the opening in her wrapper and settled over a linen-covered breast. Warm, soft flesh filled his hand, and his palm brushed against a nipple that instantly hardened. Roxanne didn't protest his audacity, but moaned in pure pleasure, a soft, deep moan against his mouth. He raked his palm over the hardened nipple, stroked his thumb across the giving flesh of her full breast, and she arched into him with a quick intake of breath. She came apart in his arms, losing herself to the sensations of touch.

When the pull of her wrapper impeded his progress, he reached down and blindly, unthinking, untied the sash. It fell open, giving him freer access. His unimpeded hands raked over her ribs, and came back up to her neck, brushing lightly over pebbled nipples as he explored the wondrous curves of her body.

He could feel Roxanne weakening, her knees shaking and her arms trembling. She was soft in his arms, unresisting, boneless. If he let her go now she would surely sink to the ground. Taking a single step, he pressed her back against the wall of the house. Dammit, they both needed a little support right now.

As he stroked her long throat with his thumbs he leaned forward to kiss her again. He could touch her all he wanted, he could kiss her, but there couldn't be anything more. No matter how badly he wanted her, there couldn't be anything more. A few whispered words, a couple of letters, a kiss or fifty, somehow they were all right.

But to bury himself inside her, to make love to her, was not allowed. As if in protest, his hips and his erection ground against her. Her legs parted slightly, and he pressed his manhood against her mound.

Her hands had been wrapped snugly around his waist, but boldly they began to wander as his had. Her fingers raked across his chest, flickering over his nipples beneath rough cotton. She seemed determined to touch him everywhere, to explore his body with her delicately curious hands. A palm against his ribs, fingers trailing over his chest, mere fingertips against his hip, he allowed her to touch him as she wished . . . until those hands crept up and toward his face.

It wouldn't do for her to touch his face, to run those inquisitive fingers over a scarred cheek.

He grabbed her hands firmly, manacling her wrists, and pressed them against the wall she leaned on. Lowering his head, he kissed her neck, trailed his tongue over the indentation at the base. God, she tasted sweet on his tongue. Sweet and salty. Her breasts heaved with every breath she took, and she inhaled and exhaled as if each breath was an effort, as if her body were at war.

He lowered his mouth further, and captured a linen-covered nipple in his mouth. Through the damp fabric he tasted her, drawing her nipple into his mouth and suckling gently, taking wet linen and tender flesh on his tongue and between his teeth. Roxanne, warm and soft and willing, moaned aloud and shivered deeply. He wondered if she hurt with wanting as much as he did.

No matter how much it hurt, he wasn't about to stop. This was all he could ever have of her, and dammit he wasn't going to walk away . . . to run away . . . when he could hold her for a while longer.

"I can't take this anymore," Roxanne said breathlessly.

"Yes, you can," Cyrus whispered in a very un-Calvin-like voice. She seemed not to notice as he turned his attention to her other breast and repeated the slow, sweet ritual. Tasting, sucking, nibbling. Drawing her into his mouth and pressing his tongue against her pebbled nipple. He released the grip on her wrists and settled his hands on her body, touching warm flesh through thin linen, raking his fingers across curves and valleys, memorizing every line.

His fingertips learned every angle, his palms raked over warmth and softness that arched against the gentlest pressure. When he laid his lips over hers again he felt the gentlest tremble imaginable, an uncontrollable quake that worked its way through Roxanne's body, and then his.

Her hands roamed as his did, feathering torturous caresses over his shoulders and his arms, his chest and his back, constantly moving, constantly exploring. Their movements made their coming together a dance, a sensual waltz without any music but the beating of their hearts and the rhythmic unison of their sighs.

She rocked and swayed in his arms, leaned against and into him as if she were completely, totally his. Hard and aching, he felt as if every brush of her body against his swollen manhood would send him over the edge. Still, he needed more.

Inch by inch, he worked the hem of her nightdress up, crushing the linen in his fists as his fingers reached for another handful, doing this again and again until the legs brushing against his were bare. Roxanne didn't protest. In fact, she was so lost in the long, deep kiss they shared he wasn't sure that she realized what he was doing.

Maybe he'd suffer all night, all his life, but there was no need for Roxanne to suffer, ever.

She twitched when he laid his hand on her mound, but just a little. His palm rested against her, warm and solid, sure and strong until she relaxed, accepting his presence there. She plunged her tongue deep into his mouth as if she were asking. . . .

He slipped his fingers lower to touch her intimately, to caress and tease. Her thighs parted in response. She was wet, wet for him and only him. She melted, soft and silky as his fingers smoothed over her flesh, and for a moment he actually considered . . . no, that couldn't happen.

So he stroked her with fingers that were at first easy and then more forceful, caressing and pressing, loving and insistent. Already she shook, losing control as the rhythm of her desires took over. She moved against and into him, rocking forward, closer and closer, the demand in her mouth and her hands and the body that rocked against him. When he slipped a finger inside her and the release claimed her, she cried out and shuddered, her entire body shaking, trembling in his arms.

And then she was still, curled up against him, wrapped around him.

"That was . . . " she took a deep, apparently difficult breath. "Oh my—"

Cyrus silenced her with a soft kiss. He could leave her now; he didn't want to go. There was no reason for him to stay; he didn't want to go. He would hold her a while longer, that's all, make memories to savor for a lifetime, because this would never happen again.

When he finally began to draw away, Roxanne stopped him. She held him fast with long, slender arms, crooked one bare leg around his denim clad one so that his arousal pressed against her.

"Love me," she whispered.

"Roxanne. . . ."

She slipped her hand between their bodies

and laid her palm over his engorged flesh. "You can't say you don't want me," she whispered.

He swallowed hard. "No, I can't."

"I fell in love with you as I read your letters," she whispered, and her hand began to move, to stroke gently until all rational thought was gone from Cyrus's mind. "I dreamed about this, about kissing and holding you and touching you and . . . and I even dreamed about having you inside me. Love me," she whispered again.

He had never been overcome by sensation before, had never thrown out all rational thought and allowed his body to rule. But with Roxanne's last whispered *love me*, all Cyrus's good intentions flew away.

Weak and trembly from the sensations that had wracked her body as Calvin touched her, Roxanne knew it wasn't enough. An emptiness plagued her still, a throbbing need to have him inside her. They were unfinished, undone, and she wasn't about to let him go.

She stroked the rock-hard ridge beneath his trousers, and told him everything she felt and everything she wanted, and then she whispered, "*Love me.*"

He groaned, in pain and desire. His hand joined hers over the buttons that kept him from her, and she thought, for a moment, that he was going to unfasten those buttons and take her here where they stood, fast and hard.

His hand stilled, then he manacled her wrists and removed them from his body.

"We can't," he said. "Not tonight."

He kissed her, and she could feel a faint tremble in his lips. That and his deep, ragged breathing told her how near he was to losing control, how much he wanted her. Her heart swelled with a new surge of love. He wanted *her*.

She hooked one leg around his and held him close, feeling the hard ridge beneath his trousers, the erection that had pressed against her as he held her tight. He groaned hoarsely above her, and captured her mouth again for a deep kiss that made her insides wobble.

With all her heart and soul, she knew he wanted her; and she was ready to give him everything a woman had to offer. Everything. And still he resisted.

"Love me," she whispered.

He shuddered. "Not tonight," he whispered huskily. "We have a thousand nights like this stretching before us, and then a thousand more." His breath came ragged and unsteady, every word an effort. "I won't take you on the ground, and I won't sneak like a thief into your bedroom to take something that isn't rightfully mine."

"I am yours," she whispered.

"Not yet," he muttered.

He held her tight, his head close to hers, his body very still. It was as if she could feel him taking control of his body, fighting what he wanted. A sweet, caring man, he waited for their wedding night.

Roxanne didn't want to wait. After all these years of numbness, she was alive again; she felt, she desired, she loved. She wanted Calvin to throw caution to the wind, to lose himself in sensation and need and love as she had, until nothing else mattered. Nothing.

She began to blindly unfasten his trousers, to move aside the heavy fabric that kept him from her. He protested, a small, low, grunting sound from deep in his throat. Fumbling with the buttons as she kissed his neck, she moved slowly and deliberately. He *did* want her. She *was* his.

The fastenings taken care of, she slipped her hand into his trousers to touch the hard length that had been pressing against her all night. She stroked him, as he had stroked her, with loving, teasing, erotic fingers. He groaned hoarsely above her, and captured her mouth for a deep kiss before they lowered their bodies to the ground.

Slipping her fingers beneath his waistband, she pushed his trousers over his hips, then reached down to touch his freed manhood. She quivered as she withdrew her hand from between their bodies, ready to become one with the man who had courted and wooed her, ready to take into her body the man who had brought her back into life. She wanted to see him above her, but the night was too dark.

Behind closed eyes she tried to picture beautiful, fair-haired Calvin, but her fickle mind betrayed her and it was a dark head of hair she saw, moss green, too-serious eyes as if they hovered above, watching her.

Cradled between her legs, hot and hard and ready, he hesitated. The tip of his manhood touched her with an insistent caress, but he didn't push. Already her body pulsed, aching, ready to accept him. She arched her back and lifted her hips so that he began to enter her, so that the tip of his hardness teased her entrance. She put aside all visions, thoughts of fair hair and dark, blue eyes and green, until there was only sensation. Only feeling.

And still he waited. "Love me," she whispered, and the last of his hesitation fled and with a low moan he surged to enter her, to fill her waiting body.

It was as if she'd waited all her life for this moment, the sensation of him filling and stretching her felt so right. He rocked above and inside her, withdrawing slightly and then pushing himself deeper than before, repeating the process until he stroked her each time with the full length of his hardness.

The world faded to nothing and there was only his body and hers, the sensations they created together, this night, this moment in time. Her hips rocked against his as he pounded against and into her again and again. Together they searched and climbed, breathless, sweating, mindless.

Slight tremors teased her, lightning-like flashes that coursed fleetingly through her body until at last release claimed her, wrenching her body apart with unearthly power and a pleasure so intense she cried out.

He drove deep one last time, shuddering above her as he found the same wonderful climax that continued to wash like dying waves through her body.

She closed her eyes as he drifted down to cover her, to rest his hot, sweaty, wonderful body against hers. He lay very still atop her, too still, perhaps. She lifted her hand to lay it on the back of his head. His hat had fallen off long ago, exactly when she couldn't say, and her fingers fell on silky, short hair.

"Oh," she whispered weakly. "You cut your hair."

He stiffened and lifted his head. "This afternoon," he whispered. "I hope you don't mind."

"Makes no difference to me," she sighed as she ran her fingers through the short strands. "I just wish I could see you," she said. "When we make love next time I want a hundred candles." Her voice was teasing, but she was halfway serious. "I want to see you when you become a part of me, to look into your eyes when you touch me."

She must've said something wrong, because he pulled away from her, lifting his body from hers, repairing his clothing quickly.

"I'm sorry," he whispered. "I never should've. . . ."

223

Roxanne sat up quickly. Before her she saw nothing more than a figure of a man, a dark crouching shape with his head down as he picked up his hat and placed it on his head. "What do you mean you're *sorry*?"

A tender hand touched her face. "I meant to wait, to kiss you and hold you and nothing more."

Again she thought of Cyrus, and her mind's betrayal angered her. Her own brain played nasty tricks on her, making her see and hear and think things she should not. She was *Calvin's* woman now, in every way. Her heart did a strange little flip in her chest.

She took the hand at her cheek and brought it to her mouth for a quick kiss. "If you hadn't loved me as you did, I would've spent the entire night aching and hurt and wondering what I did wrong. I don't know why you're afraid to look me in the eye when you say loving things and when you touch me, but whatever the reason . . . together we can make it better."

He took her hands in his and helped her to her feet, straightening her wrapper and tying the sash at her waist as she stood before him. Again, his head was down, the collar of his duster was up, his hat was low over his eyes. Even though her eyes had adjusted somewhat to the dark, she still couldn't see him.

She cocked her head to one side, hoping for a peek at his beautiful face. She saw nothing before he spun her around and held her tight against him, her back against his chest, his arms snugly around her.

"Are you happy, Roxanne?" he whispered, and she could hear the touch of hillbilly in his voice. Just a touch.

"Yes." She smiled in the dark.

"Then I can't be sorry."

He kissed her shoulder, feathered small kisses on her neck, and then he whispered in her ear. "I love you," the words so soft they were almost lost in the breeze that wafted by.

She hadn't thought anything would make this night more wonderful, but with those three breathy words her world was perfect. "Oh, Calvin, I—"

A hand raised quickly, and he laid two fingers over her mouth.

"Don't say it," he insisted. "Not tonight." His hands fell away from her body, the movement of those long arms slow, reluctant. "Stay right there for a minute," he whispered.

Roxanne closed her eyes and took a deep breath of cool air. Her mouth curved into a small smile. He loved her. Who could deny the deep feeling in those whispered words, the heart she heard in his voice? Her entire body tingled. Maybe Calvin would carry her to her bed and make love to her again. She wanted to make love to him all night and into the morning, to wake to his face in the sunlight. She waited, but all was silent. Too silent.

She turned around and stepped from

beneath the balcony. The night was so dark he could've been standing just a few feet away and she might not see him. "Calvin?" she whispered. All was still, and she knew, a heartbeat later, that he was gone.

Cyrus laughed as he strode down the street toward the saloon. The sound wasn't one of pleasure or mirth; it was, in fact, very close to insane.

What had he done? Ah, there was no way out of this one. Sooner or later Roxanne would find out that he had been the one to kiss her, to touch her, to bury himself inside her; Calvin would find out, and one of them would kill him.

If only she hadn't touched him, stroked him, held him. If only she hadn't whispered *love me*. . . . Dammit, he wasn't a goddamn saint!

Belatedly, a horrifying thought brought him to a momentary standstill in the middle of the street. What if Calvin and Roxanne married soon, and a few months later a baby was born? All his life he'd wonder if it was *his*, and that child—his or not—would tie him to this place forever. It was a suffocating thought.

He resumed his slow trek to Nickels' Saloon. After their fast and furious lovemaking, he'd actually broken down and told Roxanne he loved her, whispering the too true words in her ear. Then he'd had to silence her. He didn't want to hear her say, *I love you, Calvin*. Dammit.

Calvin sat at the bar, right where Cyrus had left him, still leaning over a half empty glass of whiskey. Cyrus slipped off the boy's duster and hat and retrieved his vest and dark brown hat before heading to the bar.

"Come on, kid," he said huskily, laying a hand on Calvin's shoulder. "I'll walk you home."

Calvin protested weakly, even as he left the bar and Cyrus handed him his hat and helped him into his duster and they walked through the batwing doors. When they were on the boardwalk, Calvin stopped without warning, planting himself with feet spread wide. He only swayed a little.

"I'm gettin' hitched." He slurred the words that shot a knife through Cyrus's heart.

"Of course you are." That was the plan, after all.

Cyrus had to tug on Calvin's duster to get the kid moving, and he very casually flicked away a few strands of grass at the same time. They walked to the boarding house, a trip of several blocks. Calvin tried to turn in the wrong direction a couple of times, but Cyrus was there to stop him and turn him about with an impatient hand and a muttered curse.

Finally, they reached the boarding house. Calvin said goodnight as he climbed the stairs to the front door, but Cyrus came along. They opened the front door quietly, and climbed the stairs with as much stealth as you could reasonably expect from two big men. Calvin only stumbled once, at the top of the staircase. If Cyrus hadn't been right behind him, the kid might've fallen all the way to the plank floor below.

Calvin opened the door to his room, and Cyrus caught the kid again as he started to fall.

"Calvin," Cyrus said as he closed the door. "Do you have a razor and a pair of scissors?"

Calvin closed one eye suspiciously. "Sure. What for?"

"You need a haircut."

Calvin touched his fair curls. "I do?"

Cyrus nodded. "You do."

"If you say so."

Cyrus placed a hard-backed chair in the middle of the room, and Calvin fetched the necessary implements from the dresser before lowering himself heavily to the too-small chair.

Trying to buy time—a few days, a few hours—Cyrus began to snip, fashioning the curls into a short style close to his own.

"Are you sober enough to remember a few instructions?" he asked as he cut.

"I think so," Calvin grumbled.

Blond curls fell to Calvin's shoulders and to the floor.

"When you talk to Roxanne tomorrow, she might mention a few letters you wrote to her while you were away."

Calvin turned his head and Cyrus barely missed snipping his ear. "I didn't write no letters."

Cyrus grabbed the kid's head with both hands and forced him to face front again. "I know that. I wrote a few letters for you."

Calvin tried to look over his shoulder again, and Cyrus righted his head again. "You shouldn'ta done that," Calvin said morosely.

"You're right," Cyrus snapped. "I *shouldn'ta*. But I did."

Calvin shook his head.

"Hold still!" Cyrus commanded.

"Did you put more sweet talk in them letters?" Calvin asked, still at last.

"Yes," Cyrus snapped as he snipped away. The job was almost done. When Roxanne saw Calvin she'd think he was the one she'd been with tonight. If she spoke to him. . . .

Calvin sighed, tired and drunk. "I wish you hadn't done that."

"So do I," Cyrus muttered.

"I told you I'm gettin' hitched—"

"I know, I know," Cyrus said as he brushed the last of Calvin's curls onto the floor. Calvin and Roxanne would make a handsome couple, wouldn't they? Tall and beautiful and happy, they would have a fairy tale wedding and an even happier life. "Listen carefully. When you speak to Roxanne tomorrow, she might mention something . . . strange about my visit tonight. Whatever she says, change the subject." He could only hope that Roxanne would be too reserved to say anything *specific*.

A pleasant shudder rippled through his

229

body. She hadn't been reserved tonight, not in the least. She hadn't hesitated to touch him, to tell him what she wanted. . . . Her response had been passionate and daring, intoxicating and unexpected.

Calvin raised a hand to his newly shortened hair. "Yeah, I need to talk to Roxanne tomorrow." He sounded as if he really didn't want to speak to her. "I shoulda done it tonight, but I was too . . . too scared, I reckon."

Cyrus felt a rush of impatience. Was he going to have to propose for the kid, too? "No reason to be scared," he said.

Calvin stood and shucked off his shirt. "You know, Sheriff," he said sleepily. "I figured it'd be a long while before I found the right woman and settled down. Funny how things work out, ain't it?"

Cyrus opened the door as Calvin sat on the side of the bed and tugged off his boots. "Ain't it," he whispered as he pulled the door shut.

Roxanne clutched her pillow and sprawled across the bed. She still tingled, warm and satisfied, hours after Calvin had gone.

She wished he could be with her now, stretched out beside her on the bed, perhaps holding her as he slept. If he were here maybe he would even love her again, slow and sweet this time.

Her eyes drifted closed. Behind her eyelids beautiful pictures flitted and teased her, and she smiled. She saw starlight on a white hat as Calvin hesitated at the edge of the yard, felt his skin beneath her fingertips and the deliriously wonderful pressure as he'd touched her intimately, the wonderful pressure and completeness as he'd surged to fill her. She heard, again, his soft moans in her ears, his softly whispered words. *Since first I heard the footsteps of thy soul.* His soft *I love you*.

She touched her lips, where Calvin had kissed her again and again and again . . . and as she did something strange happened.

She thought, once more, of Cyrus.

Her smile faded and her eyes flew open. What was wrong with her? Calvin was everything a woman could want; handsome, sweet, adoring, a wonderful man who wanted what she did. His love letters had touched her heart, his whispered words had healed her. He dreamed of a farm of their own, children, a life together. He was a wonderful lover.

Cyrus Bergeron was a solitary, cheerless man who turned his nose up at the very idea of marriage. Just as well. As marriage material he was definitely unsuitable. It's true he was a good man, a good friend, even—but he wore a gun, he thought children were nothing more than an awful bother, and . . . and . . . and besides, she didn't love him. She *did not* love him.

She frowned, angry with herself. Just because she thought of Cyrus at the oddest times, just because the memory of that one kiss lingered until she could sometimes think of nothing else, that didn't mean . . . that didn't mean anything at all.

She pulled the pillow over her head and stifled a scream. Calvin *loved* her; she loved him.

So why was she suddenly sure that tonight she'd made a terrible mistake?

Chapter Thirteen

She rarely met Calvin on her walk to school, but when she approached the business section and saw him standing at the side of the road, obviously waiting for her, she grinned widely and increased her step. Cutting her eyes from side to side she checked to see if they were alone. Unfortunately, she saw many citizens of Paris up and about, getting ready for another day.

Last night's momentary doubts were gone. Loving Calvin had not been a mistake. Their coming together only clarified what she already knew in her heart; this was the only man for her.

He took off his hat when she drew near, and she smiled at the sight of his newly shortened hair. She wasn't sure that the severe cut suited him, but it didn't matter. He was beautiful, still. Oh, how well she remembered running her fingers through those short, silky strands.

"Good morning," she said, and the greeting sounded somehow intimate, even though they stood in the middle of town in full view of anyone who cared to watch.

"Mornin,'" he said, glancing down at his feet as she smiled at him. "We need to talk, and I just couldn't wait another minute."

Her heart swelled, and she set aside any last little niggling doubts she might've had, any reservations. This was the man she wanted, the life she needed. Calvin bit his lower lip anxiously and cast a sideways glance in her direction, shy as always but apparently determined to have his say. Obviously last night meant as much to him as it did to her, and *finally* he was going to tell her how he felt face to face, by the light of day.

"Of course," she said softly. "You can walk with me to school."

They walked slowly, taking long, leisurely strides down the side of the street. What a beautiful spring morning, Roxanne thought as she took a deep breath. Just a hint of coolness touched the air. The chill reminded her, a little, of last night's cool breeze washing over her face and her bare legs, the chilled air she'd gasped into her lungs when Calvin had touched her. Remembering brought a warm flush to her cheeks.

Poor Calvin, he had a terrible time gathering his courage. He hemmed and hawed, and dragged his big feet as they walked down the dirt road. Roxanne smiled and waved to the people they passed, those who were setting up shop for the day, but Calvin seemed not to see them at all.

They had passed the business district and walked before a row of small cottages before he finally spoke. There weren't so many eyes on them here. Roxanne told herself that was the reason he'd waited. Such private matters should remain private, particularly for someone as timid as Calvin.

"I told you once that I wanted to get married and have kids and get myself a farm." Reticent as always, he didn't quite look her in the eye.

"You did," she said, her heart singing. This was the man who'd poured his heart into precious love letters, who'd held her close and loved her as a man loves a woman. This beautiful creature had restored her life, awakening her not with a rude shake but with a gentle hand and a heart-stopping kiss. "I think it's a wonderful plan," she said with a coy smile.

"I figured it might be a while before I found the right gal and the right piece of land, but sometimes things happen that you don't expect, they just come right out of the blue and whack you between the eyes, you know what I mean?"

"I do," she whispered. "Like last night," she lowered her voice, even though there was no one around to hear. "Last night was marvelous, Calvin. It was . . ." How could she explain when she didn't understand herself?

Calvin stopped before a bois d'arc hedge that shielded them from view. "Last night?" He looked confused, dull even, as he narrowed his eyes and wrinkled his nose.

She wouldn't let him play the game any more—distant by daylight and lover in the dark. There was no reason for him to hide anymore. Calling on a boldness she'd just recently discovered within herself, she rocked forward and laid her lips over his, ready for the explosion of power and excitement she'd experienced last night, the tingle that would warm her heart and electrify her body, the thrill that would make her weak in the knees. Her lips molded to his, soft and warm, accepting and loving, and she waited for the response that had, just a few glorious hours ago, moved her to unexpected levels.

Nothing. The kiss elicited no response at all, not in her and apparently not in Calvin, either. She opened her eyes as she took her lips from his apathetic mouth. He was blushing, beet red, and looking down at his feet again.

"Miz Roxanne, you shouldn'ta done that," he said as he took a step back.

"Last night . . . " she began.

Calvin raised his hands in the air. "I don't remember nothin' about last night," he protested. "I went into the saloon and had myself too much to drink. Woke up this morning in my own bed with my hair cut off and no idea how I got there."

"You were . . ." she swallowed hard. "Drunk?"

"Whew," he said with a shake of his head. "I was downright wobbly-ass drunk. I don't usually drink liquor much at'all, but yesterday I got so flustered. . . ."

"Flustered?" she repeated, taking her own step back. "You don't even remember what happened?"

He began to look concerned. "What happened?"

She shook her head slowly, embarrassed and more than a little flustered herself. "It doesn't matter." A hard, painful lump formed in her throat as she held back tears. She'd tasted the whiskey on his breath last night, but he hadn't acted intoxicated, not at all. On the contrary, he'd seemed very much in control.

Their passionate night had been so wonderful for her, so magical, and he didn't even remember! She was mortified at the memory of her behavior, her brazenness. Drunk or not, Calvin had still found the good sense to try to refuse her when she'd offered him everything. She felt suddenly lightheaded at the memories that had been precious moments ago and were now mortifying.

When he'd protested that she wasn't his, she'd practically begged him to ravish her. She'd touched him intimately, held on to his body and refused to let go. She'd asked him to love her . . . and he had.

237

And then he'd said he was sorry.

"Anyways," he began again. "What I wanted to tell you is that I'm getting married. Next week."

Everything went gray around the edges of her vision, and she thought for a moment she would faint. Calvin wasn't proposing to her, he was letting her go.

"Really," she said weakly.

"Yep. I met Maggie while I was staying with the cousins. She's a neighbor of theirs, the youngest daughter of a farmer out that way." His eyes lit up in a way she'd never seen, and what was left of her heart broke again. "I was smitten with Maggie the minute I laid eyes on her. Usually I'm right bashful with purty gals, but with Maggie I didn't have no trouble at'all speakin' up. Met her on Sunday, and on Monday I rode out to her Daddy's farm and asked her to be my wife."

"How wonderful for you," she said weakly, wishing for the strength to give this man a piece of her mind. She couldn't very well do that without embarrassing herself further, without reminding him of everything that had happened in the dark. "Were you . . . " she had to ask, she had to know, "thinking of Maggie last night?"

He actually smiled, his lush mouth curving into a sweet, appealing grin. "Gosh, I think about her all the time, nowadays. Sure I was thinkin' about her last night."

Dignity be damned. She took the book she

held in her hands, a weighty novel by James Fenimore Cooper, and smacked Calvin with it. The blow landed ineffectively on his arm, and when she swung again he deflected the book with a meaty hand.

"Now, there's no call to get upset. I know I said in my letter that we'd do some courtin', but—"

"Do some *courtin'*?" She swung again and this time he snatched the book from her. She wasn't just angry and hurt, she was furious. After everything he'd said and done . . .

Her fists balled at her sides, and her breathing came ragged and shallow. For a split second she felt an abysmal certainty that her life was over, that she was devastated beyond repair, that she was unbearably distraught.

Yet when she stopped long enough to look Calvin Newberry square in the eyes she realized something important, something monumentally important.

She didn't love him. Oh, she'd allowed herself to fall in love with the idea of loving again, with the sweet words and the ideal picture of a long and happy life with a loving husband at her side—but her dream was a meaningless fantasy. Like a fool she'd fallen in love with a voice in the dark, with letters that apparently meant nothing to this man, with the notion of a peaceful life with a beautiful husband and his beautiful children.

But right this minute, searching Calvin's eyes for a hint of the man she loved, she saw nothing. No thrill, no spark, no romance. No love at all. Heaven help her, she'd manufactured a man that didn't exist out of a few moments in time, out of a few words. Her breath came a little easier now than it had a few minutes ago, and the lump in her throat disappeared.

This fiasco was all her fault. Maybe she'd needed to be loved one more time, maybe she'd only wanted what he'd given her last night; warmth, touch, another body pressed against hers. She'd allowed this man to take unimaginable liberties with her, and yet when she looked into his eyes she saw *nothing*. Nothing at all.

She didn't love him.

"Give me my book," she said softly.

He held it just out of her reach. "Not if you're going to hit me with it again."

"I won't," she promised calmly.

Reluctantly, he returned her book to her. He tensed, as if he waited for her to strike out at him again. She tucked the book in the crook of her arm and looked Calvin straight in the eye, calling on every ounce of courage in her cowardly body. "I wish you every happiness."

He grinned at her, obviously relieved. "Thanks, Miz Roxanne. And you know, I hope one day you meet a man you want to marry as much as I want to marry my Maggie."

She clutched the book tightly to keep from lashing out again as she turned her back on Calvin. *Miz* Roxanne, he called her now, so formally and respectfully, as if she were an old woman. And he so *sweetly* wished her the same happiness he'd found.

"Oh no," she whispered as she continued, alone, toward the Paris Female Academy. "Never again."

Where was she? Cyrus paced on the board-walk, waiting impatiently for Roxanne to walk past. Many of her students had passed by already, arms full of books as they complained about the extraordinary amount of homework they'd been assigned, whispering—loudly—about what a foul mood their teacher had been in today.

She should've passed by now, Cyrus thought as he paced. Dammit, he should've seen her a quarter of an hour ago!

Calvin had broken the news about his impending marriage very casually, as he'd loaded a number of bags onto his horse and readied to leave Paris. Cyrus had been stunned speechless for a while, as he'd watched the kid prepare to leave town, sure that when Roxanne heard the news she would be heartbroken, dev-astated . . . especially after last night.

Calvin told him, as he climbed into the sad-dle to quiet protests from Cyrus, that he'd already told Roxanne the news of his impend-ing marriage and that after an initial bit of sur-prise she seemed not to mind at all.

Cyrus knew better. He knew, after last night, how much Calvin meant to Roxanne. She loved him!

Finally, he saw her walking down the street. Eyes straight ahead, head high, from a distance it seemed nothing was wrong.

But as she drew closer his heart sank. Her eyes were cold, dead, distant, and the hands that clutched a small stack of books were white-knuckled. She didn't seem to be paying attention to her surroundings, but stalked mindlessly, unerringly forward. If he hadn't stepped from the boardwalk to join her, she never would've seen him.

"Pretty afternoon," he said as he fell into step beside her.

"Is it?" she asked tonelessly. Her face was a bit too pale, her chin stubborn and her eyes cold. Calvin was a bigger fool than Cyrus had ever imagined if he really thought she didn't mind at all.

"Yes," he said. Her step didn't slow, and she didn't so much as glance his way.

Now, more than ever, he knew he shouldn't have gone to her last night. After everything that had happened, she was surely devastated to learn that the idiot Calvin had headed off to marry another woman. If only he'd kept his distance, if only he'd allowed her to run back into the safety of her home thinking that he didn't want her.

It would be foolish to keep talking about the weather and ignore the problem, and since Roxanne obviously didn't intend to bring up the subject, he would. Better to get everything out in the open, rather than stewing over something that couldn't be changed.

"I'm sorry things didn't work out with Calvin," he said.

She looked directly at him with cold, angry eyes. "Are you?"

He shrugged his shoulders, nervous and uncomfortable and fighting the inclination to run. He'd caused this mess, and with every attempt to help he'd only made matters worse. He had to do what he could to fix it. "I guess it just wasn't meant to be. There will be other—"

She stopped suddenly and turned on him. "Oh no," she said heatedly. "You had the right idea, Cyrus, when you said you'd never get married. I should've listened to your advice and made a similar vow myself, to stay single and unencumbered and childless. What did you say about kids? Troublesome and sassy, I think you said, among other things."

Her nostrils flared and she took a deep breath. "If having children means shackling myself to a *man*, then I'm better off remaining alone for the rest of my life." A new, almost desperate spark lit her eyes, and he wondered if she'd just this moment considered the fact that their fast and furious coming together might have resulted in a baby.

"Maybe I was wrong."

"No," she interrupted. "You were right. And if I ever ask you to introduce me to another man, if I ever mention marriage again—" she glanced

pointedly at the Colt he wore on his hip—
"shoot me."

She stalked away and Cyrus followed.
Well, he'd known this would be hard. She'd
get over it, though. She had to. "It can't be all
that bad."

She spun on him, and he was distressed to
see tears filling her angry eyes. "Not that bad?"
Her lower lip trembled, and the white-knuckled
hands that clutched her books shook. "Once, in
one of his more candid moments, Calvin told
me that pain was better than being numb." She
took a deep breath, as if she were fighting to
keep control. "He was wrong. I can live with
being numb, if I have to. I don't need the pain."

This time when she turned and walked away
he let her go.

It wasn't as easy as she'd expected to slip back
into her cold, miserable life of numbness.
Maybe she had looked into Calvin's eyes and
realized she didn't love him, maybe she had
realized that allowing herself to believe herself
in love was nothing more than a horrid mistake . . . but none of that made her heartache
any easier to take.

Why?

She paced in her dark room, the letters
Calvin had written clutched tightly in one
hand. She knew very well *why*. Calvin had
made her want love again. He'd made her realize that her life was empty and meaningless.
He'd tempted her with a future she'd never

have. Mercy, there had been moments when she *had* loved him; when he'd teased her with pretty whispered words and love letters, when he'd touched her in the dark. . . .

Coming to a sudden standstill in the middle of her bedroom, she held back a wave of panic. Allowing him to touch her had been the worst mistake of all. Swept away by lavish kisses and pretty words, she'd effectively seduced a drunken man who'd only been thinking of another woman!

What if there was a baby? *There's no baby,* she told herself. *There can't be.*

In a fit of rage she crumpled the letters in her hand. This was her fault as much, if not more, as Calvin's. Last night he'd been the one to try to call a halt to their lovemaking, the one who'd tried to keep things from starting and then had tried to keep them from going too far. Even drunk he'd *known* it was wrong.

And what had she done when he'd protested that it wasn't right? That she wasn't *his*? She'd touched him, tempted him, forced him to put his good judgment aside and make love to her. On the *ground*, for heaven's sake, as if she were an animal who had no control over her urges.

Whatever pain and heartache resulted from last night's mistake, she deserved.

She stepped onto the balcony with a tin bucket, her crumpled letters, and a single match. The rest of the world slept, but she wasn't even tired. She was cold and angry and—she sat gracelessly on the floor of the balcony—sad. She was mournful for what she didn't feel, for what she'd lost, for the lonely life she'd lead from this day forward.

She crossed her legs and set the bucket between her knees, and with a burst of anger she struck the match on the floor beside her. It flared to life and she touched the flame to a corner of one of the letters. She shook the match out and watched the letter burn, focusing her weary eyes on the low-burning flame that consumed the letter Calvin had written. When there wasn't much left she lit another letter with the flaming missive in her hand, and dropped the almost-destroyed letter into the bucket. Again, she studied the fine paper as it flickered and burned.

An unexpected wave of sadness washed over her. This devastating episode with Calvin was just something else that had to be put in the past, something else to keep her awake at night with *what ifs*.

Cyrus stood at the window, no longer able to sit and watch. His hands rested against the window frame; he needed the support. The fire before Roxanne's face illuminated her in an unearthly, eerie way that reached his heart, and he wanted, too much, to go to her and make everything right again.

He knew what she was burning, that the letters he'd written were turning to ash as he watched. Just as well. The letters were a lie, not because the words weren't true but because

Roxanne thought they'd come from another man. It was right that they burn. If only he could undo the rest of this so easily.

He'd cursed himself a thousand times in this long day. This was all his fault. He'd tried to make things right for Roxanne, and instead he'd succeeded in ruining her life, in making her miserable again. If he'd left things alone, if he'd introduced her to Calvin and then stepped back and allowed things to take their natural course, this wouldn't be happening. She never would've thought herself in love with a man who didn't really exist, a man manufactured with Calvin's face and simple dreams, with Cyrus's own words and even his body.

Dammit, he wanted to explain . . . but he couldn't. He wanted to go out there right now and stand beneath her balcony and lift his head and tell her the truth. All of it. He couldn't do that, either.

He wanted, more than anything, to claim her as his own. To love her, night after night, day after day. To give her everything she wanted; marriage, babies, forever. He wanted to make love to her by the light of a hundred candles, to sink into her while he looked into her eyes and saw a love for him and him alone.

His eyes drifted closed. Obsession, hell, he loved her and probably had for years.

His hand rose, involuntarily, to the scar on his face. He couldn't love her, couldn't look forward to night after night in her arms.

Could he? She'd said, last night, that it had

been the letters she'd fallen in love with, the whispered words. Who did she truly love? A handsome face or heartfelt words? Her dream of a safe and happy farm or the way she felt when he touched her? *Him*, not Calvin or anyone else. Not once, last night, had she mentioned Calvin's beautiful face or the safety of her ideal, isolated farm.

Instead she'd whispered about his words, in the letters and beneath her balcony, and when they'd touched . . . when they touched nothing else mattered.

He knew that in a roundabout way Roxanne did love him. She just didn't know it.

There were a thousand or more good reasons why he should stay away from Roxanne. There was only one good reason for him to consider going to her and asking for more than friendship.

Like it or not, right or not, he loved her.

Ah, actually there were two good reasons. He opened his eyes and fastened them on the occupied balcony across the way. He wanted her so badly he'd likely die without her in his life; in his bed. Going to her, pretending to be Calvin last night, had been wrong. Touching her, kissing her, taking liberties behind a mask of darkness, had been wrong. Burying himself inside her, taking everything she offered, had been wrong.

In spite of all those wrongs, loving her had been very, very right.

As he contemplated the rights and wrongs in

his life, he absently stroked the scar on his cheek. He wanted to start over, to put aside his fears and take a chance.

When Roxanne had looked at him over apple pie and said, "I want to get married," what would've happened if he'd looked her in the eye and said, "Great. Marry me." When she'd looked at Calvin Newberry with glazed, wanting eyes, he should've said, "The boy's a very nice moron." On the night of the Smiths' party he should've danced with her all night.

Ah, but there was no going back, was there? There would be no second chances to undo mistakes, no way to erase all his blunders. All he could do was start over.

He leaned forward until his face was so close to the windowpane he could feel the cold brush his cheek. *Start over*. It was the only chance they had.

Chapter Fourteen

Ada and Josiah were home, classes continued as if nothing had changed, and Roxanne forced herself to return to her old routine. She walked home from school thinking of tomorrow's lesson, the slippers that needed mending, whether they'd have chicken or beef for supper. Her eyes straight ahead, her step brisk, she ignored everything and everyone else.

In the six days—all horrendously long—since Calvin had left, she'd settled more and more comfortably into her old self. She did her job, she helped her aunt, she reached for the numbness that had gotten her through the past three years. It was best this way. If she didn't yearn for what she'd never have she wouldn't be hurt again. She had her students, her loving aunt and uncle, and she didn't need anything or anyone else in her life. Whatever foolish hope Calvin had sparked in her, a silly, stupid longing for anything more, was gone.

She increased her step, unconsciously hurrying toward the safety of home, the haven of her lonely room. Gone? That was a lie. She tried to make it true, she really did, but there was something unsettled within her, still, something that hadn't been there before. It wasn't hope, not anymore; but she definitely suffered from dissatisfaction and an unexpected agitation.

And anger—with Calvin, with Cyrus, even with Louis. Mostly she was angry with herself for allowing this mess to grow to such massive proportions.

Cyrus stood, indifferent as always, in front of the saddlery, she noticed. As she had in the past several days, she ignored him. She hadn't spoken to him since the afternoon she'd asked him to shoot her if she ever spoke of marriage again.

Of course, he hadn't spoken to her, either. He was always there at the saddlery as she walked home, or in front of the barber shop, or in front of the saloon, and he passed his time either looking at his feet or talking to some old geezer who didn't have anything better to do than bend the sheriff's ear. Today he stood alone.

Roxanne kept her eyes straight ahead, her head high and her spine straight as she blatantly ignored Cyrus. They were *not* friends, she reminded herself silently. He'd kissed her, he'd looked at her on more than one occasion as if he saw something extraordinary in her perfectly ordinary face, and she'd been foolish enough to share all her silly dreams with him. He'd confused her, and if she'd learned nothing else from her experience with Calvin it was that she didn't want or need to be confused by a man ever again.

Her steps had almost carried her safely past a silent Cyrus when she heard the cry; a faint, exasperated, "Mary Alice!"

About that time the little girl brushed past, cutting across so closely she ruffled Roxanne's brown skirt. Roxanne had to stop short to keep from plowing into the child, and when she did her books and papers slipped through her arms and went flying. One thin book landed, open and face down, at her feet, and the others tumbled this way and that. The papers scattered, caught by a sudden whiff of a breeze, as Mary Alice threw herself at Cyrus.

"Sheriff Cyrus!" the child cried with an unbridled joy that tugged at Roxanne's heart.

Cyrus braced himself and caught Mary Alice, long arms wrapping around her pale pink dress as she vaulted herself up with a giggle.

"Well, hello. If it isn't my best girl," he said softly.

Roxanne stifled an unladylike curse and dropped down to collect her books and snatch whatever papers she could. They were the girls' poems, some silly and some quite good, and she didn't want to lose a one.

"I'm so sorry," Merilee said as she came

rushing by. "She saw Cyrus and I just couldn't stop her."

Of course Merilee couldn't stop her little girl. She carried a baby on each hip, a boy on one side and a girl on the other. The twins were seven months old, now, babies but obviously heavy to carry.

"It's all right," Roxanne said. She lifted her eyes to see Cyrus with Mary Alice in his arms, heading her way. "It was just an accident." She grabbed as many papers as she could reach, and stacked her dusty books in the road.

"You're going to have to watch where you're going, young lady," Cyrus said as he put Mary Alice on her feet and began to collect a few papers that had blown up against the board-walk a few feet away. "We can't have you running down the schoolteachers."

Mary Alice collected a few papers herself, then handed them to Roxanne with a muttered, sincere apology of her own before her mother herded her toward home.

Roxanne stiffened as Cyrus came toward her, a messy stack of dirt-smudged papers in his hand. "I think this is everything," he said. His eyes fixed on her face, but they told her nothing; nothing at all.

A flutter of white caught her eye, and she turned her head to follow a single sheet of dancing paper. "Over there," she said.

Moving quickly, Cyrus rescued the lone poem, snatching it up and adding it to the stack he held.

"Here you go," he said softly as he placed the papers in her hands. She couldn't quite bear to look at him, so she stared down at the papers, instead. Well, she could add cowardice to her ever increasing list of faults. All she wanted to do was escape before she made yet another mistake.

"Thank you," she muttered, and Cyrus stepped out of her way. She took a single step before gathering her courage and spinning around to face him. "I thought you were leaving town."

"I will," he said. "Someday."

"I thought you were leaving soon," she whispered, perhaps a little desperately. "That's what you said."

"I changed my mind."

Heaven above, she felt something for him even though she knew it was hopeless. Hadn't she blundered enough without making a fool of herself over a man who obviously had no use for a wife and family? Who'd made it plain that he liked his life the way it was? Simple. Unfettered. Uncomplicated. She, on the other hand, had complicated her own life miserably by allowing a man who did not love her to take a husband's liberties. She'd let passion cloud her judgment, she'd allowed her body to rule instead of her mind or her heart.

She'd cursed herself a thousand times in the past week. What if she carried Calvin's child? And even if she were fortunate and there was no baby, how could she ever let another man touch her without remembering that night? How could she take a man into her life without telling him what a fool she'd been? And if she told, he would hate her.

Cyrus was the only man who threatened her heart, who kept alive that horrid spark of hope. If he left, if she didn't have to see him every day, perhaps she'd be able to put him in the back of her mind where she stored the rest of her regrets.

"You changed your mind," she repeated. "Why?"

"The time's not right."

She turned around with a swish of her plain skirt and headed toward home. Well, he was going to make this difficult for her, with his soft voice and his piercing eyes and his ridiculous decision to stay in Paris. Fine, she deserved whatever pain and heartache she got.

The difficulties began immediately, as Cyrus fell into an easy step beside her. "There's going to be another picnic Sunday," he said casually.

"How nice." Her voice was cold, dead, just as she intended.

Keeping pace beside her, Cyrus grumbled something she couldn't understand, but if she wasn't mistaken the words were horribly obscene. A moment later, he reached out and grabbed her arm to rudely stop her progress. It took a great juggling effort to keep her books and papers from flying this way and that all over again.

"What do you think you're doing?" she

snapped, staring cold and deep into Cyrus's eyes, and then cutting her gaze to the fingers that gripped her arm, long, dark fingers against the white linen of her sleeve. "Let go of me."

The fingers on her upper arm tightened. "No." He shook his head once to reaffirm his refusal. "Not until you hear me out."

Her heart beat too fast, and she could feel, too clearly, the pressure of those fingers against her flesh. She wanted to scream. She wanted to cry. Instead she said calmly. "Go ahead."

The fingers of one hand gripped her tightly, but not painfully, and he raised his other hand to her shoulder where it rested warmly. She no longer wanted to scream. More than anything, she wanted to fall into Cyrus's arms and cry her heart out, she wanted to throw herself at him and have him call her his best girl. She wanted to tell him everything and have him understand.

"Stop this," he whispered.

She pushed back all her insane urges and maintained her cool exterior. "I don't know what you're—"

"Stop punishing yourself," he whispered. "So you made a mistake. It's not the end of the world."

How much did he know? How much had Calvin shared with Cyrus and the others he knew? She could feel her face flushing hot and red. Calvin claimed not to remember anything about that night, but what if he'd been lying? What if Cyrus already knew everything?

"A colossal mistake," she said, her voice shaking.

"We all make mistakes," he said gently. "You're entitled to one now and then."

She felt her eyes filling with tears, her calm exterior giving way. Every panicky fear, every horror, drifted to the surface. "Not like this." Her voice shook slightly. "You just don't know—"

"It doesn't matter," he interrupted, his voice quick and soft, caressing and friendly. "I know things didn't work out like you wanted, but that's over and done with and you have the rest of your life ahead of you." His voice became gruff. "Stop . . . stop punishing yourself and everyone who cares about you."

"I'm not punishing myself, and I'm certainly not punishing anyone else," she insisted weakly.

The hand on her arm tightened, and Cyrus inched closer and closer, until she could almost hear his heartbeat, almost feel the heat pouring off his body. "You're punishing me," he whispered, and her heart skipped a beat. "Dammit, Roxanne, it kills me to see you like this."

"Why?"

"Don't you know?"

Cyrus released her and took a step back, and it came to her that like it or not she *did* know. He cared about her and always had. He had been her friend, her rock, and even though he'd protested that he didn't want marriage and children, he didn't act like a man who didn't care for family life. Mary Alice Smith adored him, and whether he admitted it or not he had a soft spot in his heart for that little girl. Perhaps his protests about marriage and children had been hollow; empty, meaningless words meant only to steer the conversation in another direction.

Had Cyrus planned to leave town because she'd set her sights on Calvin Newberry? Was he here today, still in Paris, because Calvin was gone?

Cyrus, who was a part of her painful past, who wore a gun, who was everything she *didn't* want in a man, looked at her as if he really did care—as if she could tell him anything; even her greatest mistake. How could she go back to a life of loneliness and hopelessness when he looked at her this way? Oh, she didn't need this complication, not now.

She took a deep, stilling breath, afraid to go too fast, afraid to trust her instincts. "I'm so confused," she whispered. It was the truth. She'd been so certain that Calvin was the one for her, the perfect husband, the new love of her life . . . and she'd been very, very wrong. Was it possible that her feelings for Cyrus went beyond friendship and always had?

"I know," he whispered as if he really understood.

After what had happened with Calvin, she didn't want this, didn't want any man to court and kiss and deceive her ever again. Not even Cyrus. And yet, he was her friend. Her very, very good friend. Maybe that was enough, for now.

"Cyrus?" she whispered as he backed away. "I'll be there Sunday."

He almost smiled. She almost smiled back.

"I'll make an apple pie."

This time he did smile. The curve of his lips was crooked and small, but still they fashioned a charming smile. "Wear the pink dress," he said as he turned around.

He didn't wait for an answer, but Roxanne muttered as she turned about to head for home, "Maybe I will."

Cyrus glanced anxiously at the clock sitting on the mantle in Hank Smith's study, as Hank rambled on about the twins and his sawmill business, how hard it was to find good help and how fast the babies were growing, how smart Mary Alice was and how beautiful Merilee was. The entire conversation made Cyrus very, very nervous. If he'd known this was the conversation he'd have to endure when he'd received the invitation for afternoon coffee and cake, he would've declined.

Still, he knew Hank Smith well enough to know the man was procrastinating. The lanky ex-soldier moved anxiously about the room, his Adam's apple bobbing up and down, his long, thin fingers never still. While he did glance in the direction of the chair Cyrus sat in, his eyes never lingered and he hadn't smiled. Not once. And Hank Smith had always been given to wide, frequent smiles, even when they'd been at war.

Cyrus wondered if Hank ever woke at night screaming, if he ever spent sleepless nights watching his wife and children, afraid to go to sleep. Somehow, he thought not. Wounded though he was, gentle Hank Smith was a survivor. He'd put the horrors of war behind him, and spent his days worrying about lumber and payroll, cutting teeth and making sure his children grew up tall and smart.

"Well," Cyrus said as Hank paused to take a breath, "I really should get out of here."

"Oh, not yet," Hank said anxiously. "Have another cup of coffee," he headed for the silver pot that sat on his desk, very out of place among the papers and pens and books.

"No, thank you." He stood slowly. "I've got to be going."

Hank waved an anxious hand. "Five more minutes."

Cyrus glanced at the clock again. Dammit, Roxanne was probably already home by now. He'd been sitting here for almost an hour, listening as Hank rambled on about nothing and everything. He wondered if she'd looked for him on her way home.

"Why don't you just spit it out, Hank," he finally said impatiently. "Tell me what's on your mind."

Hank looked more than a little embarrassed. "I promised Merilee that I'd speak to you about . . . about Roxanne Robinette."

Now Hank had his full attention. "What about her?"

"They used to be good friends, you know, but since I came home, things have been different."

Since the war. There was so much in that unspoken phrase. *Since I came home and Louis didn't. Since Merilee's life went on and Roxanne's stopped.*

"A lot of things are different, now," Cyrus admitted.

"Merilee still cares about Roxanne," Hank insisted. "But she doesn't know what to do."

"About what?" Cyrus asked impatiently, his teeth clenched.

Once the subject had been broached, Hank had no problem moving forward. "Merilee had begun to think that Roxanne was finally coming around, that she was finally getting on with her life. She came to the party, and was seen out and about more often, and just seemed . . . I don't know . . . Merilee used the word 'brighter,' and I guess in a pinch that'll do."

Cyrus nodded. "And?" he prodded.

"All of a sudden she's right back where she started," Hank said quickly. "Merilee's worried, and she thinks you're the only one who can talk any sense into Roxanne."

Cyrus started to protest, startled that his involvement with Roxanne was so transparent, but Hank cut him off with a raised hand and a quick word.

"I know. It's none of our business. But Merilee said she'd rest easier if I spoke to you and I promised I would." Hank looked relieved to have the encounter over with, and a little embarrassed to be caught up in this personal situation.

"Well, you've done your job," Cyrus said noncommittally as he glanced at the clock one last time. "Merilee can rest easy, now."

He turned to walk away, and didn't even stop when Hank asked, "Shall I tell Merilee you'll speak to Roxanne?"

Cyrus muttered to himself as he walked out of the front door. "What the hell do you think I'm trying to do?"

He walked quickly through the neighborhood, down one street and across another, through one yard and then another, over Thomas Eakin's fence rather than the long way around it. A few people saw him, and if they acknowledged him he waved absently and kept moving. Finally he could see his own little house, and the Pierson house across the street.

Roxanne had just reached the wrought iron gate at the pathway that led to the front door. Her back was to him, and he drank in the fine points that were so very clear to him; the cinch at her waist, where her white blouse and dark blue skirt met. The set of her shoulders. The strands of soft dark hair that brushed that slender neck.

He'd kissed that neck; he wanted to kiss it again. Now.

"Hello," he said as he crossed the street, surprised that he sounded slightly out of breath.

She spun around quickly, surprised. "Good afternoon, Cyrus," she said a moment later.

She didn't immediately turn to leave him behind, didn't turn her back and leave him standing breathless and stupid on the street.

There were many more reasons to stay away from her than there were to run *to* her. He knew that too well. Still, he was compelled to do just that; to run to her, now and forever.

She didn't smile; he didn't expect her to, not yet. But there was something in her eyes that told him she was glad to see him, something that gave him hope where he should have none.

"Is something wrong?" she asked when he continued to stand, silent, in the middle of the street.

"No, I just. . . ." *I just had to see you.* Too soon. "I wanted to remind you about the picnic Sunday."

What might have been a smile tugged at the corners of her wide mouth. "That's just two days away," she said. "Do you think me forgetful?"

"No," he said honestly. "I just don't want you to change your mind." He heard a carriage coming, the clop of horses and the squeak of wheels, and stepped out of the street and closer to Roxanne.

"I should," she said softly. "Change my mind, that is."

"No, you shouldn't," he whispered.

She shifted her books restlessly. "Cyrus, can I ask you one question?"

"Anything."

They waited while the carriage passed. Cyrus

looked into blue eyes that were not happy . . . but they weren't sad anymore, either. He'd do anything to keep that terrible sadness from her eyes. Anything.

"I've been wondering about something. Every day . . . well, *almost* every day when I walk home from school you're there. You're on the street, on the boardwalk, or walking somewhere along the route I take home." She latched blue eyes to him, as if setting herself to gauge his reaction. "Is that a coincidence?"

She seemed to hold her breath as she waited for an answer.

"No," he finally said. "No coincidence."

He'd done it; told the truth and set himself up for rejection and humiliation from the one person in the world who had the power to destroy him.

But Roxanne just nodded once, and again he was certain he saw the tug of a smile at her lips. Not a grin that said he was ridiculous for so much as thinking of her, but a warm, welcoming smile that gave him more hope than he had a right to.

She finally opened the gate and walked away from him, and he stood there and watched her go. If anything came of this he'd have to tell her, one day, about the scheme he and Calvin had hatched. He'd have to tell her that he had been the one to speak to her in the dark, to pour out his heart in those letters, to touch and kiss her. He would have to tell her that he had been the one to make love to her in the dark, to

answer her plea as she whispered an irre-
sistible *love me*.

Would he even have to tell her? If he
touched her, wouldn't she know? He knew
without question, that he would recognize her
scent and her touch on the darkest of nights,
that to feel her touch again would be too
familiar to deny. When . . . if he kissed her,
would she realize his deception?

When Roxanne was inside the house with the
door closed solidly behind her, Cyrus walked
away.

Was it possible that Roxanne would remember his touch?

Hellfire, that remembrance was likely the
only way she'd ever know the truth about that
night. He'd *never* tell her that he'd deceived her,
that he had gone to her in another man's place,
that he'd hidden behind Calvin's pretty face to
take what he'd wanted more than anything in
the world. He would never risk dousing the
spark of life he'd seen in her eyes; he'd never
risk losing Roxanne when he'd just found her.

Not even with the truth.

Scott's Mercantile was crowded, but that wasn't
unusual for a Saturday. Not only did the townspeople crowd the store, there were a number of
shoppers from nearby, ranchers and farmers
come to town to stock up on supplies.

Roxanne shopped for needed molasses and
sugar, cinnamon and flour, tea and coffee,
and tobacco for Josiah. Her list was quite

long, and already her basket hung heavily at her side. It seemed that Ada had miraculously run out of almost everything.

From the front of the store came an unexpected, quite loud, baby's cry. Roxanne flinched at the annoying sound that reminded her of her predicament. What if her foolish encounter with Calvin had left her carrying his child? She shuddered as she adjusted her basket on her arm. While there was no need to worry needlessly about something that either already was or wasn't, she couldn't help herself.

She already had a plan, of sorts. The West was growing every day, and new, burgeoning towns needed schoolteachers. If she found herself in a predicament she couldn't explain away, she'd sell everything she owned, buy a stage ticket west, and disappear.

The prospect was terrifying, but what other choice did she have?

The cry came again, this time followed by a familiar, soothing voice cooing, "Now, now."

Roxanne headed for the front of the store, and sure enough there was Merilee with a child on either hip and Mary Alice at her heels, begging for licorice in a high, whining voice. Poor Merilee had two bright spots of color on her cheeks, she was so embarrassed.

Setting her basket on the front counter, Roxanne instinctively reached out and took the crying baby. It was the boy, little Henry, she surmised as she smoothed the front of his blue shirt.

"My goodness," she said, cradling the baby in her arms. "He's so heavy."

More surprised than soothed, she supposed, the child stopped crying and looked up at her with wide, wet eyes. His lower lip trembled pathetically. His face was red from his temper tantrum, a wispy strand of pale hair stood straight up in the center of his head—and he was the most beautiful sight she had ever seen. Why had she never noticed before how absolutely beautiful he was?

"I'm so sorry," Merilee apologized. "It's past time for his nap, and he tends to get cranky when he's tired."

As if to prove his mother's point, Henry screwed up his nose and mouth and looked as if he might begin crying all over again. He didn't cry, though. Instead, he laid his head against Roxanne's shoulder and let out a long, shuddering sigh as he closed his eyes.

Roxanne savored the warm heaviness of the limp body in her arms, the complete trust and the innocence and the softness that was beyond words. "It's all right," she said, taking a glance at the other baby, a little girl with pale curls and a pink ribbon in her hair, and a pink shift that didn't quite cover her fat legs. "You certainly do have your hands full."

Merilee sighed. "Hank was supposed to stay home with the children while I shopped, but there was a problem at the sawmill and he had to head out there for the afternoon. I had hoped to have everything done by now, and get

268

the children home in time for their nap, but one thing and then another slowed me down and here I am." She lifted desolate eyes to Roxanne. "Still not finished."

Accustomed to taking charge of her classroom, Roxanne didn't hesitate here. "Mrs. Scott," she said with a nod to the shopkeeper. "Put those on my uncle's bill and have them delivered this afternoon, will you?"

Mrs. Scott nodded and began to tally the items in the basket.

Roxanne reached out and took Mary Alice's hand. "Mary Alice and Henry and I are going to head for home, while Mommy finishes her shopping."

"Oh, Roxanne, I can't ask you to do that." Merilee protested, but a spark of desperate hope lit her wearied eyes.

"You didn't ask," Roxanne said. "I offered." She balanced the baby she held and looked, almost longingly, at the other one. "I would take all three, but I'm afraid I'd drop one of the babies." She smiled. "I swear, I don't know how you do it."

Roxanne turned around, a sleeping baby on one shoulder and Mary Alice's hand in hers. She felt oddly content, even though these were not her children, even though she could not be sure she would ever have children of her own.

Deep in the darkest part of her heart, she'd always envied Merilee her family, and on a few bad days the envy had turned rather ugly, becoming more resentment than jealousy. That

Linda Jones

resentment was the reason she'd seen Merilee as little as possible over the past three years.

But at this moment, taking charge of these little ones for Merilee, just for a while, seemed only right. There was no jealousy in her heart.

She'd only taken a single step forward when a tall figure filled the doorway. She lifted her head, and smiled instinctively at the sight before her. Mary Alice squealed and yanked her hand away as she sprinted forward.

Turning to Merilee, Roxanne said, "Well, this works out just fine. Hand that baby over to Cyrus."

Chapter Fifteen

How had he gotten roped, so easily and quickly, into this duty? Little Chloe insisted on gnawing on his shoulder as she squirmed in one arm, while Mary Alice held his hand and chattered happily. Beside him, Roxanne seemed amazingly content to cradle a sleeping baby in her arms. A quick glance confirmed that Henry continued to sleep, slack against Roxanne's chest without a care in the world.

"You know," he said testily, and in a very low voice so Mary Alice wouldn't hear, "Merilee Smith could hire someone to watch her children."

Roxanne shot an amused glance in his direction. "How can you say such a thing?" She whispered so as not to disturb Henry. "A mother doesn't want a stranger caring for her babies. Most days Merilee handles everything just fine. She was just having a difficult afternoon and I offered to help."

Cyrus grumbled beneath his breath, and the baby in his arm answered by reaching out and grabbing his ear, giving a good, hard tug.

"Thank you for the licorice, Mrs. Robinette," Mary Alice said with a joyful skip.

"You're welcome," Roxanne said softly.

"I thought you were still mad at me, since I ran into you the other day and made you drop your papers." Mary Alice cocked her head so she could see past Cyrus to Roxanne.

"That was just an accident. Of course I'm not mad at you."

"You sure looked mad," the little girl said in a disbelieving voice.

Roxanne smiled softly. "Perhaps I was angry with myself." She raised a hand to Henry's fair head. "For being so clumsy," she added.

"You don't have to whisper," Mary Alice skipped forward, tugging on Cyrus's hand. "Once Henry falls asleep he's not waking up until he's good and ready, no matter what's going on around him. Why, Chloe can cry and cry and cry, right there in the same room, and Henry sleeps right through it."

Mary Alice continued her discourse on her siblings' habits, happily sucking on a whip of licorice between complaints and the occasional compliment.

Henry didn't cry as much as Chloe, she said, but when he did cry he was much too loud.

Chloe was the most fun to play with, but sometimes she liked to bite, and since she was teething she slobbered too much. Mary Alice made it clear she couldn't wait for her brother and sister to grow up.

Roxanne held little Henry with such tender care it was obvious how much she wanted children of her own. On occasion, during their slow walk toward the Smith house, she would smile for no apparent reason. Her fingers caressed Henry's spine and the back of his head as if she couldn't get enough.

Chloe clamped down on his shoulder again, and Cyrus contained a vile curse by the greatest force of will. Of course Roxanne was content; her bundle of joy didn't bite.

"Stop that," he said sternly, and Chloe answered by turning her face up and assaulting him with big blue eyes that filled instantly with tears. Her chin shook and her pink lower lip trembled, and she wrinkled her pert little nose, gearing herself up for a good cry.

"Sorry," Cyrus said in his most soothing voice. "Don't cry." He forced a smile that only pushed her closer to tears. "I tell you what," he said, shifting the baby in his arms. "Go ahead. Chew on me all you want."

Beside him, Roxanne laughed softly. "For a tough, no-nonsense sheriff, you certainly do fold easily."

He glanced at Roxanne as Chloe tried to climb over his shoulder. She was surprisingly strong for one so small. He dragged her back down and she immediately clamped her mouth to his shoulder. Thank goodness he wore his leather vest; there wasn't much skin in this particular mouthful.

"It's the big blue eyes," he confessed. "I swear, I'd rather face a loaded gun any day."

Roxanne laughed, and then she fixed her own big blue eyes on his face as they finally reached the Smith house.

Mary Alice led the way to the nursery upstairs, where both babies were put to bed. Henry, of course, simply continued to sleep. Chloe started to fuss, until Mary Alice fetched her favorite blanket. With the small quilt in hand, Chloe flashed a heart-grabbing grin at Cyrus, then closed her eyes.

Mary Alice had a tea party planned, and she took Cyrus's hand to lead him back downstairs. At the doorway to the nursery, he looked over his shoulder to watch Roxanne hover over Henry's crib.

"I'll be down in a minute," she whispered. "I just want to make sure they're napping soundly before I leave them up here all alone."

Cyrus hesitated while Mary Alice tugged impatiently on his hand. This was what Roxanne wanted; babies, family, chaos.

He'd decided long ago that he didn't need chaos. He needed peace. There had been no peace in his years on Gil's farm. In the years after he ran away, survival had been his only objective, as he worked his way from place to place, from job to job.

The closest he'd ever come to true peace had been in his early years in Paris, but the war had come along to turn his new home and everyone in it upside down.

For four years he'd felt responsible for every poorly trained boy who came along, for every sad, unfit soldier and homesick husband. There were moments when he swore he didn't want to be responsible for anyone ever again.

Making that promise to Louis had made him responsible for Roxanne's life and her happiness. Falling in love with her threatened to change everything.

She wanted children of her own, and while Cyrus had always rejected the idea of taking on that kind of obligation, he wondered, as he watched Roxanne, if it wasn't already too late. He wondered if there wasn't already a child, his child, growing inside her.

The real hell of it was, if there was a baby she didn't know it was his. What the hell had he done?

Mary Alice led him away from the nursery. Before they reached the stairwell they strolled across a long section of hallway that looked over the foyer, and there the little girl stopped to grab the rail with her one free hand and look down.

"Sometimes it makes me dizzy to look down," she said as she moved on. "Does it make you dizzy?"

She led him downstairs and directly to the kitchen, and there they arranged a plate with freshly made shortbread. When did Merilee find time to bake? The kitchen, like the rest of the house, was spotless. Merilee Smith was perfectly put together whenever he saw her, walking with her children or shopping or at church. Hank seemed to be disgustingly happy and, for a thin man, well fed, and the children were certainly well cared for. So, when did the woman sleep?

They were walking toward the parlor, short-bread in hand, when Mary Alice lifted her head. "Look down," she said loudly. "Does it make you dizzy?"

Cyrus turned about and lifted his head. Roxanne stood above, her hands on the banister, her eyes intently locked on him. His heart skipped a beat. She couldn't possibly recognize him, not like this. Still, her head tilted strangely to one side as she studied him. She looked at him, for a split second, as if she saw something that didn't quite fit. As if she were puzzled. As if he were someone else.

Merilee threw open the front door, her arms full of packages, her smile impossibly wide, and as she thanked Cyrus for his assistance, he made a quick, cowardly escape.

It was another beautiful spring day, just windy enough for a few of the children to be flying their kites, just cool enough for Roxanne to need the thin shawl she kept wrapped around her shoulders.

Getting ready for church this morning, she'd

rejected the rose-colored dress in favor of the gray she'd worn to church a hundred times, but standing before the mirror, ready to go, she'd heard Cyrus's soft voice. *Wear the pink dress.* So while Ada and Josiah waited impatiently, she'd quickly changed her dress.

The look on Cyrus's face when he'd seen her had made her bravery worthwhile. He'd looked pleasantly surprised and, a moment later, oddly cheerful. Sitting just a few pews up from her family, and on the other side of the aisle, he'd glanced over his shoulder more than once during the service. She'd pretended not to notice, of course.

Watching his back when she should've been listening to the sermon, her eyes on the set of his shoulders and the strength of his neck and the way his dark hair lay against that handsome neck, she'd recalled the moment she'd looked down from the Smiths' upstairs hallway to see him standing below. For a second, no more, she'd had the strangest feeling that she'd looked down on him just so before. There was such familiarity in the way he walked, in the way he lifted his hand when he spoke to Mary Alice. She'd quickly dismissed her foolish notions, crediting them to the softness of the moment, the warmth in her heart, and plain old wishful thinking.

Yesterday's wishful thinking put firmly behind her, the church service already forgotten, Roxanne sat beside Cyrus in Mallory Park. They had the blanket that he'd brought to themselves, and both of them were comfortably full of Ada's rolls and braised chicken and Roxanne's apple pie. Cyrus had stretched out on his side, and with his eyes half-closed he looked like he wanted nothing more than to lie back and take a nap. He looked, in fact, quite content.

She was at ease with Cyrus in a way she'd never been with Calvin. Why had she so stupidly set her cap for a man she didn't know? Calvin had never been anything to her but dreams and fantasy, escape from the lonely prison she'd built for herself. Cyrus was no fantasy; he was real and true and good, and no matter what he said he was a man who needed a woman and a family.

In truth, the only good times she'd had with Calvin had been in the dark or from a distance. By letter or by whisper. She never would've been comfortable with the big, beautiful man resting beside her, a long and comfortable silence stretching between them.

If Cyrus did truly care for her, and she was beginning to suspect that he did, was she a fool for dismissing him so easily? For deciding, without even giving him a chance, that a lawman who was a part of her past was completely unacceptable? She had begun to believe that he needed her in his life as much, perhaps more, than she needed him. If only she hadn't made such a colossal mistake with Calvin, then maybe . . . maybe. . . .

"Are you cold?" Cyrus asked.

Roxanne shook her head. "No. Are you?"

He sat up quickly, moving his long limbs with a masculine grace that was quite pleasant to watch. Strange, how lately she saw so much magnificence in this man. It was rather like suddenly finding extraordinary beauty in a sunset you'd seen every day of your life, like one day finding perfection in a simple flower that grew right outside your window.

"No. It's just that you . . . " he hesitated, crossed his long legs Indian style as he faced her. "You shivered, a little."

"Did I?"

He'd kissed her once before, and right now she wished he'd try again. He'd shocked her so much the first time she hadn't responded at all. His lips had touched hers and then quickly moved away, without giving her a chance to taste, to really feel. Next time, *if* there was a next time, she would. Not now, of course, with all these Paris eyes on them, but maybe one day, when they were all alone again. . . .

Roxanne made herself look away, setting her eyes on a group of children that ran in absolute circles. Just watching made her a little dizzy, but that was all right. What on earth was wrong with her? First Calvin and now this! She hadn't even thought of love for years, and now within a month she'd fancied herself falling in love with two different men. Surely this wasn't natural.

But she'd learned her lesson with Calvin. From now on, she would take matters slowly.

Very slowly. And if it turned out she was not carrying Calvin Newberry's child, and if she still felt this way about Cyrus in, oh, a year or two, and he still seemed interested in her, and if he didn't despise her when she told him what had happened with Calvin, then maybe . . . maybe they could have something real and lasting and wonderful.

Much as she dreaded telling him what had happened with Calvin, she had no choice. If she knew nothing else, she knew that she couldn't build her life with any man on a lie.

But how on earth would she tell him?

She jerked slightly, surprised, when Cyrus laid his hand on her shoulder. Almost immediately he moved his hand away, and she turned her head away from the running children to look at him.

"Are you all right?" he asked.

"I'm fine. I guess I was just . . . daydreaming."

Why did he look at her this way? So hard and deep she shivered again, from the inside out, as if he knew her daydreams and nightmares, her secrets and her regrets. Silly thought. No one knew her deepest, most terrible secret.

Cyrus Bergeron looked like a man who had a few secrets of his own, and a few regrets, as well. If she was right about him, about their future together, one day she'd tell him of her greatest mistake. What would happen then? Would he understand and share his own secrets, or would he despise her for her single night of indiscretion?

"Tell me more about the farm you grew up on," she said, desperate to change the direction of her thoughts.

"There's not much more to tell," he said softly.

She felt a need to know him better, to look into his heart and discover the real Cyrus. "Why did you run away when you were only thirteen?"

He shook his head slowly. "It's not a pretty story, Roxanne. You don't want to hear it."

"I do," she insisted softly.

He turned his head slightly, so that he no longer looked directly at her. She waited, patiently, for him to either fulfill her request or deny it.

"Gil liked to take his frustration out on me," Cyrus said, his voice low. "I was convenient, a responsibility he'd never wanted, and his wife didn't make such a fuss when it wasn't one of her own kids he was beating on."

"He *hit* you?" Roxanne hissed, horrified.

Cyrus turned his head slowly to look at her, to really, really *look* at her. "On occasion. He liked to take his belt and just lash out at whatever he could hit. Usually I'd just cover my face and head with my arms, and let him have at it until he got tired. If I didn't make a sound, he usually didn't last long."

"He hit you," she said again, her lower lip trembling in anger and indignation.

"One day," he continued, ignoring her soft outburst, "he found me reading one of Jean's books when I should've been shoveling out the horse stalls. He took the book away, dragged me into the house, and made me watch while he tossed it into the stove. Made me so mad," he said, leaning back again and watching the sky above. "The only time I wasn't completely miserable was when I got a few minutes to read, and he just watched that book burn while he told me what a worthless kid I was. When he took off his belt to teach me my lesson, I snatched it away from him and beat the stew out of him."

"Good," Roxanne said heartily. "That's no better than he deserved." Her anger simmered. "Son of a bitch," she muttered beneath her breath.

Cyrus rolled his head to look at her, eyebrows raised in feigned shock.

"Well," she whispered, leaning just a little bit closer. "If ever a man deserved to be called such a name, it's your despicable cousin. He *hit* you." Her eyes filled with a tear or two, tears of anger rather than of sadness.

Cyrus laid a hand on her knee. "Honey, it was a long time ago."

Honey. He seemed to realize what he'd said about the time he did. He removed his hand from her knee and sat up.

"Sheriff Cyrus!" Mary Alice threw herself at Cyrus's feet. "Edith Terry's brother Frank got his kite stuck in a tree!" Her voice was urgent, the words insistent and loud. This was a disaster of major proportions. "Can you get it down? *Please?*"

"Where is it?" Cyrus followed the line of sight Mary Alice provided with her excited, shaking finger. Sure enough, a cluster of kids gathered around a tall oak tree, and far above their heads a brightly colored kite and a long rag tail fluttered, the toy tangled in the limbs.

He glanced at Roxanne and smiled, perhaps as relieved as she was by the interruption. "If you'll excuse me, duty calls."

Roxanne watched him walk away, led by an excited Mary Alice who practically ran as she took him to her friends on the other side of the park. When they were almost there the little girl reached up and took Cyrus's hand.

Yes, Roxanne thought as she watched the endearing scene, Cyrus was a kind man at heart. Maybe he was occasionally gloomy, and maybe he was a sheriff who carried a gun, but that didn't change who he was or how she felt.

She could thank Calvin for one thing, no matter how much he'd hurt her. She was finally able to put the past in the past where it belonged, she was able to think of Louis without pain. It didn't really matter that Cyrus was a part of her past, not anymore. For that, maybe she could forgive Calvin for breaking her heart.

As she watched, Cyrus lifted his head to study the situation. Kids gathered at his feet, solemn and hopeful. If anyone could save that kite, it was Sheriff Cyrus.

He removed his hat and handed it to Mary Alice, who took the offering with awe and reverence and held it gingerly as Cyrus clapped his hands together once and lifted his head. Roxanne stared at his back, at the shape of his shoulders and the handsome taper to his waist, at the length of those strong legs.

From a standing position, he leapt into the air and grabbed the lowest limb, hauling himself gracefully from the ground and into the tree. Roxanne's heart skipped a beat. He threw one leg over the limb in a move that was sheer poetry in motion, and so very familiar.

She shook her head as he disappeared into the leaves. There weren't that many different ways to climb a tree, certainly. Just because Cyrus and Calvin both climbed trees in the same way, that didn't mean anything. From the back the graceful movement had looked disturbingly familiar, but it was just coincidence. Just one of those things. Like yesterday, when she'd looked down on him standing in the Smith's entryway and been so sure she'd seen him from that angle before.

Calvin didn't move the way Cyrus did. He lumbered, he was clumsy, at times he was uncomfortable in his own body. At least, by the light of day. . . . By night he'd been downright graceful, agile and poised. He'd been sure of himself, compelling, elegant. He had, in fact, moved much more like Cyrus than like the awkward Calvin who was so shy he could barely speak a coherent sentence in her presence. And she wondered. . . .

She shook her head and made herself look away. Wishful thinking was one thing. Fantasy was another.

It had been a nice day, a good start in Cyrus's opinion. Roxanne looked great in her brightly colored dress. The pink made her skin glow, made her look younger, happier. Maybe she wasn't really happy yet, but he had a feeling she was getting there.

She was wary but not sad. Pensive, but no longer angry. Every now and then when she looked at him she fastened her eyes on him so hard and intimately he shivered. He liked it, he liked it a lot.

What he didn't like was the growing certainty that no matter what happened he was going to have to tell her the truth about the night he'd made love to her. He couldn't allow her to go through life thinking Calvin had used and then abandoned her. Couldn't let her go through life punishing herself for his mistake, for his weakness.

But not now, not today. When the time came the truth might not exactly be welcome, and he didn't want to spoil this fine day.

They walked, side by side, toward home.

"Cyrus?" she said, and there was a lilt in her voice that warned him she'd been thinking and wondering about something. "Are you familiar with Elizabeth Barrett Browning?"

She might as well have hit him in the chest with a log. He took a moment to think, mumbling and humming under his breath. "Let me think. . . . " What had her asking such a question?

"It's just that I've been introducing the older girls to her poetry, and I wondered if you'd ever read her work. That's all."

He breathed a sigh of relief. His imagination was getting the best of him. "Oh, she's a *poet*."

"Yes," she said, apparently lost in thought. " 'The face of all the world is changed, I think,' " she said dreamily.

Cyrus bit his tongue.

Roxanne flashed him an unexpected smile. "Perhaps I can loan you one of her volumes of poetry some time. She's my favorite poet."

"Sure," Cyrus said, suddenly glad to see his house and hers ahead.

They stopped outside the wrought iron gate. As far as he was concerned, the day had been spoiled, just a little. Bringing up Browning had been a coincidence, right? Still, the *coincidence* sat in his chest like a brick. He opened his mouth to tell Roxanne goodbye and cross the street, to escape before she brought up the subject of poetry again.

She laid a hand on his arm, stopping him. The touch was familiar and jolting and arousing, and it was nothing more than her gentle hand on his forearm. She looked past him, down the street, and saw what he did—Josiah and Ada still a good distance from home but heading this way.

Roxanne opened the gate and stepped beyond, pulling Cyrus after her. Moving quickly, she slipped behind a nearby flowering hedge and placed herself directly before him, her body so close to his that if she breathed deeply her chest would brush his. He looked down at her lifted face, at her wide eyes, her full lips, her stubborn chin.

"Kiss me," she whispered.

"What?"

With a despairing sigh, Roxanne rocked forward and laid her lips on his. At first he didn't move, the action was so unexpected, so shocking. But a heartbeat later he responded, moving his mouth against hers, sucking and tasting, slipping the tip of his tongue over her lower lip.

Her arms slid around him, and without thinking he dropped the blanket he carried and took her in his arms. She molded against him, and the kiss went on and on.

When she touched him he lost control, and this unexpected embrace was no different. In an instant, there was nothing but sensation and need and hunger, there was no one in the world but the two of them. He held her tightly and, eyes closed, danced his lips over hers. Ah, she was familiar and responsive and right, she fit against him in a way no other woman ever had or ever would.

Her fingers stroked his back, her well-remembered caress threatening to send him over the edge here and now. He teased her tongue with his own, and felt her responsive shiver in his arms. He even felt the moment when her knees went weak.

She took her lips from his and fell slowly away, and Cyrus's eyes drifted open. He could see the confusion on her face, the slight tremble of her lips as she retreated from him. The kiss had been familiar to him, bringing back memories of the night they'd kissed, the night he'd touched her and made love to her, the night he'd told her he loved her and then walked away.

Was the kiss familiar to her, as well? Was that why she looked suddenly scared?

"Looks like rain," she said without so much as glancing at the cloud-filled sky.

"Yes, it does," he agreed, never taking his eyes from her as she continued to back toward the front porch.

"We may even get a storm," Roxanne said as she almost stumbled over the bottom step.

"Maybe."

She laid her hand on the doorknob, and as she did Cyrus heard voices approaching. Josiah and Ada were talking, *arguing*, about the new minister. There wasn't much time.

"Roxanne. . . ."

She threw open the door and stepped inside with a quick goodbye, leaving Cyrus to collect his blanket from the ground and make his escape before he found himself face to face with Roxanne's aunt and uncle.

She'd pled a headache and retired early, and since that time Roxanne had done nothing but pace in her room and try to convince herself that she was wrong.

Maybe she just wanted to believe that it had been Cyrus beneath her balcony, in her tree, kissing and touching her in the dark. Maybe she just wanted to believe that all this time she'd been falling in love with one man . . . not two.

Watching Cyrus climb the tree in Mallory Park had triggered these thoughts, but once she got started they kept coming.

Without stepping onto the balcony, she looked across the way to Cyrus's little house, to the window that faced her balcony. If he'd been watching for her after school, it stood to reason that he had, at least on occasion, watched her from that window. He knew she liked to spend the evening on the balcony, he knew because he'd watched a thousand nights.

The voice beneath the balcony had always been different from Calvin's usual voice. More refined, more confident. She'd known that all along, but had dismissed any discrepancies to the night and the dark and the husky whisper. She'd accepted because she'd wanted so badly to believe that she could have everything she wanted so easily.

She'd never seen his face, not after a few awkward words that first night. A few awkward words before he'd stepped beneath the balcony to collect his thoughts, only to reappear self-assured, with sweet words from behind that wide-brimmed white hat.

He'd never spoken so sweetly to her by the light of day.

And when she'd asked him to love her, what had he said? *You don't love me. You're not mine.*

Who'd written the letters? If it had, indeed, been Cyrus courting her by the dark of night, then he had also been the man to write the letters. Of this she was certain. The man who wrote the letters and the man who'd sat in the tree outside her window to woo her were one and the same.

She thought, again and again, about his kiss. When she'd surprised him that night, sneaking up behind him to finally take him in her arms, he'd taken her into the darkest possible shadows to kiss her. The smells, the sensations, the way his mouth and his body had molded so ideally to hers, all were as clear to her as if he'd just kissed her.

And how could she forget the way he'd hesitated when she'd asked him to love her, the way he'd tried—more than once—to stop what was happening between them.

The way he'd whispered *I'm sorry* as he lay, still cradled between her legs.

Cyrus had come into her mind that night, she remembered, and she'd tried to dismiss him. No wonder he'd come to mind! Something inside her knew, perhaps remembering the soft kiss he'd given her when he'd said he was leaving, perhaps unconsciously remembering his scent, his taste.

When she'd kissed Calvin the day he left, if you could call the cold brush of their lips a kiss, she'd felt nothing.

But this afternoon, when Cyrus had kissed her, it had been exciting and stirring, bringing to the surface memories she'd tried to bury deeply. The taste, the smell, the feel, the rush of her blood . . . they all were familiar.

Still dressed in her rose gown, she paced the bedroom nervously. One minute she was furious with Cyrus, so furious she cursed him silently and vowed never to forgive him. The next minute she felt more confusion than anger, wondering if she could possibly be right or if she had deceived herself once again. Finally, relief flooded through her. A moment later she'd be angry again.

She paced to the window to watch Cyrus's little house across the road. So close . . . he was so close and yet for years she'd been blind to him. Had he been the one? *Was* he the one? She had to know. She had to be certain.

Josiah and Ada had retired long ago, as had most of the residents of Paris, but a light still shone in Cyrus's house. He was awake, and she wouldn't sleep again until she knew the truth. Had he lied to her? Had he and his dimwitted deputy hatched some elaborate scheme to seduce her into marrying Calvin?

She sneaked from her room and closed the door quietly behind her. In the dark, she slipped down the stairs, feeling and remembering her way. When she stepped outside the front door and past the overhang, a few cool drops of rain hit her face and her rose colored gown. She didn't care.

Practically running, she crossed the deserted street. It was too cold to be out without a shawl at the very least, but she had nothing to cover herself with. The chill cut through her gown the way the cold rain stung her face. She didn't care. The soft light in Cyrus's window was like a beacon, guiding her in the dark. She didn't hesitate, not once, not even as she knocked soundly on Cyrus's door.

Almost immediately he threw the door open. Apparently he'd been dressed for bed, because his feet were bare and all he wore was a pair of trousers that weren't even buttoned all the way up.

She looked at his stoic face, into his calm, clear eyes, studying him, wondering. Still angry and confused she hoped, more than anything, that she was right. He waited silently on the other side of the threshold, watching her, maybe even knowing why she was here. He didn't ask her in, and he didn't shut her out.

She licked her lips and took a deep breath. " 'The face of all the world is changed, I think,' " she whispered.

Cyrus swallowed hard and his jaw clenched, making his face appear hard, unforgiving. He gripped the side of the door so that the muscles in his arms and chest flexed and hardened as if he were preparing to fight, to swing out at her and anyone else who got in his way.

He looked past her . . . perhaps to the balcony where she'd been so well wooed. And then he fastened warm, green eyes on hers and whispered back.

" 'Since first I heard the footsteps of thy soul.' "

Chapter Sixteen

When he'd seen Roxanne running across the street he'd stepped into his trousers and prepared himself for trouble; the kind of trouble people came to the sheriff with. But when he'd opened the door and seen her face he'd known. Somehow—from the kiss, no doubt—she'd found him out. How had he ever thought he could keep this from her?

He waited for her to run away in tears, her worst fears confirmed with the utterance of a few words. But she didn't run. She stood her ground and looked him in the eye, and he, who could usually read her so well, couldn't tell what she was thinking.

"It was you," she finally whispered.

The rain started to come down harder, and a gust of wind blew cold drops beneath the small overhang above his front door. It pelted Roxanne, and a few cold drops even found his chest and arms and face.

"Get in here," he said, taking her hand and drawing her into his one-room house, shutting the door on the rain and the night. As soon as she was inside and the door was closed behind her, he released his hold on her hand. "I guess you'd like an explanation."

He expected almost anything; tears, screaming, cold anger. He didn't expect what he got; a calm, serene, "Yes, I'd like that very much."

He pulled out a chair for her and she sat down, her full pink skirt and voluminous petticoats rustling as they settled around her. While she watched and waited, quiet and composed with her hands folded demurely in her lap and her face lifted expectantly, he paced before her.

The lamp and a small fire blazed low, lighting and warming the room. The curtains were tightly closed, shielding them, somehow, from everything that happened outside this room. Rain pattered against the house, a low wind howled, but here they were warm and dry.

As Cyrus paced, he searched for the words that would explain away his deception. Roxanne didn't make it easy for him; she waited patiently.

"When you started talking about getting married again I knew your long mourning had come to an end, and I was happy for you. The time had finally come for you to start a new life, to put the past behind you where it belongs." True enough, so far.

"And then you saw Calvin, and it was like . . . it was like you were finally becoming your old self again." He cut a quick glance to her, to see how she reacted. She didn't, not at all. "The look on your face when you first saw him was extraordinary. Your eyes lit up, and your cheeks flushed pink, and your mouth practically fell open."

Her eyebrows arched slightly, but that was her only response.

"Beautiful Calvin," he whispered, "with his handsome face and plans for a farm where you could be isolated and hide from the world, was everything you wanted. Everything you needed. He was your ideal man, and I did my best to give him to you."

She bristled but said nothing.

"In the beginning, I just tried to help him along, to give him a shove in the right direction." Cyrus ran a distracted hand through his hair. A shove, hell, he'd practically thrown Calvin and Roxanne together. "I never meant for my interference to go so far, I swear. I'm sorry. Dammit, Roxanne, I'm so sorry."

He stood before her and waited for her reaction, for her anger and righteous indignation, for her hatred and contempt. All deserved. But even as he waited for all that he held his breath, hoping. He had no right to ask for forgiveness, but that didn't mean he couldn't hope. . . .

297

Roxanne lifted her head to look him in the eye. "Did all of this come about simply because I said Calvin was beautiful?" She didn't wait for an answer. "Really, Cyrus, how insulting. The world is full of beauty, things to be admired for a moment or two. A sunset, a painting, a happy child. That doesn't mean. . . . " She took a deep breath, perhaps searching for control. The hands in her lap clenched, white knuckled, and crushed against pink silk. "I don't expect everything I admire to be laid at my feet," she said quickly. "I don't *want* everything I admire laid at my feet!"

He shook his head, wishing Roxanne would look away so he could. "I didn't mean—"

"Did you mean a word of it?" she interrupted. Bright tears shone in her eyes. "Was it all just . . . just a game to you?"

"I meant every word I said," he admitted, to himself as well as to Roxanne. "And every word I wrote."

She relaxed a little, her hands unclenching, her shoulders drooping. "Why didn't you just tell me the truth?" she whispered. Her eyes were too bright, but she did not weep.

She made it sound so damn easy, as if telling her the truth had ever been an option.

"You wanted Calvin," he said bitterly. "You said it yourself, more than once. The man you were looking for had to be *safe* and beautiful. I'm not safe or beautiful, Roxanne, and I never will be."

She came to her feet quickly, angry at last.

"So you tried to make the most important decision of my life for me, is that it? You took that pretty, dimwitted boy and wrapped him up in a package I couldn't resist. You . . . you. . . ." Her eyes widened as a new thought occurred to her. "Cyrus Bergeron, you *seduced* me for someone else."

"I guess I did," he muttered.

He waited for her to bolt for the door, to run out of his life. While he waited he simply looked at her, knowing this might be the last time he enjoyed the luxury, knowing that after tonight any hope he'd had for them was gone.

Something amazing happened as he watched. Her face softened, the anger fled from her eyes. The fingers that had clenched into tight fists unfurled, slowly and softly.

"But you were the man who came to me, the man who loved me."

"Yes."

"You're the man who enticed me, who courted me and touched my heart." She stood so near he could see the rise and fall of her chest, the slight tremble of her lips, the way the hands that hung at her side shook ever so slightly. "You're the man who made me want to live again. Maybe you intended to seduce me for someone else, but when the time came . . . when the time was right. . . ."

"I know," he said softly, when it seemed she couldn't finish her sentence aloud and he could no longer stand the silence, the accusation, that hung between them.

"And then you let me believe you were another man," she said, her voice strong again, "just because I was shallow enough to observe on an occasion or two that Calvin had a handsome face. Even after he left town," she added angrily. "You allowed me to believe that I'd made the most horrible mistake of my life. You sat back and let me feel *guilty* and indecent and . . . and. . . ."

He tried to come up with an argument that would excuse himself, but there was none. What he'd done was unforgivable. "I wanted to tell you. A hundred times I wanted to tell you." He made himself look her square in the eye. "Another hundred times I swore I never would. I didn't want to hurt you any more than I already had. I didn't want to chase you away," he added softly.

Roxanne reached up and laid a hand on his cheek, over the scar that reminded him every day of his failure. That wonderfully soft hand trembled, and her eyes softened. "All this, just because I said Calvin was beautiful. Just because I came up with a silly plan to manufacture what I thought I needed to move on. Beautiful and safe." She sighed once. "I think you're beautiful," she whispered. "And as for safe . . . I never felt so safe as I did when you held me and told me you loved me, and I always feel safe when you're with me."

Having her hand on him, even so innocently, was more than he could take. Everything in him tightened and tensed, and he fought the natural urge to lift his arms and hold her, to pull her body against his. His hands were hard fists at his side as he fought his own traitorous impulses. "I only wanted to give you everything you want," he whispered. "You deserve that."

"Cyrus," she said, leaning closer to him, teasing him with her scent and her warmth, with her luscious, waiting mouth and her smoldering eyes. "Ask me what I want now."

"What do you want?" He already knew the answer, the amazing, wondrous answer, as his lips drifted unerringly towards hers.

"I want you."

Roxanne sighed as Cyrus finally slid his arms around her, as he finally kissed her. Falling against his chest she melted against him, into him. She was starved for his warmth and his hard, steady body against hers, for his arms and his kiss and his love.

His lips were studiously slow and ardently tender, and she savored every brush of his mouth against hers. Just that easily he captured her. She felt him in every pore, in every thrum of her heated blood. She laid her hands over his bare back, resting her palms against skin hard and warm. The simple contact seemed electric, and as if to prove her right a crack of thunder broke the night.

Cyrus moaned, low and soft, and she caught the telling breath between her slightly parted lips just before his tongue slipped into her mouth and launched a riot of sensations that coursed through her body. She felt this kiss in her heart and her weakening knees, in her lungs and the pit of her stomach. Yes, this was right. This was perfect.

The sensations were familiar, as was the touch and smell and taste she savored. But tonight, as her body sang and thrummed and rejoiced, she could open her eyes and, by the light of the fire and a single lamp, see the face of the man who had brought her back to life.

She took her mouth from his and tilted her head back so she could do just that. A strand of dark hair fell across his forehead, and she reached up to push it back. His beautiful eyes, a warm and mossy hazel-green, were looking at her with love and desire and maybe even relief that his secret was no longer a secret.

The features of his face were strong and perhaps even brutal, in the strange light cast from the fire and the single light, his cheekbones prominent and his nose unerringly straight. His mouth damp and full. His jaw sharp and dusted with dark bristles. The scar on his face was ugly, but only because it served as a reminder of his terrible pain.

Pain that was in the past, just as her fears and numbness were in the past.

"I love you," she whispered.

"Roxanne, don't . . ." he said huskily.

"I love you," she said again. "Love me."

Cyrus answered by kissing her once again, gentle and then hard, adoring and demanding. His fingers speared through her hair and he held her close. She leaned back as he towered over her, as he held her with arms strong and powerful and wonderfully tender.

His grip was assured, his mouth demanding, his body hard and hot, overpowering with its size and strength. She was completely in his hands.

And she was wonderfully, magically safe.

His hands fluttered against her throat, and she felt the buttons there slip through his fingers until the lace and silk fell away and he brushed his fingers gently against her bare skin, burning a trail she felt even after those fingers slipped lower to brush over a linen-covered nipple. With his mouth he caressed her neck, licking and sucking at the sensitive base of her throat while his hands grazed over her body.

She arched against him, pressing her breast against his palm, craving, already, the feel of his bare skin against hers, the press of flesh she hungered for.

He was everywhere. As he kissed her lips and her neck and caressed her with tender hands, he worked the tiny buttons all the way to her waist. He slipped a hand inside the opening and peeled away inch after inch of fabric, found the laces and hooks and eyes that held her rose gown and the simple underwear beneath in place. Skin that was revealed he kissed, nibbled and stroked and sucked. A soft glow that started deep inside infused her body with heat and a splendid sensitivity to every breath, every touch, every kiss he gave her. Ribbons were untied, laces were loosened, hooks unfastened to allow her to breathe deeply.

All at once, without warning, the rose dress fell to the floor, and she stood before him in nothing but a thin chemise, one of her three petticoats, and a corset that was already mostly unlaced.

"You're very good at this," she whispered as she kicked away the dress and he finished unlacing her corset.

"I'm inspired," he said, with just a touch of husky humor, as he yanked away the corset and tossed it aside. With one hand he loosened the last remaining petticoat, and it fell to the floor to pool at her feet.

Her insides quaked and shivered as Cyrus kissed her again. This time as he kissed her, he half-walked, half-carried her to the bed. Without the skirt and petticoats between them, she could feel the evidence of his arousal, the firm ridge that pressed insistently against her. When he stopped at the side of the bed and laid a hand on her breast, to caress and tease and arouse, she reached down and touched him there, her tentative fingers barely brushing against his trousers. He groaned and stepped quickly away.

"Stay right there," he ordered huskily.

She waited; suddenly shy, half-naked, trembling with anticipation.

Cyrus moved quickly through the room,

opening one drawer and then another. What was he doing? She wanted him here, needed him, craved him. As he moved through the room she watched, admiring the artlessly graceful way he moved, the beauty of his body so different from her own. He collected something from the pantry on the opposite side of the room. With the pantry door opened she couldn't see what it was he carried, but as he came to her she could see very well.

He carried in his arms a dozen or more candles, a small brass candelabra, and a box of matches.

"I don't have a hundred," he said as he arranged the candles on the bedside table. He didn't look directly at her, but gave his attention to the task at hand. "Maybe this will do."

He lit each and every one of the candles, until a soft, warm glow washed over the bed. Roxanne smiled. Yes, this time when she touched Cyrus she would see his face, she would know the man who loved her. There would be no hiding tonight, no denial, no questions unanswered.

By the light of the flickering candles he removed the last of her clothing; the thin chemise. When she was naked he lowered her to the bed, holding her close, wrapping his body around hers so that somehow they floated down together.

She stretched across the center of the big bed, tense and hot, tingling and anxious. Cyrus lowered his head to touch his lips to hers, to take the kiss lower, to her throat, to continue the slow descent to take a pebbled nipple into his mouth. He suckled gently, drawing her into his mouth. The sensation was more than she could stand, and she bucked slightly, coming up off the bed. He didn't stop, but sucked the nipple deeper into his mouth, laved his tongue against it, sucked again. She threw her head back and closed her eyes, lost in impossible sensations that grew and whirled through her entire body.

When he left her, left the bed completely, she felt momentarily abandoned. Alone and desperate and wanting. She opened her eyes to see him standing at the side of the bed, shucking his trousers so he was as bare as she. Need rippled through her, and still she smiled up at the man she loved; the man who loved her. He had a magnificent body, hard and rippled with muscles that were usually hidden by his clothing. His arms and legs were long and powerful, his hips narrow and his belly flat. His arousal was impossibly big and hard. Just looking at it made her body throb in response.

Slowly, he drifted down to cover her, to rest atop her waiting body. It was as she remembered, only better, keener. Hot flesh met hot flesh, hungry mouth pressed to hungry mouth. When he reached between their bodies to part her thighs, she spread her legs wide without a moment's hesitation. When he touched her, where she was already wet and throbbing for him, she arched against him involuntarily and moaned aloud.

Weak and strong, she trembled with a burst of unknown power. A throbbing emptiness quaked deep inside her, a hollowness that only Cyrus could fill. She waited anxiously for the thrust that would bring her longing to an end.

His fingers continued to tease her mercilessly, and she felt a faint tremble of his lips as his kissed her. That, and his deep, ragged breathing, told her how near he was to losing control, how much he wanted her.

Her eyes drifted closed as she wrapped her legs around his and pulled him closer. Once again Cyrus was cradled between her thighs. Hot and hard and ready, he hesitated. The tip of his manhood touched her, teased her with an insistent caress, but he didn't surge to fill her. She could feel herself opening for him, and her hips rocked slightly up in invitation.

"Look at me," he whispered hoarsely, and she opened her eyes to search the face of the man she loved, the man who loved her. Flickering candlelight illuminated his face for her, danced over features strong and harsh and beautiful.

"Love me," she breathed.

With a low moan he pushed to enter her, to fill her waiting body, to stretch her impossibly and become one with her. The sensation of him filling her felt so right she sighed in contentment and held him tight. He rocked above

Linda Jones

and inside her, withdrawing slightly and then pushing to take himself deeper than before, repeating the process until he was stroking her each time with his fullest, deepest strokes.

They were no longer lost in darkness, there were no lies between them. Her eyes drifted open to find that he watched her face as he very slowly loved her, as he pushed his hard length to the hilt and held it there. Stretching her, filling her. A fine sheen of sweat covered his body and hers as he moved within her again, rocking back and forward, slowly and sweetly, unhurried as he lingered over every stroke, every breath.

Her fears gone, there was only *this*—his body above and inside hers, her body around his, the fire that grew with every stroke. Every breath. Her hips rocked against his as she moved with him, searching and climbing, needing the release that teased her with slight tremors and lightning-like flashes that coursed fleetingly though her body, promising what was to come.

Her eyes drifted closed and she wrapped her legs around his, lifting her hips, answering him as he plunged faster and deeper, moaning deep in her throat as her body reached for release until at last the culmination burst upon her, wrenching her body from the inside out with power and a pleasure that was shocking in its intensity.

She cried out, Cyrus's name on her lips as he drove deep and shuddered above her, as he found the same release that shocked her with its intensity, its power.

He drifted down to cover her, his body drained and weak, hot and slick with sweat. This time there were no doubts, no regrets, no deception. There was just love and passion, pleasure and possibility. All was right with the world. They had so many nights stretching before them, so many nights of talking and laughing and making love, just like this.

The rain came down hard now, fast and heavy. It pounded violently against the roof and the windows. Roxanne smiled. It didn't matter what went on outside these walls. Not now, not ever.

She settled her lazy hand over the back of Cyrus's head, gently ruffling the short strands. "I love you," she whispered.

He lifted his head to look down at her.

If only he would smile and tell her that he loved her, too. He'd said the words before, once, when he'd been pretending to be Calvin, but she wanted him to tell her face to face, eye to eye. He looked so serious, as if he wasn't yet sure this was a good thing. Maybe he wasn't ready to say the words face to face. It didn't matter; she knew he loved her. He'd shown her in a thousand ways.

She tried to smile for him, to tempt him with a wide, seductive grin until he put every grain of indecision behind him. One day soon he would look her in the eye and tell her he loved her, she knew it. Until that moment came she'd be satisfied to have him show her his love now and again.

Ah, what a wonderful place to be on a rainy night. She felt every breath he took, every beat of his heart, the sweat on his skin . . . and she knew that this was where she belonged.

Cyrus propped up on his elbow to watch Roxanne sleep beside him. Outside the rain continued, a constant slap against the house. Occasionally thunder rumbled, but it was far away and not a threat to their sanctuary or Roxanne's sleep.

He'd doused the candles and the lamp a while back, leaving only the dying fire to light the room and the sleeping woman beside him. She looked so peaceful. Happy. Safe.

She was no delicate flower, his Roxanne, no fragile, insubstantial dream. She was real, warm and passionate. Fearless and honest. Strong of heart and soul, relentless and gracious. Somehow she was all this, and more.

He'd always known her to be exquisitely beautiful, but until tonight he'd never had the chance to study, so closely, the bits and pieces that together made her who and what she was. Her limbs were long and shapely, graceful and strong. Even her hands and feet were long, narrow, utterly feminine. The shape of her body was perfection itself, from the elegant line of her neck to the firm swell of her breast to the gentle curve of her hips. And her face . . . well, he'd had opportunity to study her face before, but that didn't mean he didn't enjoy looking at it right now.

Her eyes were large and slightly tipped up at the corners, and as she slept long, dark lashes rested on perfect, creamy cheeks. Her brows were elegant dark wings above those eyes, and a simple lift of one or both spoke volumes. In waking hours her chin was often stubborn, as if she were ready to do war with the world. In sleep she was completely relaxed, and the lines of her jaw and chin were softer. His eyes fell, hungry already, on her full mouth, a mouth that kissed and smiled with abandon, and spoke to him of love.

Not once, as he'd loved her, had she been afraid or hesitant. She was open and honest, and ravenous for the life she'd denied herself for the past three years. She came to him with unchecked power and life and hope, for both of them.

He had expected she would never know he'd been the one to charm her, in Calvin's place, to make love to her in the shadow of the balcony where she'd spent so many nights. He'd been so sure that if she did know she would hate him for the deception. She'd surprised him, especially with her whispered, *"Ask me what I want now."*

As he watched, her eyes fluttered open. She came awake slowly, peacefully, and with a small smile, as if she'd just awakened from a good dream.

"Why are you still awake?" she asked, reaching out to lay her hand familiarly, easily, on his arm. "You need your sleep."

"I'd rather watch you," he whispered.

Her smile widened. "It can't be that fascinating," she whispered.

"It is," he answered seriously. Deep in his heart he was afraid this chance would never come again, that Roxanne would come to her senses and realize that he was not everything she wanted him to be. He reached out and brushed a dark strand of hair away from her face.

Her smile faded, and even in the near dark he could see her eyes smoldering, her lips falling apart as if asking for a kiss. He was already heavy with wanting her, but with that searing glance he hardened.

He was in no hurry. He wanted this to last all night, he intended to savor every moment, every touch, every word. "How long can you stay?" he asked, whispering. "How long before your aunt and uncle miss you?"

"Hours," she said with an enticing smile.

"Good." His fingers trailed from her cheek to her neck, to the hollow at the base of her swanlike throat, to the valley between her breasts. His hand stilled there. It looked so harsh and clumsy against her pale skin, so dark and crude. He brushed one rough palm over her breast, felt the nipple harden at his touch.

"I thought you would be furious if you ever found out," he said, watching his hand against her breast instead of looking into her telling eyes. "I was so afraid I would lose whatever chance we might have if you knew the truth."

Surprisingly, she laughed; a low, deep, laugh that faded quickly. "Just this afternoon, when I finally accepted the fact that I was falling in love with you, I decided that this time I would take it slow. That maybe in a year or two you and I might. . . ." Her soft voice faded away.

"A year or two?" he repeated, horrified.

She laughed again. "Yes. Well, that idea didn't last long." Beneath his hand she sighed and stretched, breathed deep and extended her body like a happy, lazy cat.

"Thank goodness."

She lifted a hand to his chest, and he watched the play of her pale, slender fingers on his skin. "When I first began to suspect, I thought my flight of fancy was just wishful thinking. Ah yes, if it was Cyrus who romanced and loved me, then all my problems are solved. That solution was much too easy, I assumed. Much too far-fetched. And then when you kissed me like I knew you'd kissed me before, when I put all the pieces together and they fit, I was so relieved," she whispered.

"Relieved?"

She scooted her body closer to his, rocking across the sheets in a slow, undulating motion that brought her near. "Angry, too, but relieved," she whispered, laying her mouth against his own, small, flat nipple.

Her mouth came away slowly, and she

breathed against the wet spot she'd made with her mouth. The sensation was icy cold and intense and arousing. Cyrus held back a groan. Impossibly, he grew harder.

"Relieved," she said again, "to find out that in the past several weeks I'd only been falling in love with one man, not two. For goodness sake, Cyrus, I thought I'd lost my mind."

"Two men?"

His hand slipped lower to rest against her flat belly. He could feel her quiver.

"I found myself smitten with some faceless romantic I thought was someone else, while at the same time I continued to have these entirely inappropriate thoughts about my friend the sheriff." Her hand dipped lower to brush against his hip, her light, teasing touch torture. Her lips floated close to his, but not close enough, her breast brushed his chest, the nipples raking across him as he took a deep breath.

"I wanted so much not to fall in love with you," she whispered seriously. "You were right when you said I wanted to hide from the world." Her hands became bolder and she touched him, wrapped her gentle fingers around the hard length of his manhood. "I don't want to hide anymore, Cyrus. Not from the world, not from the pain that comes from living, not from love." She brushed her lips against his, the touch light and fleeting. "I especially don't want to hide from you."

Roxanne stroked his arousal until he had to

grab her hand and move it away. He took her wrist in one hand and pressed his mouth to hers, and with a gentle nudge he pushed her against the rumpled sheets that covered their bed. She fell onto her back and he rolled with her, covering and entering her in one move.

He loved her hard and fast, mindless and with primitive abandon. Her body stroked and grabbed his, invited him, accepted him, as he pounded into her again and again. This was no tender coming together; it was a wild mating of bodies so hungry for one another that nothing but this ferocity would satisfy them. Beneath him, Roxanne lifted her hips to embrace each powerful thrust, to take everything he offered. To love him.

She shattered beneath him, shuddering, whispering his name, tightening around him, and he allowed himself the release he'd been holding back since the moment she'd touched him. He lost himself in her, in her body and her confessions of love, in her smile and her deep sighs.

He sank down to cover her sated body with his, wrapping his arms around her, laying his head against her shoulder. She idly lifted one leg and wrapped it around his, and wound one limp arm around his neck, until they were impossibly entwined.

Roxanne had been nothing but open and honest with him. She held nothing back, no part of her mind or her heart. Her honesty made his well-meant deception seem worse, more of a betrayal than he'd ever imagined. Perhaps it was time he followed her lead and attempted the truth.

"I do love you," he whispered into her ear, his breath brushing against soft, dark hair that was spread across his pillow and her pale, tempting shoulders. "More than you can ever imagine."

He lifted his head to look down at her, to look her in the eyes and open his heart to her the way she had opened her heart and her body to him. "I love you."

She kissed him, on his neck and his jaw and his face and his chest. With a gentle laugh she swayed, rolling him off her body and following his slow rotation to hover above and feather a hundred small, happy kisses over his body. He lay there, exhausted into inertia, warm and satisfied, while she held his hands to the mattress and laughed and kissed his shoulders and his neck and his chest, just above his pounding heart. There was pure joy in her laugh and her feathery kisses, such love and enchantment. Eventually, she collapsed beside him and snuggled her head against his shoulder.

"I love you, too, Cyrus. Sleep now," she whispered breathlessly, wrapping one bare leg over his. "Sleep."

Amazingly, he did.

Chapter Seventeen

He ran faster and harder than he'd ever run before, his legs pumping beneath him, his heart pounding until he thought it would burst in his chest. Raindrops pelted his face, and in the distance a boom of thunder mingled with the roar of cannons. Cyrus glanced quickly at the sky, and hard, needle-like drops stung his face. He almost stopped running; somehow he knew it wasn't supposed to be raining.

He ignored the rain and the certainty that the storm was all wrong, and kept running. Louis was in trouble. Cyrus prayed that he'd get there in time. If he could run fast enough, just this once, just this one time, everything would be right again. His legs were so weak they shook beneath him, threatening to collapse with every pounding step. The harder he tried to run the weaker his legs became. They trembled beneath him as he pushed himself to be stronger, faster.

The Yankee beast lunged and swung his meaty arms, and Louis was killed. Louis's eyes remained opened, his mouth still moved, but he was dead. Suddenly, too late, Cyrus was there. He threw himself between the boy and the Yank, and the bayonet swung up and across his face. This time there were cold raindrops mixed with the warm blood, and as he fell he saw a streak of brilliant lightning that matched the clap of thunder above.

"Louis." Cyrus turned away from the lightning to face his friend, the boy who was dying. His heart beat so hard he felt it pounding, thudding against his chest. He could barely breathe. No matter how many times he tried to stop the tragedy it always ended this way. He was never fast enough.

Louis fastened angry eyes on Cyrus. He was dying, he was weak, but energy and fury and an unearthly light flickered dangerously in his eyes. "Why did you let this happen?" he whispered in a croaking voice that was full of rage and pain. Bloody hands reached up and grasped Cyrus's shirt, and Louis hauled himself up to place his mouth against Cyrus's ear. "Did you want Roxanne so badly that you let me die?" he whispered hoarsely. "Did you kill me so you could sleep next to my wife?"

"No," Cyrus whispered, horrified. He tried to make Louis release his grip, to pry the strong,

bloody hands away from his shirt. But Louis's fingers were like steel. They refused to relax and fall away.

"You let me die so you could fuck my wife, didn't you Cyrus?" Louis whispered. "So she could lie naked in your bed, and you could touch her and whisper into her ear." Louis's breathing was raspy and weak, but his words were clear and condemning. "Did you think that with me gone she would love you?"

"No," Cyrus tried to say, but he couldn't hear his denial for the clap of thunder above.

"You could've saved me," Louis said clearly as he dropped back and closed his eyes for the last time and his hands finally fell away. "Maybe no one knows that but you and me, maybe no one else will ever know, but that doesn't make it any less true."

"I tried . . ."

"You could've saved me."

A loud boom of thunder that shook the house awakened Roxanne, but it was Cyrus who kept her awake.

The last embers of the fire gave off a touch of light in the dark room, and she could make out his dimly lit form. Covered with sweat, he tossed beside her on the bed, his legs moving slowly, his hands reaching out blindly, his head rolling from one side of the pillow to the other. He'd already thrown the quilt on the floor, and as she watched he turned to her and flung one arm out wildly, his fisted hand missing her head by mere inches.

Another flash of lightning lit the room momentarily, the bright light shining through the curtains strongly enough to illuminate his tortured face for her. Her heart constricted at the sight of his evident torment.

"Not fast enough," he mumbled.

She reached out a tentative hand to touch him, to awaken him from the nightmare. He looked so unlike the Cyrus she knew and loved, so frantic and furious, that she hesitated for a moment before laying her hand on his shoulder.

Her initial touch and whisper of his name had no effect. None at all, and that scared her. What if he didn't wake up? The nightmare that terrorized him would go on and on. She dug her fingers into his shoulder and shook him slightly, raising her voice as she called to him again. As the seconds ticked past and he didn't respond, she became more and more frightened.

"Cyrus, please," she said, shaking him again, harder this time. "Wake up."

He came up so quickly and unexpectedly that she was nearly thrown back. He cried out once as his arms came up in a defensive motion to clear everything and everyone away from his tense body, and a flailing fist landed on her shoulder as she scooted to the edge of the bed.

She could see the moment Cyrus became aware, the moment the nightmare left him and he knew where he was. He became suddenly, completely still, motionless but for the rise and fall of his chest, silent but for the sound of his breathing. He raked his hands through sweat dampened hair, took a deep ragged breath, and closed his eyes.

"Cyrus," she whispered, reaching out to touch his arm, to offer him a little bit of comfort.

He flinched, and when his head snapped up he looked at her as if he'd forgotten she was there, as if finding her naked in his bed was a shock.

"Are you all right?" She reached out to touch him again, but he moved away, leaving the bed quickly before she could so much as lay a comforting hand on him. "It was just a bad dream, that's all."

He reached for his trousers where he'd left them on the floor, and with his back to her he stepped into them and pulled them up. "The problem is," he whispered as he fastened the buttons, "I don't know anymore what's dream and what's memory." His voice shook, a little.

She made a small move, as she prepared to leave the bed and go to him, but he stopped her with a raised hand. "Stay there," he whispered as he gathered the quilt from the floor and covered her with it. He didn't touch her face, or her hair, or lean over to kiss her. He just covered her.

Roxanne gathered the quilt around her and sat up, facing a Cyrus she didn't know. With an easy hand she massaged her shoulder, there where he'd hit her as he came awake. It had been a glancing blow, but since she had a tendency to bruise easily she imagined she'd have a mark there in the morning.

He watched the gentle motion of her hand. "I hit you, didn't I?" he whispered.

"No," she said quickly, and then he settled his eyes on her so hard and deep she shivered. "Well, just a little, and it was an accident." She tried to smile, but he looked so devastated she couldn't quite pull it off.

"I hit you," he said softly, and this time it sounded as if he were talking to himself, not to her at all.

She dropped her hand, not wanting to remind him of the glancing blow for another second. "Tell me what the nightmare was about," she said. "Together we can make it better, I know we can."

He didn't seem anxious to comply. Leaving her side, he lit the lamp and brought it to the bedside table, placing it among candles that had burned away to almost nothing before he'd extinguished them long ago.

"I don't think so," he whispered as he stalked beside the bed, occasionally glancing at her so intensely, so sadly she felt the glare on her skin. As if to protect herself, she clung to the quilt, hugged it to her body.

Finally, he stopped pacing and stood beside the bed. "God in Heaven, what was I thinking?" His voice was soft and uncertain.

She reached out and took his hand, and this

time he let her hold it. "Is this about us?"

He sat beside her on the bed, his weight making the mattress dip so that she rolled toward him. He didn't even seem to notice when her hip settled against his. "There is no *us*, and there can't ever be."

She would've been insulted, heartbroken, if he didn't sound so desolate himself. "It's much too late for that," she whispered. "You can't deny what's happened, what already is."

He locked his eyes to hers. "I should've left town when I realized what was happening, but it never occurred to me that it would go this far. I never dreamed that you would end up. . . ." He looked at the rumpled bed where they'd passed the night. "Here."

A shiver of unpleasantness ticked her spine. "What are you trying to say?"

"Tonight was a mistake," he said harshly. "This whole masquerade, with Calvin and the letters and the whispered deception, was a mistake."

"Tonight was not a mistake," she insisted. "And as for the rest," she tried to slip up and forward to kiss him, but he leaned away from her in a move that spoke of clear, unmistakable rejection. She dismissed it. "I've already forgiven you for that."

He took his hand from hers, breaking that tender connection, and glared grimly at her. "Maybe you have, but you'll never forgive me for this." He pointed at the scar on his face, the old wound perfectly illuminated by the nearby lamp.

Roxanne reached up and laid her hand over the damaged cheek, and this time Cyrus didn't move away. He allowed her to touch and caress the scar, to rest her hand on his face. "Do you really think me so vain that I'm bothered, or ever will be bothered, by something so trivial as a scar? I love you—"

"Don't," he said, wrapping strong fingers around her wrist and removing her hand from his face. "It's not the scar," he said in a grave whisper. "It's what the scar means, what it reminds me of."

Nothing could be so bad that she'd give up what she'd found with Cyrus. "It doesn't matter—"

"I was with Louis when he was wounded," he said crisply. "He asked me to tell you that he was thinking of you when he died. It was a simple enough request, but I never found the courage to do that for him."

Cold fear knotted in the pit of her stomach. She didn't want Louis's memory to come between them. She'd just learned to put him in the past, to accept that he wasn't coming home and that she had the right to live her life without him.

"I can understand why honoring that request would've been difficult for you."

The fingers at her wrist were tight, almost too tight. "I could've saved him," he whispered. "If I'd been fast enough that day I could have saved him for you. I tried." He released the grip at her wrist and leapt from the bed to begin

324

pacing again. "At least, I *think* I tried. Goddammit, I don't know anymore. All I know is that every time I look in the mirror and see this scar, I'm reminded that when it counted, when it really counted, I wasn't fast enough. Cyrus, with his fast hands and fast gun and quick reflexes, couldn't run quite fast enough that day."

Roxanne gathered the quilt securely about her and left the bed, dragging it with her. "I know you," she said angrily. "I know you well enough to be absolutely certain that if you could have saved Louis you would have. It's not your fault that he died. Don't punish yourself for something that's not your fault." She raised one of the hands that held the quilt at her bosom, and laid it on Cyrus's back. "It happened a long time ago."

He didn't turn to take her in his arms, but he didn't step away from her touch, either. His back was incredibly tense, and she rubbed her thumb against a knotted muscle.

"Sometimes it feels like yesterday."

"I know," she whispered, planting a kiss on his shoulder.

"If I could've given my life for his, I would've done it," he whispered. "For you."

"Don't say that." A chill wracked her body, and it had nothing to do with the coolness of the night air. "I did love Louis, but I know now that I loved him as a child loves another child. We thought we were all grown up, but we weren't." She took a deep breath. The words and memories caused pain, but this was what she needed, what they both needed; to let go of the past and embrace the future. "I love you the way a woman loves a man. My heart is deeper than I'd ever imagined, and you fill it. You, Cyrus, not a memory."

For a few long moments they stood there. Lightning and thunder no longer shook the night, and the rain had slackened to a steady, light drizzle.

"I held him as he died," Cyrus whispered.

"I know," Roxanne breathed against his shoulder.

"Louis, your husband, a boy who loved you with all his heart, asked me to tell you that he was thinking of only you when he died." He sighed and then shuddered. "Then he asked me to take care of you, to make sure you were happy."

A coldness grabbed at the pit of her stomach again. "He did?"

Cyrus nodded. "He said it was up to me now, to take care of you, and I had to say yes, I had to promise him that I would. . . . "

Roxanne stepped back, allowing her hand to fall away. Cyrus Bergeron took his promises seriously, and she imagined he would rather die than fail. All those days he'd been there, standing silently on the street or the boardwalk, quiet and attentive. . . .

"Is that why you watched me, all these years, why you were always there?"

"Yes," he breathed.

"Is that why you tried to *give* me Calvin after I was foolish enough to admire him from a distance?"

"Yes," he whispered, without hesitation.

She tried to swallow but there was a knot in her throat, a large, bitter knot. Knowing Cyrus as she did, this was beginning to make sense. She didn't like it.

"Is that why you pretended to be Calvin, whispering sweet words and writing those letters, to make me happy?"

"Yes."

She shivered, suddenly cold all over. "Was any of it true?" *Do you love me?* The question she couldn't bring herself to ask stuck in her throat.

"I don't know," he admitted with a low breath. "I believed it, every word, but—"

"But what?" she asked, her voice suddenly cold.

He didn't answer.

"Tell me," she said, her voice controlled once again. She shivered to her bones, but her voice was cool, icy and lifeless. "What was tonight about? A promise to my dead husband? Were you just trying to fulfill some . . . some obligation?" She felt, all of a sudden, like a pitied whore. "Did you take me into your bed because I was foolish enough to tell you that I wanted you, and since you'd promised Louis—"

"No," he responded quickly. "Tonight was wonderful and I wouldn't trade it for anything." He turned to face her again. "But tell me, Roxanne," he said coldly. "Tell me you won't look at me one day, that you won't wake up one morning and see this scar and think *If he'd only been a little faster. If he'd tried a little harder. If he'd taken care of Louis the way he said he would.*"

"I never should've asked that of you," Roxanne whispered, suddenly horrified at the memory of that request and what had come of it.

"But you did, and I promised, and I failed you."

"You did your best—" she began, her whisper so low it was little more than a breath of air.

"Did I?" Cyrus interrupted harshly. "How can you be sure? What if I loved you even then, and when the time came I failed you because somewhere in the darkest part of my soul I wanted Louis to die?"

She shivered hard. "I don't believe that of you."

"I didn't either, until tonight." He stepped into his boots, grabbed a slicker from a rack near the door and his hat from the next peg over. He slipped the slicker over his bare chest and set the hat on his head. "Did I try hard enough? Did I let him die? Maybe you can live with the doubt," he said as he opened the door onto darkness, "but I can't."

Roxanne stared at the closed door, and listened to the soft rain as she hugged the quilt to her. He hadn't said so, but she knew that Cyrus expected her to be gone when he returned.

He hated the rain, but not as much as he hated looking into Roxanne's face now that he'd finally told her everything. *Everything*.

He stood beneath a tree that protected him from most of the rain, but still he was wet. Dammit, he hated to be wet. Most of all he hated it when his feet and head were soaked, and right now his boots were damp and water ran off the rim of his hat in a steady stream.

During the war they'd marched through rain, been wet and cold for days at a time, crossed rivers keeping only their rifles dry. He'd been hungry, gone without sleep for days, worn rags on occasion, and still it seemed to him the worst hardship of war was being wet. Sometimes he still had nightmares about crossing endless rivers, feeling the wet material stick to his skin as he left the water behind, boots squishing, trousers clinging . . . it was a stupid, senseless fixation he couldn't shake any more than he could shake his dreams of Louis.

Tonight's nightmare remained with him, and Louis's accusation echoed through his brain. If only he could remember more about that day, if only he could separate the damned nightmare from reality. He'd tried to save Louis, hadn't he? He'd done his best. He just hadn't been fast enough. Not that day.

You let me die so you could fuck my wife, didn't you Cyrus? The vulgar accusation echoed through his brain, making him question everything. When had he become obsessed with

Roxanne? When had he fallen in love with her?

His heart still pounded too fast, as if he really had been running instead of sleeping. Dammit, he couldn't live like this, ecstatic one minute, falling asleep with the woman he loved beside him; a moment later reliving the most horrible day of his life and hearing Louis's tortured, *"Did you let me die?"*

He'd hit her, dammit. Coming out of that cursed nightmare he'd *hit* her. That alone told him there was no future for them, no way he could leave the past behind and start a new life. What if one night he came awake to find he'd really hurt her? Remembering some of the nightmares that plagued him on occasion and the way he woke from them, that horrible thought wasn't an impossibility.

He would not hurt Roxanne any more than he already had, and he sure as hell wouldn't ask her to live with his demons.

Roxanne, in her pink dress once again, left his house and ran across the street. She didn't have far to go, but he watched every step she took, every hurried jump over puddles and low plants that got in her way. She held her skirt off the ground, so that her ankles and calves were exposed as she took graceful leaps this way and that. The lightly falling rain didn't seem to bother her, not at all.

He moved from beneath the tree so he could watch her slip through the front door of the Pierson house, waited until she'd had time to reach her room, and then he lifted his head to the balcony. He was almost certain he saw a flash of pink there, a hint of color just inside the shelter of the room.

Ah, he did love her. Every word he'd said and whispered and written was true. In the past few weeks he'd known more moments of peace and happiness than he'd ever thought to know, and all because he'd finally admitted that he loved Roxanne.

But he couldn't make her happy. Together their lives would be moments of heavenly bliss broken by haunted nightmares and unspoken accusations. Eventually she would doubt him, as he doubted himself, and then maybe they wouldn't even have those moments of bliss anymore. They'd both be miserable.

He started walking toward his little house, knowing what he had to do. It didn't matter that he loved Roxanne, any more than it mattered that she thought she loved him. He'd been right all along; it was time to move on.

Chapter Eighteen

Roxanne did her best to hold her eyes wide open, in spite of her exhaustion, as her students read aloud. April Henley was reading from Dickens's *Tale of Two Cities*.

Her only rest had come last night in Cyrus's bed; no more than two hours. After she'd returned to her own room, sleep had been impossible. Her mind spinning, she'd laid in her cold, wide bed and stared at the ceiling, wondering how everything could've gone so wrong so fast.

She wanted to believe that whatever had shaken Cyrus last night would seem different to him, better, by the light of day. She didn't believe for a minute that he'd allowed Louis to die, and she didn't want to believe that he'd let the war that was over and done with come between them. Not now, not when they were so close to love and happiness and everything they wanted. Everything *she* wanted, anyway.

She'd looked into Cyrus's eyes as he'd touched her, as he'd told her he loved her. She'd seen the truth there, had heard it in his soft words. It wasn't possible that such depth of feeling grew from nothing more than a promise to her dying husband, that everything that had happened between them, *everything*, was nothing more than an obligation. Cyrus did love her. He had to.

"Mrs. Robinette," April said softly.

Roxanne lifted her eyes to the student who held the open book in her hands. "Yes?"

"Isn't it someone else's turn to read? My throat is dry."

"Of course." Roxanne chose another student to take April's place. These were her best students, the older girls who had a love for reading and writing. Usually she enjoyed this class immensely, even when everything else seemed hopeless. But today . . . today her heart wasn't in her teaching. Today her heart was battered and broken, and she couldn't even think clearly.

As Betsy took up where April had left off, Roxanne turned her eyes to the window. It had started to rain again, and drops pattered against the glass and made the view—tall trees and fine homes beyond the well-kept lawns— seem foggy and indistinct. Josiah had delivered her to school via carriage this morning and had promised to pick her up in the afternoon, since the rain continued to fall softly and intermittently. She wouldn't have minded the walk, in her waterproof hooded cloak and oldest boots, but Josiah had insisted. She hadn't been able to find the heart to argue with him, not even over such a small detail.

She wondered, foolishly she imagined, if Cyrus would be standing in the rain this afternoon, waiting for her to pass by.

Likely not.

Cyrus sat across the table from the slick, citified gambler who'd been ruining Hamlin's business. Almost as soon as Sir Latimer had left, this man had shown up. He called himself Johnny Black, and every time Cyrus had seen him he'd been dressed dramatically, all in black, a color to match his long hair and his last name.

Black smiled across the small round table, shuffling the cards in his hands with an ease that comes from hundreds of hours of practice. The cards ruffled and danced, whispered and crackled. "What can I do for you, Sheriff?"

Cyrus found himself in no mood to play games. "I hear you've been cheating at poker."

Black's smile died quickly, and the cards stilled. "That's a mighty serious charge, Sheriff."

"Yes, it is."

"Has someone made an accusation?" Black glanced quickly over the room that was nearly deserted at this time of day. There were a few customers enjoying a drink or a conversation, but not one looked in their direction. They were all terrified of the gambler with good luck and a deadly reputation. Black returned his cold gaze to Cyrus.

"I hear things," Cyrus said, casually leaning back in his chair.

Johnny Black raised his eyebrows almost elegantly and resumed shuffling. "Rumors, Sheriff. Ugly, insubstantial hearsay. Those rumors were started, no doubt, by someone who's jealous of my string of good luck."

Cyrus leaned forward and placed his folded arms on the table. "You know, I really don't give a damn if you cheated or not."

The gambler bristled again as Cyrus used the word *cheated*.

"All I care about is that you're disrupting the peace in my town, and I want you gone. Today."

Johnny Black's brilliant smile returned, but the gleam in his eyes remained calm and deadly. "Are you here to run me out of town, Sheriff?"

"Yes." No one watched, but Cyrus was well aware that everyone in the room listened. "But I really don't want any trouble today. I'm in no mood for it."

"Neither am I."

"So I tell you what," Cyrus fastened his gaze on the cards that flew through Black's hands. He was good. Fast and careful. Ah, and the rumors were not completely groundless. There was a card up the gambler's left sleeve. Cyrus caught a glimpse of the very corner, no more than an edge. Most men would've missed it.

"We'll draw for it," he said. "One card. I win, you leave town this afternoon and never come back. You win, and not only do you get to stay, I'll talk Hamlin into letting you have, rent free, the best room he's got above stairs."

"Cyrus!" Hamlin cried out, his distress evident.

Cyrus didn't look in Hamlin's direction, but raised one hand to silence the owner of Nickels' Saloon. "Deal?"

Black beamed. "Absolutely."

Cyrus reached across the table. "I deal."

The gambler stopped shuffling, made a production of tapping the deck on the table to bring it to perfect order, and then offered the cards on his palm.

How many countless nights, during the war, had he passed playing cards? Too many to count. So many that he got sick of it and didn't play anymore. As he took the deck with one hand he dropped it onto the table, undoing Black's efforts at bringing perfect order to the deck.

"Sorry about that," Cyrus muttered as he gathered the cards into a pile. Black helped, a smirk on his pretty face. The silly smile remained, unchanged, even as Cyrus slipped a finger into a ruffled cuff and covertly swiped the card the gambler had concealed there. "I haven't done this in a while."

At the bar, Hamlin groaned and placed his head in his hands.

At first Cyrus shuffled the cards slowly, getting a feel for the way they moved against his fingers and landed in the palm of his hand. Gradually, he began to shuffle faster and faster, until the cards flew through his fingers every bit as fast as they had through the gambler's.

"Well, what do you know about that?" Cyrus asked with a grim smile. "This isn't so hard after all."

Black's grin was gone. He didn't much like the sight of those cards moving in such expert fashion in someone else's hands. When the cards were well shuffled and Black was suitably impressed, Cyrus slapped the deck onto the center of the table.

"Go ahead," he ordered curtly.

Johnny Black reached out and cut the deck, his hand hovering over the cards unsteadily before he divided the deck into two uneven piles. Cyrus reassembled the deck before tossing a single card at the gambler and then dropping one to the table before him.

"You first," Cyrus muttered, his fingers tapping the back of his own face-down card.

Black tossed his card over and glanced down at the jack of hearts that fluttered into place. His smile returned. At the bar Hamlin Nickels, who was a gentle, peace-loving man, uttered a filthy curse.

Cyrus shot a quick, sharp glance to the barkeep. Ah, the man had no faith, no confidence in his sheriff. His thumb teased the corner of his own card. "A jack. That's pretty good," he muttered.

"Yes it is," Black said confidently. "How about we finish this?" He pointed at Cyrus's card and wiggled his fingers in an almost feminine way.

Without looking down, Cyrus flipped over his own card to reveal the ace of spades Johnny Black had been keeping up his ruffled, lacy sleeve. "Well what do you know," he said softly. "I win."

Angry and surprised, Black locked dark eyes with the man who'd beaten him with his own card. Beneath the table, Cyrus laid a hand over his Colt. There was nothing more dangerous than an angry, surprised man.

But Black's anger fled quickly. "Well, Sheriff, aren't you clever?"

Cyrus said nothing as the gambler rose from his seat, straightening his cuffs and then collecting his long-tailed jacket from the back of the chair. He looked beyond the batwing doors to the gray day beyond.

"It's raining again," Black said with evident distress. "Surely you don't expect me to leave town in this miserable weather."

Cyrus maintained his seat. "I'll be happy to give you a slicker, if you don't have one," he said softly. "Compliments of the city of Paris."

Black glanced over his shoulder and grinned at Cyrus as he took his leave, pushing through the swinging doors. "No thank you, Sheriff. I'll

Linda Jones

manage." He looked to the wet, dreary street before him. "A little rain never hurt anyone."

It rained for three days straight, until the streets were nothing but mud and standing water, and the creeks and streams rose, threatening to overflow.

In Paris, Texas, people stayed at home and watched the waters rise and prayed for the rain to stop.

Roxanne kept to her room, on this third day when it was too nasty even for the Paris Female Academy to open its doors. From here, she could occasionally look through the wide balcony doors to the small brick house across the street. She saw Cyrus come and go, swathed from neck to foot in a long slicker, his head covered with his wide-brimmed brown hat. He never so much as glanced in her direction.

As of this morning, she knew there was no baby. She should be relieved, but the emptiness inside her was no relief. It felt too much like grief.

So close. She and Cyrus had come so close to finding what they both obviously wanted. What had happened to ruin their chance? A nightmare? Not a nightmare. The truth. At least, the truth as Cyrus saw it. She didn't accept, not for a moment, that he had allowed Louis to die. He might be able to kill when he had to, he might be a dangerous and feared soldier at heart. But he would not allow a man to die for his own gain, not even unconsciously.

340

What bothered her most, what kept her awake at night listening to the rain and haunted her in the hours she was confined to this house, was Cyrus's promise to a dying Louis. His devotion, his friendship, his love. Was any of it real? All this time, as he'd watched over her so intently and kissed her and loved her . . . had he only been fulfilling that promise?

Cyrus Bergeron took vows and responsibilities seriously. He would do anything to fulfill a promise, risk his life to keep his word. His inability to keep his long-ago promise to her, that he would keep Louis safe, bedeviled him still.

Did he say he loved her only because he knew it was what she wanted to hear?

Did he think himself in love with her because he felt, Heaven forbid, obligated?

In the past three days she'd started, more times than she could count, to make her way boldly across the street to tell Cyrus that she didn't care about the past anymore, that she didn't care that he carried a gun, that she didn't care *why* he loved her.

Something always stopped her. Maybe she wasn't quite sure of her own feelings just yet.

Then again, maybe she was simply afraid that Cyrus would reject her, and she wasn't strong enough to withstand his rejection. Not yet.

He needed time. That's all. So did she.

He didn't own much, and packing everything into two saddlebags wouldn't take any time at all. Anything that wouldn't fit into the saddle-bags or into a roll behind the cantle would be left behind.

The rain grated on Cyrus's nerves. When would it stop? By the end of the week his business here would be taken care of and his deputy, Will Haller, would take his place in the office of sheriff. As soon as he knew that Roxanne wasn't with child, he would be able to ride away from Paris with no obligations, no regrets. But dammit, he didn't want to ride off in the rain, not if he could help it.

With the rain falling so persistently, he hadn't seen even a glimpse of Roxanne since she'd left his house in the early hours of Monday morning. He didn't know if she'd gone to school that rainy day or not. For once, he hadn't been there to watch.

But he did know the rain made it impossible for her to step onto the balcony at night. Perhaps that was just as well. If she stepped into the moonlight and he saw her from his window, he might be compelled to stand beneath her one last time, to look up at her as he spun a fantasy world for her by the darkness of night.

Fantasy by moonlight, reality by sunlight, nightmare behind closed eyes. They were all woven together until he didn't know what was real and what was fabrication. All he knew was that Roxanne would be better off without him.

Roxanne picked at her stew and nibbled on a biscuit. When Ada and Josiah asked if she was coming down with a cold, she said yes. Better a small lie than a truth that would shock and dismay them both.

They talked about the rain until she thought she would scream. They talked about the new minister until she wanted to toss her bowl of stew across the table. They talked about new pieces for the furniture store until she wanted to lay her head on the table and cry.

She did none of these things, of course, because she realized that her aunt and uncle had nothing to do with her desire to scream and cry. Cyrus did this to her, not inane dinner conversation.

Josiah finished off his stew, his spoon scraping against the bowl with an irritating rasp as he shook his head. "I still can't believe Cyrus is leaving. This town won't be the same without him."

"What?" Roxanne's head snapped up. "What do you mean Cyrus is *leaving*?"

"Oh, that's right," Ada said softly. "You weren't down for dinner last night when Josiah first mentioned it. Seems the sheriff has decided to move on." She sighed. "It's so difficult to find and keep a really good lawman these days. Why, do you remember—"

"He can't leave," Roxanne whispered, interrupting her aunt's reminiscence.

Ada and Josiah both stared at her expectantly, eyes wide with surprise.

"I love him," she said. "He *can't* leave."

"Oh dear," Ada sighed.

Roxanne stood quickly. "I'm going over there right now," she said, to herself as much as to her aunt and uncle. She should've done this days ago, she should've stayed in his bed after he'd run from her, stayed until she convinced him that his fears were false.

"That's not wise," Ada said primly. "It's after dark, after all, and it's still raining quite hard. Besides, it's really not proper for you to be in Cyrus's company unchaperoned. If you still feel the need to talk to him tomorrow," she said, "your Uncle Josiah can take you to the jail." She wrinkled her nose. "Though that's really not a fitting place for a lady like yourself. Maybe we can invite him to supper tomorrow night," she added cheerily, as the solution came to her.

"I'm going over there right now," Roxanne said, determined. "And I'll tell Cyrus that I love him, and I'll do whatever I have to do to make him stay."

"Oh, my," Ada said, fanning herself furiously with her napkin. "This is just too scandalous. Josiah, make her sit down and behave."

Josiah sputtered, more than a little embarrassed. Ada fanned herself briskly and rolled her eyes, as if she might faint.

Roxanne smiled, content at last. No matter what Ada and Josiah thought, she knew with all her heart that this was right. "And if I can't convince Cyrus to stay in Paris," she said calmly, "I'll follow him when he leaves. I'll pack a bag and buy a horse and no matter where he goes, I'll be there."

Ada emitted a distressed sound that bordered somewhere between a laugh and a sob, but Josiah, bless him, lifted his head and gave her an uncertain smile. "So, you really love him, eh?"

Roxanne nodded. "I do."

"Cyrus Bergeron," he said thoughtfully. "He's a fine fella." The statement held more than a small amount of approval.

"I know." Roxanne smiled.

"But Roxanne . . ." Ada began, her voice high-pitched and unsettled. "You can't just throw yourself at the man. It's . . . it's not *done*."

"I don't have any choice." Roxanne left the table and headed for the front door. Outside a mere sprinkle of rain fell, a soft shower that would not hamper her on her short walk across the muddy street. She didn't want to delay even long enough to collect a hat or a shawl to cover her head. She couldn't afford to take precious time to think about her pride or her dignity, or what she would do if Cyrus said no.

The road was a sticky mess, and her shoes were ruined long before she reached his front door. There was even a goodly amount of mud on the hem of her skirt, even though she had tried to hold it out of the street as she made her way toward the yellow light in the window of Cyrus's brick house.

When she reached the front door she didn't even stop to knock, but opened it quickly, before she could change her mind. Cyrus sat before the fireplace, and he jumped to his feet as the door swung open.

"Leaving?" she said as she stepped inside and slammed the door.

She watched his face harden and his eyes close to her, as if he had prepared himself for this moment. There was no emotion on his face, not even a hint of regret.

"Soon," he said softly. "I wanted to talk to you first, to make sure there was no . . . that we hadn't. . . ."

This was the Cyrus she remembered coming home from war; stoic, indifferent, ancient-eyed. What had he seen with those eyes? She would never know. She didn't want to know.

"There's no baby," she whispered.

Cyrus closed his eyes. "Thank God."

"You don't have to sound so relieved," she said angrily.

"I couldn't leave not knowing." His soft voice displayed no regret, no joy.

"You can't leave. Your place is *here*." She took a step toward him, moving into the light the fire and the single lamp cast. Some of the iciness of his expression melted.

"You're wet." It seemed he shivered.

She looked down at her rain-splattered green skirt and white blouse, at the muddy hem that almost brushed the bare plank floor. A strand of damp hair fell past her cheek. "Just a little."

He offered her his chair by the fire and

346

grabbed a folded towel from the top of a small dresser. It was then that she spotted the stuffed saddle bags, and as her eyes roamed the room she saw that it looked empty already. Surfaces were bare, and the room had lost some of its warmth. As if Cyrus had left it already.

Without a word he began to dry her hair, rubbing the warm dry towel gently over her scalp and neck. His hands were tender and heavy, comforting against her wet head. He touched her with the ease of a man who knows a woman, and yet with a distance that broke her heart. For a while she sat there silently and allowed him to tend to her with loving, gentle hands. He did love her. If she knew nothing else, she knew that Cyrus loved her.

"Don't go," she said as he moved the towel to her neck.

"It's for the best." His hands brushed her shoulders and then her arms, as he warmed her from the inside out.

"Best for who?" she asked. "For you?"

Cyrus dropped his hands and backed away. "Does it matter?"

"Yes." Roxanne left the chair by the fire and walked toward a retreating Cyrus. "It matters very much. Best for who?" she asked again.

"Best for you," he whispered.

He dropped the damp towel on the table and lowered his eyes. His body was tense. His neck corded, his hands knotted into fists, and she knew he was fighting this horrible decision. He didn't want to leave her any more than she wanted him to go.

"Well, you're not getting rid of me that easily," she said, taking another step toward him. She set her pride and her fear of rejection aside, knowing that if she didn't she wouldn't have anything but her pride to keep her warm at night. "I didn't wait for you all this time only to give you up without a fight." She balled her fists in frustration. "Blast you, Cyrus, I never knew you were such a coward."

He lifted his eyebrows slightly. It was likely no one had ever accused Cyrus Bergeron of cowardice. "A coward?"

"Yes," she said, feeling a new surge of strength. "A coward. Otherwise you'd fight for us. You fight for everyone else, why not for what we could have?"

He lifted his eyes to her; determined, cold eyes. "I'll be leaving by the end of the week."

If he wouldn't fight for them, she would. "Fine. I'm coming with you."

Cyrus shook his head slowly. "What are you doing? Why are you so damned and determined to punish us both?" He settled those emotionless eyes on her, and she felt a chill that touched her bones. "You don't need me anymore, Roxanne. You've left the past behind, and in a few weeks or a few months you'll meet a man and you'll fall in love again and he'll give you everything you want."

"I'll meet another man," she repeated incredulously.

He nodded once. She stepped closer, lifted her face, and placed her hands on his chest. His heart beat beneath her fingers as she tilted her head up to lay her lips on his. Perhaps this was all he could understand, this physical connection they had. If she had to be bold and remind him of what he was throwing away, she would. She kissed him.

He didn't turn away from her, but delivered a passionless response. The meeting of their mouths was warm, friendly, bittersweet; the kiss of two friends parting.

The arms that wound around her were gentle—too gentle, as if he was afraid to hold her any tighter. He held his body rigid, distant, even as he allowed his mouth to continue touching hers. It was the kiss of a stranger.

She pulled her lips from his and backed away. That simple embrace, that lukewarm kiss, told her everything she needed to know. Cyrus didn't want her. The unwelcome knowledge hit her cold and hard in the gut. Her worst fears were true.

Everything that had brought them to this place, the sweet words, the watchful eyes, the love letters . . . even the way he'd loved her . . . had been his way of fulfilling his promise to Louis. Nothing more.

"I'm a complete idiot," she whispered, backing away.

"No, you're not," Cyrus whispered. He tried to give her a smile, but it didn't work. "You're a strong, beautiful woman and your life is only going to get better."

"Without you," she whispered.

The false smile faded. "Without me."

She backed toward the door. "You're finished here, aren't you? You loved me until I could feel again, you shook up my life until I knew I wanted more than numbness and memories, and now you're walking away." He didn't deny her accusations. "You fulfilled your promise to Louis, and now you're free to leave, is that it?"

"You're going to be all right, Roxanne," he whispered as she laid her hand on the door handle. "You're stronger than I ever suspected, and you're going to be just fine."

She shook her head as she opened the door and ran out into the rainy night.

Chapter Nineteen

His bags were packed and on his horse, his house was closed up and Will Haller had said he'd keep looking for a buyer. Cyrus had told Will that he'd send word of his new location when he was settled, but he didn't think he would. A clean break was for the best.

The rain had finally stopped, but its effects were seen all around Paris. A few low-lying houses were flooded, the streets were a muddy and often impassable quagmire, the creeks and streams were filled to their banks and in some cases beyond. What had once been mere trickles of gently flowing water had become wildly rushing rivers.

A day or two of sun would make a world of difference, but Cyrus wouldn't be here to see it.

He double-checked the buckle that held his

saddlebags in place. It was early, still, but not so early that the sun and a few early risers weren't up and about. He had to get started. At any minute Roxanne might come walking down this muddy street, on her way to school. He'd looked her in the eye and kissed her and sent her on her way once, knowing it was for the best. He didn't think he could do it again.

A few of the folks who were on the street and the boardwalk nodded and said goodbye, but most of them stayed clear. He'd already been asked, several times, for a reason for his resignation, and his vague answers had left the nosy interrogators unsatisfied. His leaving was sudden and unexpected, he knew, and many of the town's residents were confused. They seemed to feel he was deserting them, somehow.

"Cyrus!" He lifted his head to see a limping Hank Smith and a hysterical Merilee hurrying down the street. Something was wrong. Hank walked faster than usual, in a way that made his limp look pronounced and painful, and Merilee seemed not to notice that her skirt and petticoats dragged through the mud.

"What's wrong?"

"Is she here?" Merilee asked breathlessly as she and Hank looked up and down the street, into spaces between buildings they passed, and then, expectantly, at him.

"Who?" he thought, his mind immediately going to Roxanne.

"Mary Alice," Hank said as they reached Cyrus. "She heard us talking over breakfast about you leaving today, and she got very upset. She wanted to find you to say goodbye, but Merilee was feeding the babies and I was eating my breakfast, and . . ." he stopped, breathless. "When I went to look for her just a few minutes later, she was gone. We thought maybe she'd decided to come here on her own, so we left Henry and Chloe with the neighbors and hurried on down to catch you."

"I haven't seen her." A niggling concern settled inside his chest. Dammit, he couldn't ride out of town not knowing where Mary Alice was, without making sure she was safe in her parents' arms. He hitched his horse to the nearest post. "But she can't have gotten far."

Merilee breathed a sigh of relief, as Cyrus agreed to help them search for her daughter. "Mary Alice could be anywhere," she said. "That child never walks in a straight line. She's always wandering this way and that." Merilee was so nervous her voice was unnaturally fast and high, as she tried to make idle conversation. "Why, if I send her from the kitchen to the parlor to fetch something for me, she's likely to take a detour through her bedroom and the pantry and the front porch."

Cyrus led the small search party down the middle of the street, walking over a high spot where the surface was driest. It made sense that Mary Alice had stopped somewhere between her house and here. Her parents had made the mistake of walking in a straight line in their search. The little girl had probably made one of her detours; to a friend's house or the park or toward some unusual and beautiful sight that had caught her eye.

A beautiful sight caught *his* eye. Roxanne walked straight toward him, chin high and eyes—even from this distance—cool and angry. Just as well.

Merilee took a few quick steps toward her friend. "Have you seen Mary Alice this morning?"

"No." Roxanne's anger fled quickly. She looked every bit as concerned as Merilee. "Is she missing?"

Merilee nodded her head quickly. "She wanted to say goodbye to Cyrus, and Hank and I were both busy so she just left the house on her own. I can't believe she did that," she said with tears in her voice. "Why, as soon as I give her a big hug and a kiss I'm going to tan her hide."

Roxanne gave him a quick, cutting glance that said very clearly that this was all his fault. "I'll help you look for her."

The four of them continued down the road, Roxanne retracing her steps until they reached the next cross street. Cyrus turned right and the others followed. Mallory Park was down this road, and so was Mary Alice's notorious little friend Edith Terry.

"So, today's the day," Roxanne said in a low, biting voice. "I didn't know."

"Yep," Cyrus muttered, his eyes straight ahead.

Their steps carried them further and faster than the Smiths, and they soon distanced themselves from the pair.

"So you were just going to leave without a word," she accused.

"We've already said everything that needs to be said." It started to rain again, and the wind howled. Cyrus glanced to the darkening sky. "I figured it would be best if I just left. No need to make a fuss."

"Oh, no," she said in a voice that was sure to carry much too far. "No need to make a *fuss*."

Hank and Merilee surely heard. Not that it mattered; he'd be gone as soon as he found Mary Alice.

Cyrus kept his searching gaze straight ahead, but he could feel Roxanne's eyes on him. They burned, they prodded, they intruded . . . and he cherished every uncomfortable minute, because he knew he would never feel it again.

The rain and the wind picked up, but no one made a run for cover. The change in weather only made Merilee and Hank worry more, so that they hurried to catch up. Their little girl was out in what could turn out to be another vicious storm.

A faint cry, far away and indistinct, intruded, and Cyrus stopped suddenly. "Did you hear that?"

"I did," Merilee whispered. "That was Mary Alice, I just know it. Where is she?"

Cyrus moved forward, increasing his step, breaking into a slow run. Hank struggled to keep up, and Merilee and Roxanne held their skirts off the ground and ran. The sound came again, a slightly more audible and terrifying wail that sent a shiver up his spine.

Mallory Park waited straight ahead; the trees, the expanse of wet grass, the flowering hedges, and all of a sudden he saw her. Mary Alice hung precariously from the railing of the bridge that spanned the creek. Rising waters had weakened the structure so that it canted dangerously to one side, the support beams loosened or gone, the structure shaking as rushing water buffeted it. Mary Alice hung above the water, her arms straining, her head lifted as she cried out for help.

Cyrus broke into a flat-out run. The others tried to keep up, but they soon fell behind; Hank hampered by his bad hip, the ladies held back by their long skirts that dragged through the mud, and by the wind and rain that pushed them back. His hat flew away. Merilee screamed.

The same mud and rain and wind that hampered the others tried to pull at Cyrus, grabbing his boots and hanging on, pushing against him, making his effort more difficult. He fought the forces of nature that seemed to grow more determined with every passing second; the wind harsh, the rain nearly blinding as it pelted his face. Reality became too much like the dream, where invisible fingers tried to hold him back.

Can't be too slow this time. The air in his

lungs burned, his legs pumped so hard the world around him became a green and gray blur. Mary Alice turned her head and saw him, and she screamed again; louder this time.

"Sheriff Cyrus!"

Even from here he could see that she was barely hanging on. Her little fingers clutched the railing tenuously, her feet dangled mere inches from rushing water, the wind that tried to push her back grabbed at her hair and her pale yellow dress, like a living monster that tried to yank her away from the safety of her family.

He ran hard and fast. *Fast enough?* He ran until he was no longer aware of the mud beneath his feet or the rain or the wind or the people who were, by now, far behind him. Everything else stopped, until there was only him and Mary Alice, and the space between them.

The bridge cracked and shuddered, and Mary Alice screamed as her lifeline, the thin railing, shook and shuddered.

"Hold on," Cyrus whispered. Almost there. He could see the grain of splintering wood, the white knuckles of Mary Alice's tiny hands, the chocolate brown of her eyes.

She slipped, until it looked as if only her fingertips kept her from falling into the rushing water. *Not fast enough.* As Cyrus reached the bank of the normally serene creek Mary Alice fell. Without so much as slowing his step he lunged toward her.

His arms found her as they both fell with a jarring splash into the water. What had once been a creek was now a river that rushed swiftly, carrying them quickly away from the damaged bridge. He struggled to keep Mary Alice's head above water. She screamed once, and then worked her arms around his neck and held on tight.

Cold water pushed and pulled at him, the current impossibly strong. His head bobbed, and a torrent of the icy water flooded his mouth, threatening to choke him. Mary Alice's head was above his, but she felt the cold as surely as he did. Her entire body shivered, the thin arms around his neck shook almost violently.

All he had to do was find a place to grab on to, a way to get Mary Alice onto the bank. Rushing water and rain lashed against his face, and through it all he searched for a way to the bank.

"Hold on tight!" he shouted into Mary Alice's ear. He knew she heard through the thundering rush of water because her little arms tightened around his neck. He kept one arm around her—the water rushed all around them, unmercifully strong, and he didn't trust even her strongest grip—and with the other he tried to steer them toward the bank. It wasn't easy, but the edge of the rushing water got closer and he was able to reach out and grab at solid land. A clod of mud and grass came apart easily in his hand and they continued to drift.

He saw the roots of a tree ahead, roots that

had grown through the ground and over the edge of the bank. When they drifted near, he reached out and grabbed a root. The water continued to lash them, but at least they were no longer being swept away. He hung there for a moment, head down, Mary Alice snug against him, cold water rushing all around. He couldn't move. Every ounce of energy in his body was drained, every muscle screamed.

He heard the ominous crack above, and for a moment he thought the sound was simply another clap of thunder. He lifted his head and saw the heavy limb above his head shudder and shake and dip.

He looked up to see Roxanne running straight for him. Merilee and Hank were behind her, struggling to keep up. The limb cracked again.

"Come on, sweetie," he whispered, and Mary Alice raised her head. "You're all right, now."

He heaved, with the arm that held onto the root, and raised them both out of the water.

"Cyrus!" Roxanne shouted, her voice an unmistakable warning.

He looked up as the branch cracked again, louder than before. It was coming down. He just had time to shove Mary Alice away before the limb crashed down upon his head.

The schoolteacher in her took over, and Roxanne began to issue orders as she and Hank dragged an unconscious Cyrus away from the water. Merilee carried Mary Alice and ran for shelter, and Hank hurried back toward the square to the doctor's office.

Roxanne checked Cyrus's head. She sat on the wet ground and leaned over him so the rain didn't pelt him directly in the face, and she examined his head with her fingers. She found a nasty lump on one side, and her hand came away bloody.

She reached beneath her skirt to rip away a long length of her single petticoat, folding it into a thick square and pressing it firmly over the gash in his head, doing her best to stop the bleeding.

He still hadn't moved or so much as opened his eyes.

"Damn you," she muttered. The wind that had been so horrific for a time had subsided to a brisk, steady breeze, so her words were quite clear. "Don't you dare die."

The rain slowed and then stopped, as the last of the brief but violent storm moved east. "Don't you dare," she whispered.

He opened his eyes slowly, as if the effort pained him. "Is she all right?" he asked in a raspy whisper.

"Mary Alice is fine, and Hank has gone for the doctor."

Cyrus tried to sit up, but the effort was short-lived. He sank back to the ground and closed his eyes. "If Mary Alice is fine, then why does she need a doctor?"

"The doctor is for you." She laid a hand on

his chest. "You took quite a nasty blow to the head."

"I don't need a doctor," Cyrus insisted stubbornly. "I just need to . . . to lie here for a minute and pull myself together."

"Of course," she said testily, never easing the pressure on his wound. "Let's see, you nearly drowned, and a limb that might've killed you fell down on your head. I'm sure a few minutes of rest will mend everything." She snorted. "Ridiculous. You're going to let the doctor take care of you, and I won't stand for any argument."

He cracked one eye open and looked up at her. "You sure are bossy, you know that?"

"Only when it's necessary."

He took a deep breath and closed that one condemning eye. "Goddammit, I'm wet," he muttered. "I hate being wet."

Roxanne refused to leave Cyrus when Hank arrived with the doctor and half a dozen others. Hamlin Nickels brought a wagon around, and even though it lurched and rocked through the mud, Cyrus was able to ride away from the scene of the incident. She insisted on taking him to her house so she could care for him there, but Cyrus, in one of his more lucid moments, opened his eyes and glared at her and said if he was going anywhere it would be home.

Close enough, she decided.

She ran to her own house to change into dry clothes only because the doctor and Hank refused to allow her to be present as they stripped the wounded man and dressed him in dry clothes of his own before putting him to bed. But she made quick work of her task, and was back at Cyrus's side as the doctor examined his wound.

"Looks pretty bad," the doctor said as he applied a thick, dry bandage.

"I could've told you that," Roxanne snapped.

The doctor, who was a good friend of Josiah's, gave her a cutting glance to put her in her place. "Let him rest, and later on today try to get him to take a little broth. Nothing heavy."

"I can do that," Roxanne said. "Anything else?"

The doctor shook his head as he gathered up his medical bag. "All we can do is wait and see. I'll check in on him again this evening." He closed the door easily on his way out, and Roxanne gave her full attention to the man on the bed. He slept again, breathing steadily and deeply.

"He saved Mary Alice," Hank said with a mixture of relief and wonder and horror.

"Yes, he did," Roxanne whispered.

Still in his wet clothes, with his damp hair stuck to his head, Hank paced at the end of the bed. "I haven't seen a man run like that since . . ." he stopped abruptly.

Roxanne lifted her head. "Since when?"

He shook his head. "Doesn't matter."

She had a feeling, from the way he said it, that it did matter. "Was it Cyrus?"

"Yes."

"In the war?"

Hank shifted his feet uncomfortably. "I don't talk about the war much. And I don't think you want to hear this particular story."

"I do."

He laid sad eyes on her. "Louis was there."

Her heart constricted. "I know."

Hank's story began the same as Cyrus's, but it was different in many respects. In Hank's version, Cyrus was much too far away from Louis to be of any help, and the killing blow had been struck while Cyrus still fought another Yankee. When he'd turned and seen that Louis was wounded, he'd begun to run. Hank shook his head in wonder. He'd never seen a man run that fast before, like the wind rushed beneath his feet, like he had wings. He'd never seen a man run that fast since, until today.

"He thinks he could've saved Louis if he'd been faster," Roxanne said.

Hank shook his head. "Impossible. He did kill the Yankee who did Louis in, but not before . . ." He raised a hand to his face. "Not before he was wounded."

How many nightmares had it taken for Cyrus's memories to become so confused that he didn't know what was real and what was not? How many tortured nights had he dreamed of that battle?

Roxanne reached out and took Cyrus's hand. The fingers she gripped were cold, inert, and she gave them a little squeeze hoping for a response. Nothing. "Have you ever spoken to Cyrus about that day?" she asked softly.

"No," Hank said, aghast. "We don't talk about the war."

"It's very painful, I'm sure." She continued to hold Cyrus's hand. "But he needs to hear the truth from someone who was there."

"He knows—"

"He blames himself for Louis's death."

"No," Hank was horrified. "Cyrus was always the best of us. He saved my life more than once, and Louis's, too. How could he possibly blame himself?"

Not caring that Hank hovered over her shoulder, Roxanne leaned over and kissed Cyrus on the cheek. "Did you hear that, my love? You've let a nightmare take the place of your memories. You've blamed yourself all this time, and it's not true."

"I'm going to go home and check on Merilee and Mary Alice," Hank said in a gruff voice. "I'll be back shortly."

"No rush," Roxanne said, her eyes on Cyrus's sleeping face. "I'm not going anywhere."

She leaned closer, and as she did she heard Hank quietly leave the house, closing the door behind him. "I love you," she whispered. "Remember. Remember what really happened so we can have a life together."

The hand she held moved. The stirring she felt was little more than a tremble, as Cyrus's fingers seemed to try to clutch hers. And then he was still again.

* * *

He ran, and this time nothing held him back. The battle continued around him, but he was somehow distant from it. Up ahead, Louis did battle with a Yankee. They were evenly matched, one small, young, frightened man against another. There are no monsters here.

Cyrus ran unimpeded, his legs pumping without pain and without effort. The sun and the wind didn't only surround him, they carried him. He flew across the battlefield.

As he reached Louis everything disappeared; the Yankee, the battle, the field littered with dead and wounded bodies. Louis was whole and smiling. There was no bayonet swinging up and into Cyrus's face. There was no blood, no death, no screams.

"I thought you'd never get here," Louis said with a grin. His rifle changed to a walking stick, his uniform into a regular suit of clothes.

"Me, either." Cyrus looked down. His uniform had changed, also, into the clothes he wore on an ordinary day in Paris. His rifle was gone, and in its place he carried a crooked cane that still bore the marks of the tree it had once been a part of; a knot near a bend in the center, a bit of bark showing on the grip. He looked behind him, expecting the battle to reappear at any moment, but all was peaceful.

Louis turned to look over the next hill. "I'm going to head over that way," he said, pointing his walking stick straight ahead. "Looks pretty *over there." He glanced over his shoulder, that happy grin still on his face.*

It wasn't real. Cyrus knew, as always, that this was just a dream. It was just a dream. It was memory and doubt and terror and expectation, the curse of a lifetime, his own personal hell. But in this dream, everything was different. The war was gone . . . no, it wasn't gone, it was over. Somehow he knew this was the last time he'd dream of Louis.

Louis started to walk away, toward that pretty hill, and Cyrus followed. It was his job to watch over the boy, right? He'd promised Roxanne, after all, he'd given her his word.

But before he'd taken two steps Louis looked back. "I'm going on alone, Cyrus. You can't go with me." He grinned and glanced over the next hill before turning back to Cyrus and winking devilishly. "You take good care of our girl, you hear?"

Cyrus stopped in his tracks and watched Louis walk away. At first he felt panic. Complete, utter panic. And then, as Louis disappeared, the panic was replaced with a peace so warm and complete he knew he'd never felt anything so heavenly. It was over. By God, the war was finally over.

His eyes flew open. He lay in his own bed and his head hurt like hell. A little light, as on any cloudy day, broke through the curtained window. Roxanne sat by the bed. Her head listed to the side, her eyes were closed, a frown marked her worried face. And she was the most beautiful sight he'd ever seen.

Take good care of our girl.

He reached out and touched her knee. She jumped when he touched her, but her frown was quickly replaced by a bright smile.

"You're awake," she whispered as she covered his hand with hers and leaned forward. "Thank heaven. I thought you were going to sleep all day."

His head pounded, he wanted to drift off to sleep again, every muscle in his body ached . . . but he felt strangely *good*.

Roxanne grinned brightly. "You're quite the hero, you know. The Smiths have been here twice this afternoon already, checking on you. All of them. Half the folks from town have stopped by to make sure you're all right. Hamlin said he'd take care of your horse and baggage, so you don't have to worry about that. Oh, and Maude Hipp is baking you a chocolate cake, and Aunt Ada is making her famous pot roast."

"Women are always trying to feed me," he mumbled.

"You have no idea," Roxanne said softly. "Elizabeth Fowler is making you some fresh calf's-feet jelly, and she swears it will heal you faster than any doctor's medicine."

Elizabeth Fowler? He'd always been so sure she hated him for the simple betrayal of surviving when her boys had not.

"Jane Rice asked me to tell you she's making you another lemon sponge cake," she said, a less-than-kindly tone slipping into her voice, "and Rose Wells delivered some special tea, along with her best wishes." Roxanne leaned slightly closer. "You can have none of it, not even a crumb of cake, until the doctor and I both say so."

"Yes, ma'am," he muttered obediently.

She smiled at him, a wan, tired attempt at a cheerful expression. You've given everyone a scare, Cyrus. Mary Alice is especially distraught that you were hurt helping her. She's been quite worried about you." Her smile faded. "So have I."

"I'll be fine," he raised a tentative hand to the bandage on his head. "Guess I won't be traveling for a few days, though." He squinted one eye shut as a bolt of pain shot through his head.

Roxanne took her hand from his. "I guess not."

The nightmares were gone, he knew that. There would be no more waking up screaming in the middle of the night, no more long nights where he sat at the window afraid to fall asleep. Louis, and the memories of that day, weren't going to haunt him anymore. The nightmare was over, finished, healed.

He settled his gaze on Roxanne's face, on her worried eyes and the wonderful, stubborn set of her chin.

He loved her. He would always love her, and she was looking at him right now as if nothing else mattered but love. Not memories; good or bad. Not promises; kept or broken.

Take good care of our girl.

Chapter Twenty

Cyrus sat at the table, refusing to spend another minute in that damn bed. His head hurt. Hell, even his *hair* hurt, but he would survive. He had a hard head.

Once the doctor had assured Roxanne that he would recover, she'd reluctantly left him to Hank's able care. It was obvious that she hadn't wanted to leave, but he'd insisted. Dammit, he couldn't even think clearly when she was in the same room. How could he be expected to make a rational decision while she hovered over him as if every breath might be his last?

After she'd gone, Cyrus had insisted to Hank that he didn't need a caretaker, but the man persisted in sticking around. Just to be sure, he said, that no unexpected complications cropped up. They'd seen their fair share of nasty head injuries in the past, enough to know that they couldn't take a quick recovery for granted.

Cyrus had reluctantly agreed to allow Hank to stay; but by God if the grateful father thanked him one more time for saving Mary Alice he was going to kick the scrawny man out—headache or no headache.

Hank joined him at the table, his own cup of tea in his hands. Cyrus would've preferred coffee, or better yet whiskey, but together Roxanne and the doctor had commanded that he stick to tea and broth for the time being. He'd tried to argue with them; after all he was no invalid. But agreeing was easiest, and since he likely wouldn't be here much longer. . . .

Cakes and pies and breads—gifts from the residents of Paris—crowded one end of the table. He stared at one particular pie, a fine-looking custard. He wasn't hungry, didn't even like custard pie all that much; but this pie had been made by Elizabeth Fowler, a woman who had delivered it herself along with the disgusting-looking calf's-feet jelly and a softly spoken inquiry into his health.

He'd always been so sure she wished him dead, that every time she looked at him she remembered her boys and cursed fate for being so unfair, allowing him to live while they did not.

"Cyrus, I think we need to talk," Hank said sheepishly.

Cyrus withheld a groan that had nothing to

do with his aching head. "You would've done the same thing if you'd gotten there first," he said impatiently. "I just—"

"This isn't about Mary Alice," Hank interrupted. "Though I do thank you again—"

"Don't."

Hank stared into his cup of tea, a pale, sweet beverage he obviously didn't like any better than Cyrus did. He rotated the cup, swirling the warm liquid, and then he set it down and dipped his spoon into the tea, splashing and stirring. He stalled for time, looking as if he truly agonized over what was to come.

"I think we need to talk about the war," he finally said, cutting anxious eyes upward to look at Cyrus's face. "About Louis."

Cyrus left his chair quickly . . . too quickly. His head spun and he stumbled once as he escaped from the table. Hank came out of his own chair and followed. When the meddling bastard tried to catch Cyrus's arm, Cyrus vigorously shook him off.

"Go home, Hank," he muttered. "I'll be fine. I don't need a damn nursemaid."

"I'm not your damn nursemaid," Hank said testily. "I'm your damn friend. Sometimes I think you've forgotten that."

Cyrus glared, to no avail.

"We left here together, years ago," Hank continued. "We fought together, then we came home and tried to leave it all behind. I don't want to go back there," he whispered. "But I

think you've got yourself some very wrong
ideas and I need to set you straight."

Cyrus didn't head for the bed, but turned
around and headed for the pantry in the far
corner. "Wrong ideas?"

"Yep. Roxanne says—"

Cyrus spun around, and the expression on
his face silenced Hank. "Roxanne says *what*?"
he whispered.

Limping more than usual, Hank returned to
his seat at the table. He looked every bit as miserable and exhausted and drained as Cyrus felt.
Surely he didn't want to talk about this anymore than Cyrus did.

With a deep sigh, Hank placed his head in
his hands, palms covering his eyes as if he
could find comfort in the darkness. "Don't you
want to know the truth?" he asked softly.

Cyrus shuffled to the pantry and fetched a
half bottle of whiskey. His saddlebags had been
so full there hadn't been room for everything.
He'd chosen carefully, taking only what he
could carry, only what he had to have. What a
stroke of luck that he'd left this bottle behind.

Dammit, if they were going to sit here and
talk about the *truth*, he was going to need
something a lot stronger than tea.

Roxanne sat on the end of the bed and stared
past open balcony doors to the complete darkness beyond. Now that the crisis was over she
trembled and felt physically ill. Her stomach

knotted painfully, and she'd been close to tears all evening.

She could've lost Cyrus. When she'd seen the limb come crashing down on his head she'd been scared and angry, but there hadn't been time for panic and hysteria. Right now, she had nothing *but* time.

Her worst fear was that she'd lose one she loved again. Unfortunately, the only way to make sure that never happened was not to love at all. Too late for that. For better or for worse, Cyrus had worked his way into her heart and there he was going to stay. Whether he remained in Paris or left for parts unknown, whether he loved her back or not, whether he ever again touched her or not . . . she loved him.

Her fears were not unfounded; her worries were not irrational. Losing Cyrus to a bullet or an illness or a tree limb would destroy her, but so would living without him.

What was she supposed to do, shelter her heart until there was nothing left to guard? Become a nun and close herself off from the world? Not that the Presbyterians *had* any nunneries . . . not that it mattered. She didn't want to guard her heart so closely that she numbed it forever. Not anymore.

She went to her desk and lit a candle. Paper and ink and a pen were gathered from the bottom drawer, and she placed them all before her, flexing her fingers and wrinkling her nose as she searched the deepest part of her heart.

What do you say to a man to make him stay when he's determined to leave? How many ways can you say *I love you*?

Candlelight flickered over the blank sheet of paper for much too long, but when the idea finally came to her she smiled. She put pen to paper.

In spite of the hours he'd slept yesterday, Cyrus passed a long, peaceful night. He slept, dreamless, and woke more rested than he'd been in a very long time. In spite of the pain in his head, he felt strong and contented and whole; as if a piece of him that had been missing had been restored in the night.

How had he let his memories get so twisted? As Hank had talked about that day on the battlefield in Tennessee, a conversation that had been painful for both of them, the memories came flooding back; real memories, clear as day. Not nightmares, but reality. The truth.

He hadn't let Louis die. He'd been there as the boy had passed, he'd promised to watch over Roxanne, but the killing wound had been delivered before Cyrus started running.

No one ran that fast.

He walked around the room for a few minutes, working the kinks out of his legs. He still hurt all over, he still ached *everywhere*. So why did he feel so damn good? He dressed quietly, and then sat the edge of the bed.

Hank slept, as he had all night, in a hard-backed chair. His long, lean body looked uncomfortably twisted. His jaw went slack, his mouth fell slightly open and he snored softly.

Hank had bad memories of his own, and a bum leg to remind him every day of that battle in Tennessee. Neither the memories nor the old wound kept him from claiming the life he wanted, from having a loving family and a nice home. They didn't stop him from living.

A brief, very light knock on the door sounded as it swung open, and Merilee entered with Mary Alice in tow. They carried two baskets, Merilee's larger basket filled with ham and sausage and biscuits, and Mary Alice's smaller one containing three jars of jam. Strawberry, peach, and blackberry, she told him as she placed the jars, one at a time and with the greatest of care, on the table.

Merilee woke Hank with a gentle hand on his shoulder, a smile and a soft *good morning*, and Mary Alice came, basket and all, to the bed where Cyrus sat.

"I have something for you," she said, reaching into the basket to retrieve one last item. "It's a letter," she said needlessly as she offered it, her eyes impossibly big. "Uhhh . . . from *me*."

Cyrus looked down at the fine, even writing on the envelope. *Sheriff Cyrus* was written there in a neat cursive hand that certainly did not belong to a not-quite-six year old.

"Well, thank you," he said, staring down at the letter.

Mary Alice climbed onto the bed and sat

beside him, reaching up a small, tender hand to touch the bandage that encircled his head. "Does it hurt?"

He opened his mouth to say *like hell*, but thought better of it. "Just a little."

"I'm glad you caught me yesterday," she said, her only show of emotion a slightly trembling lower lip. "I can't swim a lick."

"Well, maybe it's time you learned."

"That's what Daddy says. He said he'll teach me to swim this summer."

"Good."

"You know," she said thoughtfully as she came up on her knees and draped an arm over his shoulder. "Being in the creek was scary, but it was kinda fun, too." She glanced at her mother and lowered her voice. "I was really scared until you got there, but after you caught me I wasn't scared at all. The water moved so fast, I felt like I was flying."

Cyrus smiled. "It was pretty fast."

"Maybe we can do it again sometime, but without the tree falling on you," she whispered.

Mary Alice scrambled off the bed to help her mother put breakfast on the table. Hank came slowly out of his chair, exchanging good morning hugs and kisses with his family, studying the fare before him and declaring himself hungry as a bear.

Cyrus dropped his eyes, opening the envelope to withdraw the single sheet of paper. He began to read, fully expecting a formal thank-you note from Merilee.

Dear Sheriff Cyrus,

How do you thank a man for saving your life? For making the rain and the wind and the storms go away, for pulling you from a deep, dark whirlpool that threatens to drag you down so deep you're sure you'll never find your way to the surface? It isn't easy.

You may think I say I love you just because you saved me, but that isn't the case. I love you because of who you are, for your kindness and your good heart, for your strengths and your weaknesses. They make you who you are. I love you because you're a man who tries to save everyone but himself. I love you so much I want to be the one to save you.

So I'm asking, no I'm ordering you to stay in Paris. There's a Fourth of July dance coming up in just a few weeks. I'll expect you to be there, and I'll expect you to dance with me and no one else. I have a new blue dress I've never worn before, and I think you'll like it.

We need you here, all of us. Stay.

Love,
Your best girl

Cyrus folded the letter and placed it in his pocket.

"I'm going for a walk," he said as he stood.

"Before breakfast?" Merilee said.

He shook his head. "I'm not very hungry."

"Well, you need to eat," she said as if she was

speaking to one of her children. "And I'm not sure that you're ready to be up and walking—"

Hank reached up, took Merilee's wrist in his hand, and pulled her down into her chair. "Leave the man alone, Merilee, and eat your breakfast."

"Well I just—" she began defensively.

"Leave the man alone," he repeated slowly.

"Yes, dear," Merilee said demurely.

Cyrus was halfway to the door when Mary Alice piped up. "I must write a pretty good letter."

Roxanne knelt in the dirt. She was too restless to do much of anything, but the mindless task of pulling weeds from Aunt Ada's flower garden suited her mood. Tall, green weeds came easily from the wet ground, and with her gloved hand she pulled weed after weed after weed.

From this garden she couldn't see Cyrus's house. That was the reason she'd decided on this particular chore, after all. To sit in her room and watch his front door and just *wait* would be torture.

What if she'd made a mistake? What if no matter what she said, Cyrus was determined to leave? She yanked much too hard at a flimsy looking weed. If he had his mind set on leaving her behind, there was nothing she could do. Nothing.

Mary Alice should have delivered the letter by now. She wondered what Cyrus thought of

it, if he was amused or embarrassed or unim-
pressed, if he was touched at all. Last night it
had seemed such a good idea, to use one of his
own tricks against him in a way he was sure to
understand. But now . . . now she wasn't so
sure.

A raspy, distant noise intruded into her
thoughts, but she dismissed it easily. It was
just a bird, she thought, or maybe a cat, pranc-
ing in the vegetable garden on the other side of
the house and celebrating the end of the rain.

She ripped viciously at a weed and tossed it
aside.

Cyrus represented everything she feared. He
was now, and probably always would be, a
lawman who carried a gun. Every day of his
life he would face the possibility of real danger.

And as if that weren't enough, he was an
undeniable part of a past she wanted only to
forget. Nightmares of the war might haunt him
forever. Memories she could never understand
would be with him always.

With Cyrus there would be no safe, isolated
farm where she could hide from the worries of
the world; no easy, gentle safety; no shelter
from the cruelties of life. He belonged here in
Paris, where the people needed him.

Ah, fear or no fear, none of that mattered.
She knew now that danger was everywhere, for
everyone. No one was truly safe. As for the
nightmares, well, if they came she should be
there to soothe him, to make the past fade for
him as he had made her fears fade. She needed

to be at his side to tell him, to show him, that the past and the uncertain future were nothing compared to a night in the arms of the one you loved. There was only today, always.

"Roxanne!"

Her musings faded at the sound of that familiar voice bellowing her name. Dropping the handful of weeds and tugging off her gloves, she stepped quickly around the back of the house. He called her name again, louder this time, and she dropped the gloves as she ran.

Cyrus stood beneath her balcony, his face lifted, a stark white bandage wrapped around his dark head.

"What's wrong?" Her heart clinched as his head snapped around and he saw her standing there. "You should be in bed. Did the doctor say it was safe for you to just get up and walk around as if nothing happened?" Her worries melted away as he smiled at her and fastened clear, bright eyes on her face.

"I thought maybe you'd still be in your room this time of morning," he said softly. "Maybe I hoped you would be, so I could say this from a safe distance."

Her heart clenched in her chest. He'd come to say goodbye.

"I called softly, the first few times," he said. "When you didn't come to the window I thought . . . I thought maybe—"

"I've been pulling weeds in Ada's garden," she explained. "I didn't hear you."

He nodded his head, and if she wasn't mistaken he looked a little relieved. Did he really think that after all that had happened she would sit in her room and ignore him? That she was still capable of hiding?

"I said a lot of things to you," he said softly. "From this very spot. I concealed my face, disguised my voice so you would believe the words came from someone else."

She took a single step forward. Oh, this didn't sound like goodbye, not at all.

"What on earth is going on out here?"

Frustrated, Roxanne closed her eyes at the sound of Ada's harsh voice.

"Sheriff!" Ada said as she rounded the corner, holding her shawl tight against the morning chill. "My goodness, what on earth are you doing shouting like a band of wild Indians? Is something wrong?"

Cyrus turned his head to look at Ada, and smiled. "No. Nothing's wrong. I just need to talk to Roxanne."

Ada flashed a smile of her own. "Well, it's much too chilly to carry on a conversation out here. You two come on inside and I'll make a fresh pot of coffee. Josiah is getting dressed but he'll be down shortly. You two can discuss—"

"No," Cyrus said softly and firmly. "I need to talk to Roxanne right here." He pointed to the ground at his feet, and then glanced up at the deserted balcony above his head. "Yes, right *here*."

"Well, I . . ." Ada said as she backed away. "I

suppose I should get back inside and make Josiah's breakfast. If you want that coffee. . . . "

Roxanne hurried her aunt along with a loving smile and a soft shooing motion of her hand. Ada uttered a low "Oh, my," and disappeared around the corner of the house.

Cyrus returned his attention to her, staring so hard she could feel it. "I wrote letters. I stood here, on this very spot, and opened my heart." He lowered his voice. "I even touched you. Loved you. And all the time I pretended to be the man I thought you wanted. I accused you of wanting to hide from the world, and all this time I was hiding myself behind another man's pretty face."

The morning sun illuminated his face, a face she had learned to love so well. Maybe they'd both been hiding, each in their own way, but there was no disguising anything by the light of day. She saw the truth in his eyes, the uncertainty that flickered there still, and love. Yes, she saw love.

"Even though I allowed you to believe that it was another man who courted you, everything I said, every word I wrote, was true."

"Every word?"

He actually gave her a very small smile. "Every word. Remember the night I told you what I think and feel and want?"

"Yes." She whispered, taking another step toward him. She remembered very well.

"I still think you're an extraordinary woman," he said. "I feel alone and empty when you're not with me, blessed when you're at my side. And I want. . . . " He took a deep breath and fastened his eyes to hers. Even from this distance she could feel the heat and intensity of his stare. "I want to wake up every morning for the rest of my life to see your face. I want a house full of babies, fat and sassy and loud kids who'll chew on me and pull my hair, and disobey me and make me worry." He smiled. "That all sounds pretty good to me right now, because I know what comes with it. I love you, Roxanne. Marry me."

She ran, closing the distance between them in a heartbeat and throwing her arms around his neck.

"Tell me this isn't your head wound talking," she whispered. "Swear that you won't come to me in a day or two and tell me your brain was addled by the tree limb landing on it and you're only talking nonsense."

He smiled at her. "I mean every word."

She rested her body against his, felt as much at *home* in his arms as she'd ever felt anywhere.

"You know," she confessed softly, "when I decided that I was tired of living alone, that I wanted a husband and children and a new life, I started searching all around me for the perfect man. And all the time here you were, right under my nose."

"I'm not perfect," he whispered.

"You are to me," she breathed against his lips. "Say it again," she ordered with a smile.

"The whole thing?"

"Just that last part." Her lips hovered close to his.

"Hmmm." His arms tightened. "You mean the part about fat, sassy babies who'll chew on me?"

She raked her mouth across his. "No, but I did enjoy that part."

"I love you, Roxanne," he said without hesitation. "Marry me."

"I thought you'd never ask," she said with a sigh, and then she settled her mouth over his.

Epilogue

September

He refused to tell Roxanne where they were going, no matter how many times, how sweetly, how *insistently*, she asked. She'd seen past the "picnic" ruse as soon as the wagon had passed the city limits, just a couple of miles back.

"But Cyrus," she said, trying the demure approach again. "Can't you at least tell me where we're going?"

"We're here," he said, pulling the wagon to the side of the road.

While she studied the vast and beautiful nothingness that surrounded them, he set the brake on the wagon and collected the picnic basket and blanket from the back. He assisted

Roxanne from her seat, holding on to her just a second or two longer than was absolutely necessary. Grasping the basket and quilt together, he took her hand and led her away from the road.

They passed a thick copse of trees, hardwoods and pines, and walked down a small hill and into a clearing. Cyrus studied the area for a moment, then dropped Roxanne's hand and spread the blanket in the middle of the grassy field. "Here, I think."

"Here *what*?" she asked, exasperated again.

He smiled at his wife. "Have a seat. You really shouldn't allow yourself to get all excited, not in your condition."

She rolled her eyes, but she *did* sit down on the blanket. Not even far enough along to show yet, she didn't always appreciate his deference to her "condition." She told him, again and again, that carrying a baby was not a disease.

"I can't believe you're so secretive. And speaking of secrets," she said as she settled herself comfortably on the blanket. "You never did tell me who you were dancing with at Merilee's party. Behind the tree?" she said to remind him.

"I told you the last time you asked," he said as he sat down beside her. "I wouldn't want to get my dance partner in any trouble."

"I promise not to tell," she said, as she always did when she asked.

"You wouldn't approve," he said with a smile. "You'd say she's too young for me."

She grinned. "So it *was* Jane Rice. I knew it. Really, Cyrus. . . ."

He shook his head. Maybe one day he'd tell her it was Mary Alice who'd danced with him in the dark . . . but not today. It had become a game, where Roxanne got jealous and then tried to kiss the truth out of him. One thing led to another, and . . . no way was he giving this game up any sooner than he had to.

"Don't you want to know why we're here?" he asked.

"Of course," she sighed.

"I'm thinking two stories," he turned from her and gestured to the trees. "Downstairs a parlor, and a big kitchen, and a study so I can work at home on occasion, and maybe a nice big dining room for all the family dinners we'll have. Four bedrooms upstairs," he said, lifting his hand further as if the house already stood before them. "Maybe a balcony or two."

"The house we have now is plenty big enough for the two of us and a baby," she said softly. "I don't need—"

He silenced her protest with a kiss. "Good, because it'll probably be a year before I actually get this house built. After that—" He pressed her down to the blanket and kissed her again—"I imagine we'll outgrow that little brick house pretty fast."

She smiled. "A balcony, you say."

"Or two. I have a few fond memories of balconies."

"Oh you do?" she purred.

He touched his mouth to hers again, tasted her sweet lips and her tongue. As they kissed their bodies realigned, inch by inch, until he towered above her. Her arms encircled his neck, one leg wrapped familiarly around his thigh. He laid with her just this way every night, only now a thickness of annoying clothes kept his flesh from hers.

Everything he wanted was right here; the woman he loved and desired and needed, the child they'd made. This was his family, his home, his sanity. Nothing else mattered. Nothing.

He unbuttoned Roxanne's blouse and laid his mouth on her throat, her chest, her breasts. She closed her eyes and sighed, a deep sigh of contentment that he felt himself, as if her breath touched his very soul.

Unhurried, he savored the taste of her flesh and the way her entire body quivered beneath his hands. A soft breeze wafted over their bodies, pushing strands of dark hair across Roxanne's face.

He opened her blouse all the way down to the waistband of her skirt, and pressed his nose against her belly. "You'd better not bite," he whispered.

"Are you talking to *me*?" Roxanne asked, unbridled joy in her voice.

"No." He laid his hand on her flat stomach. "I'm talking to *her*. The other night, when we had dinner with Merilee and Hank, Chloe damn near took a chunk out of my shoulder. A little nibble now and again is one thing, but that bite was downright vicious. I decided right then and there that our little girl is not going to bite."

She laughed at him. "And what if it's a little boy?"

"If it is, then he won't bite, either." He kissed her stomach, pressing his lips against her warmth and softness. "But I think this one is a girl. I just . . . feel it."

Roxanne's hands settled in his hair, and for a long, precious moment they lay in perfect silence.

He'd only had one nightmare in the two months and twelve days since the wedding. *One*, and it hadn't been that old familiar horror where Louis died in his arms. It had just been a dream. He'd come awake in the night with the sounds of some long-ago battle ringing in his ears, looked at Roxanne sleeping beside him, and the nightmare had faded to nothing. Minutes later he'd fallen asleep once again.

Maybe he'd never be completely rid of the nightmares, but by God he could live with *anything* as long as he had Roxanne to wake up to.

He kissed her stomach again, lazily raised his head to kiss her breasts and then her neck. His lips razed over her flesh, and in a heartbeat the precious moment changed. He wanted her, needed her.

When he pushed her skirt high her thighs drifted open. When he touched her intimately, she took his face in her hands and kissed him deeply, searchingly, with all the passion and love and soul she possessed.

Raindrops began to fall, soft rain that whispered in the trees and pelted the ground and the blanket around them, landing on his back and his head.

Roxanne opened her eyes. "It's raining," she said, disappointment in her voice.

"Yes, it is," he whispered, moving forward so that he sheltered her face from the drops, kissing her again as he freed his aching flesh and surged forward to fill her, to envelop himself in her heat and her love.

He loved her slow and easy, while rain fell over and around them. Warm rain soaked his body as he rocked into her welcoming heat again and again, while he whispered, "I love you," against her mouth.

She shattered beneath him, her warm body clenching around him, releasing, squeezing again as she whispered his name. The rain came down harder as he plunged deep one last time and allowed himself release, pumping his seed and his heart and his soul into her waiting, welcoming body. In that instant he felt Roxanne inside him, as surely as he was inside her. She was forever in his blood. In his heart.

He protected her body from the rain with his, not minding so much that he was drenched to the skin, that his hair dripped rainwater onto his neck and his face, and his shirt and pants were soaked through. A little rain never hurt anybody.

The rain eased to a drizzle, and he rolled away from Roxanne to lie on his back. He closed his eyes and allowed the soft drops to pelt his face. Roxanne laid her head on his chest and cocked a leg and her full skirt over his thighs, and he placed a hand on her wet hair.

"So, what do you think?" he asked.

She laughed and kissed his chest, soaked shirt and all. "I think I love you."

"About the house," he clarified.

She lifted her head, propping her chin on his chest and looking him in the eye. "There really is going to be a house? I thought maybe you just brought me out here to seduce me."

"That, too," he admitted. "But yeah. There's going to be a house."

Roxanne rolled onto her back and rested her head on his shoulder. The rain stopped, but for a few errant drops that fell softly on them now and again, as they lay together on the wet blanket surveying the sky and the trees and the grassy land around them.

"So," she finally whispered. "This is home."

Cyrus smiled at a clearing sky and gathered Roxanne close. "Yes. Yes it is."

Masquerade

Katherine Deauxpille, Elaine Fox, Linda Jones, & Sharon Pisacreta

In the whirling decadence of Carnival, all forms of desire are unveiled. Amidst the crush of those attending the balls, filling the waterways, and traveling in the gondolas of post-Napoleonic Venice, nothing is unavailable—should one know where to look. Amongst the throngs are artists and seducers, nobles and thieves, and not all of them are what they appear. But in that frantic congress of people lurks something more than animal passion, something more than a paradise of the flesh. Love, should one seek it out, can be found within this shadowy communion of people—and as four beauties learn, all one need do is unmask it.

___4577-X $5.99 US/$6.99 CAN

Jackie & The Giant

LINDA JONES

It isn't a castle, but Cloudmont is close: The enormous estate houses everything Jacqueline Beresford needs to quit her life of crime. But climbing up to the window, Jackie gets a shock. The gorgeous giant of an owner is awake—and he is a greater treasure than she ever imagined. It hardly surprises Rory Donovan that the beautiful burglar is not what she claims, but capturing the feisty felon offers an excellent opportunity. He was searching for a governess for his son, and against all logic, he feels Jackie is perfect for the role—and for many others. But he knows that she broke into his home to rob him of his wealth—for what reason did she steal his heart?

___52333-7 $5.99 US/$6.99 CAN

The Indigo Blade
Linda Jones

Penelope Seton has heard the stories of the Indigo Blade, so when an ex-suitor asks her to help betray and capture the infamous rogue, she has to admit that she is intrigued. Her new husband, Maximillian Broderick, is handsome and rich, but the man who once made her blood race has become an apathetic popinjay after the wedding. Still, something lurks behind Max's languid smile, and she swears she sees glimpses of the passionate husband he seemed to be. Soon Penelope is involved in a game that threatens to claim her husband, her head, and her heart. But she finds herself wondering, if her love is to be the prize, who will win it—her husband or the Indigo Blade.

___52303-5 $5.99 US/$6.99 CAN

Dorchester Publishing Co., Inc.
P.O. Box 6640
Wayne, PA 19087-8640

Please add $1.75 for shipping and handling for the first book and $.50 for each book thereafter. NY, NYC, and PA residents, please add appropriate sales tax. No cash, stamps, or C.O.D.s. All orders shipped within 6 weeks via postal service book rate. Canadian orders require $2.00 extra postage and must be paid in U.S. dollars through a U.S. banking facility.

Name_____
Address_____
City_____State_____Zip_____
I have enclosed $_____ in payment for the checked book(s).
Payment <u>must</u> accompany all orders. ❑ Please send a free catalog.
CHECK OUT OUR WEBSITE! www.dorchesterpub.com

Cinderfella

Linda Jones

The daughter of a Kansas cattle tycoon, Charmaine Haley is given a royal welcome on her return from Boston: a masquerade. But the spirited beauty is aware of her father's matchmaking schemes, and she feels sure there will be no shoe-ins for her affection. At the dance, Charmaine is swept off her feet by a masked stranger, but suddenly she finds herself in a compromising position that has her father on a manhunt with a shotgun and the only clue the stranger left— one black boot.

___52275-6 $5.99 US/$6.99 CAN

Linda Jones
On A Wicked Wind

Hurled into the Caribbean and swept back in time, Sabrina Steele finds herself abruptly aroused in the arms of the dashing pirate captain Antonio Rafael de Zamora. There, on his tropical island, Rafael teaches her to crest the waves of passion and sail the seas of ecstasy. But the handsome rogue has a tortured past, and in order to consummate a love that called her through time, the headstrong beauty seeks to uncover the pirate's true buried treasure—his heart.

___52251-9 $5.99 US/$6.99 CAN

Dorchester Publishing Co., Inc.
P.O. Box 6640
Wayne, PA 19087-8640

Please add $1.75 for shipping and handling for the first book and $.50 for each book thereafter. NY, NYC, and PA residents, please add appropriate sales tax. No cash, stamps, or C.O.D.s. All orders shipped within 6 weeks via postal service book rate. Canadian orders require $2.00 extra postage and must be paid in U.S. dollars through a U.S. banking facility.

Name_____
Address_____
City_____State_____Zip_____
I have enclosed $_____ in payment for the checked book(s).
Payment <u>must</u> accompany all orders. ❏ Please send a free catalog.

NO ANGEL'S GRACE

LINDA WINSTEAD

From the moment Dillon feasts his eyes on the raven-haired beauty, Grace Cavanaugh, he knows she is trouble. Sharp-tongued and stubborn, with a flawless complexion and a priceless wardrobe, Grace certainly doesn't belong on a Western ranch. But that's what Dillon calls home, and as long as the lovely orphan is his charge, that's where they'll stay.

But Grace Cavanaugh has learned the hard way that men can't be trusted. Not for all the diamonds and rubies in England will she give herself to any man. But when Dillon walks into her life he changes all the rules. Suddenly the unapproachable ice princess finds herself melting at his simplest touch, and wondering what she'll have to do to convince him that their love is the most precious gem of all.

_4223-1 $5.50 US/$6.50 CAN

Dorchester Publishing Co., Inc.
P.O. Box 6640
Wayne, PA 19087-8640

Christmas Spirit

ELAINE FOX
LEIGH GREENWOOD
LINDA WINSTEAD

Three Heartwarming Tales of Romance and Holiday Cheer

Bah Humbug! by Leigh Greenwood. Nate wants to go somewhere hot, but when his neighbor offers holiday cheer, their passion makes the tropics look like the arctic.

Christmas Present by Elaine Fox. When Susannah returns home, a late-night savior teaches her the secret to happiness. But is this fate, or something more wonderful?

Blue Christmas by Linda Winstead. Jess doesn't date musicians, especially handsome, up-and-coming ones. But she has a ghost of a chance to realize that Jimmy Blue is a heavenly gift.

___4320-3 $5.50 US/$6.50 CAN

Dorchester Publishing Co., Inc.
P.O. Box 6640
Wayne, PA 19087-8640

Please add $1.75 for shipping and handling for the first book and $.50 for each book thereafter. NY, NYC, and PA residents, please add appropriate sales tax. No cash, stamps, or C.O.D.s. All orders shipped within 6 weeks via postal service book rate. Canadian orders require $2.00 extra postage and must be paid in U.S. dollars through a U.S. banking facility.

Name_____
Address_____
City_____ State_____ Zip_____
I have enclosed $_____ in payment for the checked book(s).
Payment <u>must</u> accompany all orders. ❑ Please send a free catalog.

Daughter of wealth and privilege, lovely Charlaine Kimball is known to Victorian society as the Ice Princess. But when a brash intruder dares to take a king's ransom in jewels from her private safe, indignation burns away her usual cool reserve. And when the handsome rogue presumes to steal a kiss from her untouched lips, forbidden longing sets her soul ablaze.

Illegitimate son of a penniless Frenchwoman, Devlin Rhodes is nothing but a lowly bounder to the British aristocrats who snub him. But his leapfrogging ambition engages him in a dangerous game. Now he will have to win Charlaine's hand in marriage–and have her begging for the kiss that will awaken his heart and transform him into the man he was always meant to be.

——52200-4 $5.99 US/$6.99 CAN

Dorchester Publishing Co., Inc.
P.O. Box 6640
Wayne, PA 19087-8640

Please add $1.75 for shipping and handling for the first book and $.50 for each book thereafter. NY, NYC, and PA residents, please add appropriate sales tax. No cash, stamps, or C.O.D.s. All orders shipped within 6 weeks via postal service book rate. Canadian orders require $2.00 extra postage and must be paid in U.S. dollars through a U.S. banking facility.

Name_____
Address_____
City_____State_____Zip_____
I have enclosed $_____ in payment for the checked book(s).
Payment <u>must</u> accompany all orders. ❏ Please send a free catalog.